THE PENGUIN CLASSICS

FOUNDER EDITOR (1944–64): E. V. RIEU

IVAN TURGENEV, Russian novelist, was born in Oryol in 1818, and was the first Russian writer to enjoy an international reputation. Born into the gentry himself, and dominated in his boyhood by a tyrannical mother, he swore a 'Hannibal's oath' against serfdom. After studying in Moscow, St Petersburg, and Berlin (1838–41), where he was influenced by German Idealism, he returned to Russia an ardent liberal and Westernist. He gained fame as an author with a series of brilliant, sensitive pictures of peasant life. Although he had also written poetry, plays, and short stories, it was as a novelist that his greatest work was to be done. His novels are noted for the poetic 'atmosphere' of their country settings, the contrast between hero and heroine, and for the objective portrayal of heroes representative of stages in the development of the Russian intelligentsia during the period 1840–70. Exiled to his estate of Spasskoye in 1852 for an obituary on Gogol, he wrote *Rudin* (1856), *Home of the Gentry* (1859), *On the Eve* (1860), *Fathers and Children* (1862), but was so disillusioned by the obtuse criticism which greeted this last work that he spent most of the rest of his life at Baden-Baden (1862–70), and Paris (1871–83). His last novels *Smoke* (1867), and *Virgin Soil* (1877), lacked the balance and topicality of his earlier work. He died in Bougival, near Paris, in 1883.

RICHARD FREEBORN is at present Professor of Russian Literature at the School of Slavonic and East European Studies, University of London. He was previously Professor of Russian at Manchester University, a visiting Professor at the University of California in Los Angeles, and for ten years he was Hulme Lecturer in Russian at Brasenose College, Oxford, where he graduated. His publications include *Turgenev, A Study* (1960), *A Short History of Modern Russia* (1966; 1967), translations of *Home of the Gentry* (Penguin Classics, 1970) and *Rudin* (Penguin Classics 1975), and a couple of novels.

Ivan Turgenev

SKETCHES FROM A HUNTER'S ALBUM

SELECTED
AND TRANSLATED BY
RICHARD FREEBORN

PENGUIN BOOKS

Penguin Books Ltd, Harmondsworth, Middlesex, England
Penguin Books, 625 Madison Avenue, New York, New York 10022, U.S.A.
Penguin Books Australia Ltd, Ringwood, Victoria, Australia
Penguin Books Canada Ltd, 2801 John Street, Markham, Ontario, Canada L3R 1B4
Penguin Books (N.Z.) Ltd, 182–190 Wairau Road, Auckland 10, New Zealand

—

This translation first published 1967
Reprinted 1972, 1974, 1975, 1977, 1979, 1981

—

Copyright © Richard Freeborn, 1967
All rights reserved

—

Made and printed in Great Britain
by Richard Clay (The Chaucer Press) Ltd,
Bungay, Suffolk
Set in Monotype Bembo

Contents

Introduction

TURGENEV's *Sketches* were originally published in the Russian journal *The Contemporary* between 1847 and 1851. In 1852 they were published for the first time in a separate edition – a circumstance which led to Turgenev's arrest and subsequent exile to his estate of Spasskoye. Much later, during the last decade of his life, he added further *Sketches* to those already published, with the result that the total number of such *Sketches* reached twenty-five. Of these only a baker's dozen are included in this selection, though those translated here are generally acknowledged to be among the most representative and important. It is because this is not a complete translation that it has been given the general title *Sketches from a Hunter's Album*, rather than the slightly more usual – and perhaps slightly less accurate – title: *A Sportsman's Sketches*, *A Sportsman's Notebook*, etc. The Russian title to the work (a title, incidentally, which it acquired only by accident) is usually transliterated as *Zapiski okhotnika* and means literally: *Notes of a Hunter*. The possible aura of Gamesmanship or sportiness which such a title evokes is so inappropriate to the manner and spirit of the original that I felt it preferable to introduce the word *Album* into the title, for Turgenev's work is essentially an album of pictures drawn from Russian country life in the period prior to the Emancipation of the serfs, in 1861. The Appendix also contains two recently discovered fragments of *Sketches* which have not, to my knowledge, been previously translated into English.

Ivan Sergeyevich Turgenev was born in Oryol, some two hundred or so miles south of Moscow, in 1818. He spent his boyhood on his mother's estate of Spasskoye. Here he naturally learned about the injustices of the serf system, in addition to learning from the frequent beatings which he received at his mother's hand how cruel and brutalizing such a system could be. He survived the tyranny which his mother exercised in her household, but the experience taught him to detest all tyrannies, especially the tyranny of serfdom and the accompanying political tyranny of Tsarist absolutism. A period at Berlin University at the end of the 1830s gave the young Turgenev an opportunity to study Western Europe, with the result that he returned to Russia in 1841 as a man of convinced Westernist views. Westernists, it should be explained, were those members of the Russian intelligentsia who were committed to the belief that Russia should be westernized, following the initiative already taken in this respect by Peter the Great at the beginning of the eighteenth century, as opposed to the Slavophils who wished to reject Western influences and based their hopes for Russia on the presumed superiority of things Russian.

Although Turgenev had been writing poems and articles since the middle of the 1830s, it was not until 1843 that he published his first successful work, a long narrative poem entitled *Parasha*. He was praised for this work by the critic Vissarion Belinsky, and it was partly due to Belinsky's influence that Turgenev began to devote himself to realistic depiction of the inadequacies in Russian society. Thus he became not only a chronicler of his own generation and his own society, but also a critic of his own generation's Hamletism and of the fundamental injustice of serfdom on which Russian society was based. Yet there was something accidental, or only partly intentional, about Turgenev's assumption of such roles. Intending to be a poet, he had by the latter part of the 1840s begun to demonstrate that he had remarkable talents as a writer of prose; intending to write a series of 'physiological' sketches of urban life on the lines of Gogol's *St Petersburg Stories* or Dostoyevsky's *Poor Folk*, he found himself writing about the Russian countryside in which he had grown

8

up; intending, in a moment of despair, to abandon literature for good, he left a short work entitled *Khor and Kalinych* in the editorial offices of the newly resuscitated journal *The Contemporary*, and the success of the work when it was first published early in 1847 (*The Contemporary*, No. 1) persuaded Turgenev to return to literature and marked the beginning of the *Sketches* which were to bring him lasting fame.

A representative of the new Russian intelligentsia, as much at home in Paris or Berlin as in Moscow or St Petersburg, a man of noble birth, liberal inclinations and cultivated tastes, extraordinarily gifted and well-read, Turgenev possessed an urbane charm which made him excellent company in any society. Though he admired women, he never married. His emotional life was dominated by the attachment which he formed for the famous singer Pauline Viardot, whom he met during her first visit to St Petersburg in the 1843-4 opera season and with whom he was to remain on terms of close intimacy until his death in 1883. Whether or not he was her lover is a matter on which a great deal of speculative comment has been expended, but it is characteristic of a certain contrariness in his nature that he should also have been on very amicable terms with Pauline's husband, Louis Viardot. For our purposes, this second relationship is more important, because Louis Viardot and Turgenev were not only in love with the same woman they were also in love with hunting, and it is very likely that a little collection of hunting memoirs entitled *Souvenirs de chasses* which Louis Viardot published in 1846 gave Turgenev the idea for his own Sketches.

Other Russian writers had, of course, written about the peasantry – Radishchev, Pushkin, Gogol – and there were also such European writers as George Sand or Maria Edgeworth upon whom Turgenev could have modelled his own work. Strictly speaking, however, his *Sketches* are not modelled on anything save his own experience. He wrote most of them while he was outside Russia between 1847 and 1851, either

9

while travelling in Europe or during a period spent on the Viardot estate of Courtavenel outside Paris. The fact that he was drawing on memory may account for the brilliant lustre, so evocative and even nostalgic, which surrounds the best of them; equally, perhaps, it may be that some of the luxuriance of the countryside about Courtavenel shines through the richness of the nature descriptions. Yet it must be stressed that these *Sketches* were composed largely fortuitously. They grew out of the success of *Khor and Kalinych* and the fact that his mother failed to provide him with adequate financial means. While writing them he was also busily engaged in attempting to make a reputation for himself as a dramatist – an attempt which culminated in the writing of his only important play, the five-act comedy *A Month in the Country*. These *Sketches*, therefore, are not all of a piece. In some respects, they are occasional pieces, experiments in a particular kind of portraiture, tracts for the times cast in the mould of literature, trial sketches for his future work as a novelist. The order which he finally chose for them, which is the order followed in this translated selection, does not observe a strict chronology and is evidence of the fact that he was never inclined to regard them as truly completed. Despite this, his *Sketches* have long been acknowledged to be masterpieces which occupy a very special place in Russian literature.

Khor and Kalinych illustrates many of their most characteristic features. It introduces the author in the role that he is to assume throughout his work – the role, that is, of intelligent, interested but uncommitted observer. The observation has two discernible aspects to it: there is the lucid, clearcut, pictorial aspect contributed by Turgenev, the writer and artist; and there is what might be called the sociological aspect, which involves a Turgenev who cannot help being a member of the nobility, of the landowning class, and who to that extent is both a stranger in the world of the peasants and a frankly curious observer anxious to describe this world to his readers. For fear of censorship and no doubt for reasons of taste, Turgenev does not attempt to lay undue emphasis on the fact of serfdom, but the propagandist element in his portraits of the two peasants, Khor (the polecat) and Kalinych, is evident enough. They can be said to represent differing types both of personality and, loosely speaking, of literary portraiture. Such differentiation serves not only to emphasize the individual human qualities in the two peasants but also anticipates Turgenev's later preoccupation (in his lecture of 1860) with the division of human beings into those who are predominantly Hamlet-like or those who are predominantly Quixotic by nature. Apart, though, from laying stress on the intelligence of both the peasants, on their individuality as well as their 'typical' differences, this first *Sketch* also illustrates what is, in general, to be regarded as Turgenev's usual attitude – so far, at least, as these *Sketches* are concerned – towards the nobility. The portrait of Polutykin, kindly enough in itself, is not without that laconic and slightly mocking tone which Turgenev so often uses in describing the nobility. On these grounds alone, there is good reason for supposing that the tendentiousness in these *Sketches* is rather more anti-establishment than overtly pro-peasantry.

Khor and Kalinych also sheds light on such common features of peasant life as the 'eagles' who exploit the peasant women, the itinerant scythe traders and the strict hierarchy which governs the relationship between Khor and his family, despite the good-natured bantering between Khor and his son, Fedya. Naturally, Turgenev's interest in Khor's character and family life is matched by an equivalent curiosity on Khor's part; their mutual ignorance is sufficient comment in itself on the division which exists between master and peasant. Such comments as Turgenev's about the conviction, derived from his talk with Khor, 'that Peter the Great was predominantly Russian in his national characteristics', or Khor's caginess when Turgenev taxes him on the subject of purchasing his freedom are further reminders of the divisive half-truths, even illusions, which make communication and understanding between the classes so difficult. In other words, Turgenev's conviction that the Russian peasantry can be used as an argument in favour of Westernism seems to be as much special pleading based on ignorance or first impressions as is Khor's apprehension that he would tend to lose his individuality when he became free. It is, in fact, rare for Turgenev to attempt to argue or, in a strict sense, converse with the peasants; he is content to prompt them into speaking about themselves, framing the encounter and recorded speech with passages of commentary or description which establish both the circumstances and the atmosphere, though this framework also tends to objectivize and, in so doing, to distance the human appeal of the encounter. It is a distancing, of course, which usually has the effect of making the casual encounter seem doubly significant, as though a lyric poem had been born of an anecdote, a work of art from a snapshot. But the distance, let it not be forgotten, is really due to ignorance.

The simple, almost anecdotal charm of the first *Sketch* is followed by the more explicitly condemnatory tone of *Yermolay and the Miller's Wife* (*The Contemporary*, No. 5, 1847). Zverkov's attitude towards the peasantry, especially in regard to Arina, is the nub of this episode. The reader is not explicitly asked to contrast Turgenev's attitude to Yermolay with Zverkov's treatment of Arina, but this is the most likely moral to be drawn: it lays bare at one stroke the inhumanity of the system. Arina seems to have been based on fact, for Turgenev's mother apparently treated one of her maidservants in a similar fashion. Yermolay, Turgenev's frequent hunting companion, is also drawn from life – a serf, Afanasy Alifanov, belonging to one of Turgenev's neighbours. Turgenev purchased his freedom and later gave material help to his family (though Yermolay is not endowed with a family in this

Sketch). Descendants of Alifanov (Yermolay) still live at Spasskoye, or so it was reported in 1955.

The realism of Turgenev's manner, whether it be taken as respect for the observed fact or, in a more special sense, as the ability to focus the lens of his writer's eye with such precision that the subject acquires a dramatic immediacy, is admirably illustrated by *Bezhin Lea* (*The Contemporary*, No. 2, 1851). The opening description of the July day is an example of Turgenev at his most brilliant. A special magic haunts the picture that Turgenev offers us and suggests that such beautiful July days are a part of innocence, of boyhood, clothed in the magic of recollection. The reality, then, is the night in which Turgenev encounters the peasant boys around their fires, hears their stories of hauntings and darkenings of the sun. Serfdom here is not represented as a problem of social relationships; it is a presence, like the darkness, surrounding and enclosing the boys' lives. The drama of flickering fire-light and darkness has a quality of sorcery that illuminates the darkness and light in the boys' minds, dramatically holds them in the writer's eye, photographs them for ever for the reader's gaze. Then, after the mystery of the night's experience, comes the splendour of the morning and Turgenev's always clear-minded insistence on the ephemerality of life with the announcement that Pavlusha had been killed in falling from a horse. The colour words, the visual richness, the simplicity of the anecdote so magnificently re-created and the finely etched characterizations of the boys leave a residue of wonder.

Equally rich in descriptive detail is the story of Turgenev's meeting with *Kasyan from the Beautiful Lands* (*The Contemporary*, No. 3, 1851). Kasyan, supposedly an adherent of some unnamed religious sect, is one of the most remarkable peasant portraits in these *Sketches*. His quasi-biblical speech is the vehicle not only for a protest against the shedding of blood; it is also a means of expressing his own repudiation of established society in the name of that dream-world of folk-lore 'where no leaves fall from the trees in winter, nor in the autumn neither, and golden apples do grow on silver branches and each man lives in contentment and justice with another'. But this *Sketch*, composed at a time when Turgenev's proselytizing Westernism had been somewhat modified as a result of the Paris revolution in 1848, is not as explicit a plea for justice as is *Bailiff* (*The Contemporary*, No. 10, 1847). *Bailiff* was written in May and June of 1847, though the final place and dating which Turgenev gave to it (Salzbrunn, in Silesia, July 1847) was his way of acknowledging agreement with the sentiments expressed by Belinsky in his famous *Letter to Gogol*. Belinsky, convalescing at Salzbrunn, wrote his letter in violent reaction against the obscurantist Slavophil ideas which Gogol had professed in a curious work entitled *Selected Passages from a Correspondence with Friends*. Turgenev was in Salzbrunn during part of Belinsky's convalescence, and the latter's plea for justice in Russian social and political life, as expressed in the *Letter to Gogol*, later became Turgenev's sole religious and political credo. Of all the *Sketches* which Turgenev wrote, *Bailiff*, with its exquisitely savage portrait of the foppish tyrant Penochkin and its equally acute study of his bailiff, is by far the most outspoken attack on the exploitation of the peasantry. A month or so later, in August 1847, he also probably wrote *Two Landowners*, which provides more evidence of the sickeningly callous treatment meted out by landowners to their serfs. Possibly because this *Sketch* was so critical, Turgenev did not publish it separately but included it among his collection of *Sketches* when they were first published as a separate edition in 1852.

The value of these *Sketches* as socio-political tracts for the times hardly needs to be emphasized. Their effect was such that they made a very real contribution to the movement for emancipating the serfs after the Crimean War. Yet they are probably better understood nowadays as one of the stages in

Turgenev's development as a writer, revealing some of the themes and *motifs* which recur so frequently in his work and imbue it with a significance that is as much philosophical as social or political. *Death* (*The Contemporary*, No. 2, 1848), for example, implies clearly enough that there is another kind of injustice apart from the injustice of social inequality. The isolation of the human personality in relation to nature and eternity exercised Turgenev more deeply, in the final analysis, than did the social or political issues of his time. *Death* illustrates his concern for the way peasants die, with no particular emphasis laid on the morbid aspects of such a subject; but it illustrates more clearly the compassion that he feels for the wretched Avenir, the 'eternal student', whose sensitive, enthusiastic nature proves to be as superfluous in life as it is in the context of Russian society. Viewed in relation to its essentially ephemeral character, as Turgenev undoubtedly viewed it, the human personality becomes valuable for the beauty which it exhibits in life.

Beauty is the theme of *Singers* (*The Contemporary*, No. 11, 1850) in the sense that it is the beauty of Yakov's singing which so touches the hearts of his listeners that he is universally acknowledged to be the winner of the competition. Such beauty, though, is no more than momentary. Turgenev chanced upon it in taking refuge from the heat of the day and refused to idealize the episode by omitting the drunken scene at the end. Apart from depicting the peasants as endowed with a culture of their own, this *Sketch* seizes upon a moment of epiphany in which Yakov's singing and the tearful desperation of the boy's final cries seem to embrace the full range of peasant heartache. Unlike *Singers*, though first published simultaneously, *Meeting* deals explicitly with an emotional problem and is the only attempt Turgenev made in his *Sketches* to describe such emotions among the peasantry. The glitter of the natural scene at the beginning reflects and sets in relief the expectations of the peasant girl awaiting her lover, just as the final breath of autumn is an orchestration of her tears, but for once the touch is a shade too sentimental, the artlessness betrays a shade too much of the artifice that contributed to its making.

Hamlet of the Shchigrovsky District (*The Contemporary*, No. 2, 1849) is a study in the Hamletism of Turgenev's own generation. As an anatomy of provincial society, the opening description of the dignitary's arrival and the ensuing dinner is one of the most uproariously sardonic passages to be found anywhere in Turgenev's work, matching, if on a more sophisticated and therefore less obtrusive level, the most satirical passages in Gogol. The anonymous Hamlet's recital of misfortunes and misalliances which follows may be considered equally sardonic in tone, but in the end, as the wretched Vasily Vasilyevych sticks his tongue out at himself in the mirror, the tragedy of his superfluity reflects the tragic loss of illusions and fond hopes experienced by Turgenev's generation. The preoccupation with self so characteristic of this Hamlet cannot fail to be comic, but his final reconciliation is in its own way as bitter an acceptance of social inequality as is the peasant's subservience to his master.

It is a short step to another study in reconciliation and acceptance, although in the case of *Living Relic*, which first appeared twenty-five years later, in 1874, in a collection of stories published to raise funds for famine victims in the Samara Province, the tone is not sardonic but religious, and the reconciliation of Lukeria to her travail is that of a saint enduring a solitary martyrdom. None of Turgenev's *Sketches* is more beautiful or moving than this lucidly simple portrait. Lukeria's humble, philosophical acceptance of misfortune must in part be due to Turgenev's pessimistic view that life involved such submission to fate. This readiness to submit, so characteristic both of Turgenev himself and of so many of his fictional characters, forms the crux of another *Sketch* first published in 1874, *Clatter of Wheels*. Though Turgenev's fears prove to be unfounded at the moment of crisis, the *Sketch* has a nice blend of humour and tension interlaced with characteristic passages of nature description. Finally, *Forest and Steppe* (*The Contemporary*, No. 2, 1849), which was always the concluding piece in the several editions of the *Sketches* to appear during Turgenev's lifetime, reminds us that the hunter's milieu was the forest regions, not the 'limitless, enormous steppe no eye can encompass'.

The Appendix contains translations of two fragments first published in 1964 (*Literaturnoye nasledstvo*, vol. 73, bk 1) which relate to 1847 and 1848 and in combination – it is assumed that Turgenev intended to combine them – would probably have proved to be as outspokenly critical as *Bailiff* or *Two Landowners*. As it is, these fragments are interesting for their terse and pungent thumbnail sketches of two different types of despotic landowner. *The Russian German* perhaps also helps to explain something that may seem puzzling to a twentieth-century English reader – namely, the ease with which Turgenev was able to range far and wide on his hunting trips without any apparent fear of trespassing on other people's property. His assumption of such a prerogative is one mark of the time-span that separates his age from ours.

Regardless of the fact that these *Sketches* belong to an age that is now quite remote, the wryly humorous detachment, visual honesty and poetic sensibility with which Turgenev imbued them have served to maintain the freshness and distinction of their literary appeal. In his novels, especially *Fathers and Children*, he was no doubt to achieve greater things, but his *Sketches* were his first major achievement. He was aware both of their value and their imperfections, as we know from a letter that he wrote to his friend Annenkov in 1852:

I am glad that this book has come out; it seems to me that it will remain my mite cast into the treasure-chest of Russian literature, to use the phraseology of the school-book. . . . Much has come out pale and scrappy, much is only just hinted at, some of it's not right, oversalted or undercooked – but there are other notes pitched exactly right and not out of tune, and it is these notes that will save the whole book.

Turgenev's verdict, though understandably erring on the critical side, has proved to be a just one. A translator can only hope that he has been able to reveal the justice of it in his translation, despite the many temptations placed in his way to oversalt or undercook the poetry, simplicity, irony and beauty of the original Russian.

Khor and Kalinych

WHOEVER has happened to travel from Bolkhov County into the Zhizdra[1] region will no doubt have been struck by the sharp differences between the nature of the people in the Orlov Province and those in Kaluga. The Orlov peasant is a man of little stature, round-shouldered, gloomy, given to looking at you from under his brows and used to living in miserable huts of aspen wood, working on the *corvée*[2] principle, taking no part in trade, eating poorly and wearing bast shoes; whereas the Kaluga peasant, who pays quit-rent, is used to living in spacious fir huts, has a tall build, looks at you boldly and merrily with a clean, clear complexion, trades in grease and tar and wears boots on feast days. An Orlov village (I am talking about the eastern part of the Orlov Province) is usually situated among ploughed fields and close to a ravine which has somehow or other been transformed into a muddy pond. Apart from some wild broom, which is always ready to hand, and a couple of emaciated birches, there won't be a tree visible for miles and hut will nestle against hut, the roofs strewn with rotten straw. A Kaluga village, on the other hand, will be surrounded for the most part by woodland; the huts, more independent of each other and straighter, are roofed with boards; the gates can be tightly closed, the wattle-fencing round the yard has not collapsed and fallen inwards to offer an open door to any passing pig. And for the hunter the Kaluga Province provides more in the way of game. In the Orlov Province the last areas of woodland and 'plazas'* will disappear in five years or so,

---

* In the Orlov Province large solid masses of bush are known as 'plazas'; the local Orlov dialect is noted for a wide variety of original, sometimes very apt, sometimes rather ugly, words and turns of phrase.

19

and there is no marshland whatever; while in the Kaluga Province wooded areas stretch for hundreds, and marshland for dozens, of miles, and that noble bird, the grouse, still thrives, the great-hearted snipe is plenteous and the noisy partridge both delights and frightens the hunter and his dog with its explosive flight from cover.

While out hunting in the Zhizdra region I became acquainted with a small Kaluga landowner, Polutykin, also a passionate hunter and, consequently, an excellent fellow. Admittedly, he had acquired one or two weaknesses: for instance, he paid court to all the rich young ladies of marriageable age in the province and, being refused both their hands and admission to their homes, confessed his grief heartbrokenly to all his friends and acquaintances while continuing to send the young ladies' parents gifts of sour peaches and other raw produce from his garden; he was fond of repeating one and the same anecdote which, despite Polutykin's high opinion of its merits, simply failed to make anyone laugh; he was full of praise for the works of Akim Nakhimov[3] and the story *Pinna*;[4] he had a stammer; he called his dog Astronomer; instead of *however* he used to say *howsoever*, and he introduced in his own house a French cuisine, the secret of which, according to his cook's ideas, consisted in completely altering the natural taste of each dish: in the hands of this culinary master meat turned out to be fish, fish became mushrooms, and macaroni ended up dry as powder; moreover, no carrot would be permitted in a soup that had not first assumed a rhomboidal or trapezoidal shape. But apart from these minor and insignificant failings Polutykin was, as I've said, an excellent fellow.

On the day of our meeting Polutykin invited me to spend the night with him.

'It'll be about five miles to my place,' he added, 'a long way on foot, so let's drop in on Khor first of all.' (The reader will permit me to overlook his stammer.)

'And who is this Khor?'

'One of my peasants. He lives not far from here.'

We set off for his place. Khor's isolated settlement stood amid woodland in a clearing that had been given over to cultivation. It consisted of several frame dwellings of fir linked by fences. An overhanging roof, supported by thin pillars, ran along the front of the main hut. We entered and were met by a tall, handsome young man of about twenty.

'Hello, Fedya! Is Khor at home?' Polutykin asked him.

'No, Khor's gone off to the town,' the young man answered, smiling and displaying a row of snow-white teeth. 'Would you like the cart got ready?'

'Yes, my good fellow, harness the cart. And bring us some *kvas*.'⁵

We entered the hut. No cheap pictures, such as are made in Suzdal, were stuck on the clean, beamed walls; in one corner, before a heavy icon in its silver frame, a small lamp was kept burning; the table, constructed of lime-wood, had recently been scrubbed and wiped clean; and among the beams and the window-frames there were neither scurrying cockroaches nor lurking, contemplative beetles. The young man soon appeared with a large white jug full of good-tasting *kvas*, a large portion of good wheat loaf and a dozen salted cucumbers in a wooden bowl. He placed these refreshments on the table, leaned against the door and proceeded to watch us smilingly as we ate. We had barely finished when the cart drove up to the porch. We went out to find a curly-haired, red-cheeked boy of about fifteen sitting in the driver's seat and restraining with difficulty a frisky, piebald stallion. Around the cart there stood six or so young giants, all very similar to each other and to Fedya.

'They're all Khor's boys,' Polutykin remarked.

'We're the Khor lads,' echoed Fedya, who had followed us out on to the porch, 'and there aren't all of us here – Potap's in the forest and Sidor's gone to the town with the old man. Now watch out, Vasya,' he continued, turning to the young driver, 'remember you're driving the master! See you go quietly over the bumps or you'll smash the carriage and upset the master's stomach!'

The remaining Khor brothers grinned broadly at Fedya's witticism.

'Let Astronomer be seated!' exclaimed Polutykin pompously.

Fedya, not without a show of pleasure, lifted the uneasily smiling dog into the air and deposited it on the floor of the cart. Vasya gave rein to the horses and we set off.

'And that's my office,' Polutykin said suddenly, pointing to a tiny, low-walled house. 'Would you like to see inside?'

'Certainly.'

'It's not used now,' he said, climbing down, 'but it's still worth looking at.'

The office consisted of two empty rooms. The caretaker, a bent old man, ran in from the yard at the back.

'Good day, Minyaich,' said Polutykin, 'and have you any of that water?'

The ancient caretaker made off and at once returned with a bottle and two glasses.

'You try it,' Polutykin said to me. 'It's some of my good spring water.'

We each drank a glassful, while the old man regaled us with low bows to the waist.

'Well, it's time now, it seems, for us to be off,' my new friend remarked. 'In this office I got a good price from the merchant Alliluyev for ten acres of woodland I once sold him.'

We took our seats again in the carriage and in half an hour were entering the forecourt of Polutykin's mansion.

' Tell me, please,' I asked him at dinner, 'why is it that Khor lives apart from your other peasants?'

'He lives apart because he's one of my clever ones. About fifteen years ago his hut burned down and he came to my late father and said: "If you please, Nikolay Kuzmich, allow me to settle on some of the marshland in your forest. I'll pay you a good rent for it." "And what do you want to settle in a marsh for?" "That's my business, sir; all I ask, Nikolay Kuzmich, sir, is that you don't use me for any kind of work, but name whatever rent you think is right." "Fifty roubles a year!" "Thank you, sir." "No falling down on the rent payments, mind you!" "Of course, sir, no falling down. . . ." And so he settled in the marshland. And from that time he's become known as Khor the Polecat.'

'I suppose he's got rich?' I asked.

'He's got rich. He now pays me a hundred silver roubles a year in rent, and I'll probably raise that a bit before long. Many times I've said to him: "Buy yourself off, Khor, buy your freedom!" But he, wily polecat that he is, always assures me he's got nothing to do it with, no money, nothing. He's a sly one!'

On the next day, directly after morning tea, we set off on a hunting expedition. On our way through the village Polutykin ordered the driver to stop at a squat little hut and called out loudly:

'Kalinych!'

'At once, sir, at once!' a voice cried from the yard. 'I'm just doing up my shoe.'

We went on at a walking pace and just beyond the village we were caught up by a man of about forty, of tall, thin build, with a small head bent well back on his shoulders. This was Kalinych. At the very first glance I took a liking to his warm-hearted, ruddy and slightly pock-marked face. Kalinych (as I learned subsequently) was accustomed to go out on a daily hunting trip with his master, would carry his bag, sometimes also his gun, note where a bird had fallen, act as water-carrier, gather wild strawberries, build shelters and run behind the buggy; indeed, without him Polutykin was helpless. Kalinych was a man of the happiest and most amenable disposition. He hummed endless tunes to himself, glancing around him on all sides in a carefree way and talking slightly through his nose, smiling, screwing up his light-blue eyes and giving frequent tugs at his scanty, wedge-shaped beard. He had a habit of walking slowly but with long strides, leaning a little on a long, thin stick. In the course of the day he more than once chatted with me and showed no servility towards me, but he looked after his master like a child. When the intolerable midday heat forced us to seek shelter, he led us into the depths of the wood to the place where he kept bees. Here he invited us into his little hut, adorned with tufts of dry, sweet-scented herbs, prepared fresh hay for us to lie on and then placed a kind of net sacking over his head, picked up a knife, a pot and a lighted brand and went out to his bees to cut out a honeycomb for us. We drank down the warm transparent mead like spring water and fell asleep to the monotone humming of the bees and the leaves' talkative rustling.

I was awakened by a gentle gust of breeze. I opened my eyes and saw Kalinych. He was sitting in the half-open doorway whittling a spoon. For a long while I looked admiringly at his patient face, as unclouded as an evening sky. Polutykin also awoke, but we did not get up at once. After a long walk and a deep sleep it is very enjoyable to lie quietly in the hay while one's body relaxes and dreams, one's face burns with a slight flush and a sweet drowsiness presses on the eyes. Finally we arose and again set off on our wanderings until evening.

Over supper I again turned the conversation to Khor and Kalinych.

'Kalinych is a good man,' Polutykin told me, 'diligent, obliging, a good peasant. Howsoever, he can't keep his holding in proper order because I'm always taking him off with me. He goes hunting with me every day. You can judge for yourself what happens to his holding.'

I agreed with him, and we went to bed.

Next day Polutykin had to go into town on business connected with his neighbour, Pichukov. Pichukov had ploughed up some of Polutykin's land and on this ploughed land he had also administered a beating to one of Polutykin's female serfs. I went out hunting alone and just before evening turned into Khor's place. On the threshold of his hut I was met by an old man – bald, small in stature, thick-set and broad-shouldered; it was Khor himself. The sight of this polecat aroused in me considerable curiosity. The cast of his features reminded me of Socrates: the same high, protuberant forehead, the same small eyes, the same snub nose. Together we entered the hut. Once again Fedya brought me some milk and brown bread. Khor sat down on a bench and, stroking his curly beard with the utmost calmness, proceeded to converse with me. He was evidently a man aware of his standing in the world, for his speech and his movements were of a measured slowness and he gave occasional chuckles through his long whiskers.

We touched on such subjects as the sowing, the harvesting and the life of the peasantry. He seemed to be in agreement with me on most things, but after a while I began to have apprehensions of my own, feeling that I wasn't saying the right thing, since everything I said began to sound so strange. Khor sometimes expressed himself in a rather puzzling fashion out of caution, I assumed. Here is an example of our conversation:

'Listen, Khor,' I was saying to him, 'why don't you buy yourself off from your master?'

'But why should I? Now I know my master and I know the rent I must pay. Our master's a good man.'

'But surely it's better to be free,' I remarked.

Khor gave me a sideways glance.

'That's for sure,' he muttered.

'Then why not buy yourself off?'

Khor gave a little turn of the head.

'What, sir, am I to use to buy myself off with?'

'Surely, old man, you've got . . .'

'If Khor was among free people,' he continued in a low mutter, as though speaking to himself, 'then everyone without a beard would be a bigger fish than Khor.'

'Then cut off your beard.'

'What's a beard good for? It's just like grass, you can cut it if you want to.'

'Well, then?'

'It's like this – Khor'll straightaway find himself among merchants. They live a good life, that's for sure, and they wear beards.'

'Don't you also do some trading?' I asked him.

'We do a wee bit o' trading, a bit of oil here, some tar there. . . . What about it, sir, can I order them to harness up the cart?'

You're one who knows his own mind and keeps a strong rein on his tongue, I said to myself. 'No,' I said out loud. 'I don't need the cart. I'll be going hunting in this region tomorrow and, if you'll allow me, I'd like to spend the night in your barn.'

'With pleasure, sir. Are you sure you'll be all right in the barn? I'll get the women to lay down a sheet for you and a pillow. Hey, women, come along!' he shouted, getting up. 'And you, Fedya, you go along with them. Women are a stupid lot by themselves.'

A quarter of an hour later Fedya showed me the way to the barn with his lantern. I flung myself down into the fragrant hay and my dog curled up at my feet. Fedya wished me good night; the door creaked and banged to behind him. I was unable to go to sleep for a long time. A cow came up to the door and breathed loudly once or twice; the dog gave it a dignified growl; a pig strolled by, grunting in its preoccupied way; a horse somewhere close by began to chew the hay and snort. . . . Finally I fell asleep.

Fedya awoke me at first light. I had grown to like this gay, lively young fellow very much, and so far as I could tell he was also Khor's favourite. They made very good-natured fun of each other. The old man came out to meet me. Whether it was because I had spent the night under his roof, or for some other reason, he treated me now in a much more kindly fashion than on the previous day.

'The samovar's ready for you,' he said with a smile. 'Let's go and have some tea.'

We took our places round the table. A buxom girl, one of his daughters-in-law, brought in a bowl of milk. One by one his sons came into the hut.

'What a fine, grown-up crowd you have!' I remarked to the old man.

'Yes,' he murmured, biting off a tiny piece of sugar, 'it doesn't seem like they've got much complaint to make against me and the old woman.'

'And do they all live with you?'

'They do. That's how they want it.'

'And they're all married?'

'There's one of 'em not married yet,' he answered, indicating Fedya who was as usual leaning against the door. 'Vaska's young yet, and he can wait a bit.'

'What do I want with marriage?' Fedya protested. 'I'm all right as I am. What good's a wife? To have howling matches with, eh?'

'There you go again . . . I know what you're up to! You've got those silver rings on your fingers and you're all the time sniffing round the girls out in the yard. "Give over, you ought to be ashamed!"' the old man continued, mimicking the servant girls. 'I know your sort, you'll never do a hand's turn you won't!'

'What good is there in a woman, I ask you?'

'A woman is a worker about the house,' Khor remarked importantly. 'A woman looks after a man.'

'And why do I need a worker about the house?'

'You're one for having other people pull the chestnuts out of the fire, that's why. I know your sort.'

'If that's so, then marry me off, eh? Come on now, say something!'

'Enough now, enough! You're a joker, you are. Just look how we're upsetting our guest. I'll marry you off, never you worry . . . Now, sir, please don't be annoyed: as you can see, he's just a child and he hasn't had time to pick up a lot of sense yet.'

Fedya just shook his head.

'Is Khor at home?' a familiar voice called from beyond the door, and Kalinych entered the hut carrying a bunch of wild strawberries which he had collected for his friend, Khor the polecat. The old man greeted him warmly. I looked at Kalinych in astonishment because I confess I had not expected such 'niceties' from a peasant.

That day I went out hunting four hours later than usual, and I spent the next three days at Khor's place. I became pre-occupied with my new acquaintances. I don't know how I had won their confidence, but they talked to me without any constraint. It was with pleasure that I listened to them and watched them. The two friends were not a bit like each other. Khor was an emphatic sort of man, practical, an administrator, hard-headed; Kalinych, on the other hand, belonged in the company of idealists, romantics, men of lofty enthusiasms and lofty dreams. Khor understood the realities of life – that is to say, he had built a home for himself, saved up some money, arranged things satisfactorily with his master and other responsible authorities; whereas Kalinych walked about in bast sandals and got by somehow or other. Khor had raised a large, obedient and united family; whereas Kalinych had at one time had a wife, of whom he was terrified, and no children. Khor could see through my friend Polutykin; whereas Kalinych simply worshipped his master. Khor loved Kalinych and would always give him protection; Kalinych loved and respected Khor. Khor spoke little, gave only occasional chuckles and kept his thoughts to himself; whereas Kalinych would express himself heatedly, although he never sang like a nightingale as the lively factory man is liable to. . . . But he possessed certain innate talents which Khor himself was willing to recognize; he could charm away bleeding, terror and rages, and he could cure worms; bees obeyed him because of his light touch. While I was there Khor asked him to lead a newly purchased horse into the stables, and Kalinych fulfilled the old sceptic's request conscientiously and with pride. Kalinych was closer to nature, whereas Khor was closer to people and society; Kalinych never liked thinking things out for himself and believed everything blindly, whereas Khor had reached a high pitch of irony in his attitude to life. He had seen much, knew much, and I learned a lot from him.

For instance, from the stories he had to tell I learned that each summer, before the harvesting, a small cart of a particular kind appears in the villages. A man in a caftan sits in the cart and sells scythes. If the payment is in cash, he asks a rouble and twenty-five copecks in silver coinage or a rouble and fifty copecks in paper money; if it's to be on credit, he asks three paper roubles and one silver rouble. All the peasants, of course, buy on credit. Two or three weeks later he reappears and demands his money. By this time the peasant has just harvested his oats and has the necessary with which to pay. He accompanies the trader to a tavern and there they complete their business. Some of the landowners took it into their heads to buy their own scythes for cash and distribute them on credit to their peasants for the same price. But the peasants seemed dissatisfied with this, and even succumbed to melancholy over it; they were deprived of the pleasure of giving each scythe a twanging flick, of putting their ear to it and turning it about in their hands and asking the rascally salesman twenty times over: 'Well, now, that's a bit of a wrong'un, isn't it?'

Much the same sort of trickery occurs during the buying of sickles with the sole difference that in this case the women also become involved and sometimes force the trader to give them restraining slaps for their own good. But the womenfolk suffer most grievously of all in the following instance. Those responsible for supplying material to the paper factories entrust the buying of rags to a particular species of person, known in certain districts as 'eagles'. Such an 'eagle' is given two hundred paper roubles by a merchant and then sets out to find his prey. But, in contrast to the noble bird after which he is named, he does not fall boldly and openly upon his victim; on the contrary, this 'eagle' uses cunning, underhand means. He leaves his cart somewhere in the bushes on the outskirts of the village and then, just as if he were some casual passer-by or bum on the loose, makes his way through the back alleys and backyards of the huts. The women can sense his approach and creep out to meet him. The business between them is quickly completed. For a few copper coins a woman will hand over to the 'eagle' not only the meanest cast-off rag but frequently even her husband's shirt and her own day skirt. Recently the womenfolk have found it worth while to steal from each other and to unload their ill-gotten hemp or homemade sacking on the 'eagles' – an important augmentation and consummation of their business! The peasants, for their part, have pricked up their ears and at the least sign, at the merest hint of the approach of an 'eagle', they resort briskly and vigorously to remedial and preventive measures. In fact, it's downright insulting, isn't it? It's their business to sell the hemp, and they do indeed sell it, though not in the town – they would have to drag themselves to the town for that – but to itinerant traders who, for want of a proper measure, consider that forty handfuls are equal to thirty-six pounds in weight – and you know the size a

Russian can give to his handful or his palm when he's in real earnest!

I, inexperienced as I am and not a 'countryman' (as we say in the Oryol district), had had my fill of such stories. But Khor did not do all the talking; he also asked me a great deal. He knew that I had been abroad, and his curiosity was aroused. Kalinych betrayed no less interest, but he was chiefly affected by descriptions of natural scenery, mountains, waterfalls, unusual buildings and large cities. Khor was concerned with questions of administration and government. He took things one at a time: 'Are things there like they are here, or not the same? Well, sir, what's you got to say about that?' Whereas during the course of my recital Kalinych would exclaim – 'Ah, dear lord, Thy will be done!' Khor would be quiet, knitting his thick brows and only occasionally remarking: 'That wouldn't likely be the thing for us, but t'other – that's the proper way, that's good.' I cannot convey all his queries, and, besides, there's no need. But from our talks I derived one conviction which my readers probably cannot have expected – the conviction that Peter the Great was predominantly Russian in his national characteristics and Russian specifically in his reforms. A Russian is so sure of his strength and robustness that he is not averse to overtaxing himself: he is little concerned with his past and looks boldly towards the future. If a thing's good, he'll like it; if a thing's sensible, he'll not reject it, but he couldn't care a jot where it came from. His sane common sense will gladly make fun of the thin-as-a-stick rationalism of the Germans; but the Germans, in Khor's words, were interesting enough folk and he was ready to learn from them. Owing to the peculiar nature of his social station, his virtual independence, Khor mentioned many things in talking with me that even a crow-bar wouldn't have dislodged in someone else or, as the peasants say, you couldn't grind out with a millstone. He took a realistic view of his position. During my talks with Khor I heard for the first time the simple, intelligent speech of the Russian peasant. His knowledge was fairly broad, after his own fashion, but he could not read; whereas Kalinych could.

'That rascal's been able to pick up readin' and writin',' Khor remarked, 'an' 'e's never had a single bee die on 'im since he was born.'

'And have your children learned to read and write?'

After a pause Khor said: 'Fedya knows.'

'And the others?'

'The others don't.'

'Why not?'

The old man did not answer and changed the subject. As a matter of fact, despite all his intelligence, he clung to many prejudices and preconceived notions. Women, for example, he despised from the depths of his soul, and when in a jovial mood derived amusement from them and made fun of them. His wife, an aged and shrewish woman, spent the whole day over the stove and was the source of persistent complaints and abuse; her sons paid no attention to her, but she put the fear of God into her daughters-in-law. It's not surprising that in the Russian song the mother-in-law sings:

> O, you're no son o' mine,
> You're not a family man!
> 'Cos you don't beat your wife,
> You don't beat your young one . . .

Once I thought of standing up for the daughters-in-law and attempted to solicit Khor's sympathy; but he calmly retorted that 'Maybe you like to bother yourself with such nonsense. . . . Let the women quarrel. . . . You'll only be worse off if you try to part them, and it isn't even worth dirtying your hands with it.' Sometimes the bad-tempered old woman crawled down from the stove and called in the dog from the yard, enticing it with: 'Come on, come on, nice dog!' – only to belabour its scraggy spine with a poker, or she would stand under the awning out front and 'bark insults' at whoever passed by, as Khor expressed it. Her husband, however, she feared and, at his command, would climb back on to her perch on the stove.

But it was particularly curious to hear how Kalinych and Khor disagreed when talking about Polutykin. 'Now, look here, Khor, don't you say anything against him while I'm here,' Kalinych would say. 'Then why doesn't he see that you've got a proper pair of boots to wear?' the other would object. 'To hell with boots! Why do I need boots? I'm a peasant....' 'And I'm also a peasant, but just look...' Saying this, Khor would raise his leg and show Kalinych a boot that looked as if it had been cobbled from the skin of a mammoth. 'Oh, you're not an ordinary peasant!' Kalinych would answer. 'Well, surely he ought to give you something to buy them sandals with? After all, you go out hunting with him and every day you'll need new ones.' 'He gives me something to get bast sandals with.' 'That's right, last year he grandly gave you ten copecks.' At this Kalinych would turn away in annoyance and Khor would burst out laughing, his tiny little eyes almost vanishing completely.

Kalinych had quite a pleasant singing voice and could strum a little on the balalaika. Khor would listen and listen, and then he would bend his head to one side and begin to accompany in a plaintive voice. He particularly liked the song: 'O, mine's a hard lot, a hard life!'

Fedya never let pass an opportunity to poke fun at his father, saying, 'Well, old man, what've you got to complain about?'

But Khor would rest his cheek on his hand, close his eyes and continue complaining about his hard lot. Yet at other times no one was more active than he: he would always be busying himself with something – repairing the cart, making new fence supports or taking a look at the harness. He did not, however, insist on exceptional cleanliness, and in answer to my comments once remarked that 'a hut ought to have a lived-in smell'.

'But,' I remarked in return, 'look how clean it is out at Kalinych's where he keeps bees.'

'Bees wouldn't live there, see, sir, unless it was clean,' he said with a sigh.

On another occasion he asked me:

'Do you have your own estate, sir?'

'I do.'

'Is it far from here?'

'Sixty or seventy miles.'

'Well, sir, do you live on your estate?'

'I do.'

'But mostly, I reckon, you're out enjoying yourself with that gun?'

'Yes, I must admit that.'

'And that's a good thing you're doing, sir. Shoot them black grouse as much as you like, but be sure and see you change your bailiff often.'

On the evening of the fourth day Polutykin sent for me. I was sorry to have to say good-bye to the old man. Together with Kalinych I took my place in the cart.

'Well, good-bye, Khor, and keep well,' I said. 'Good-bye, Fedya.'

'Good-bye, sir, good-bye, and don't forget us.'

We drove off. Dawn had just set fire to the sky.

'It's going to be beautiful weather tomorrow,' I said, looking at the bright sky.

'No, there'll be rain,' Kalinych contradicted. 'Look how the ducks are splashing about, and the grass has got a strong smell.'

We drove through bushy undergrowth. Kalinych began to sing in a low voice, bouncing up and down on the driver's seat and gazing all the while at the dawn.

The next day I was gone from under Polutykin's hospitable roof.

Yermolay and the Miller's Wife

IN the evening the hunter Yermolay and I set off for 'cover'.
But perhaps not all my readers know what 'cover' means.
Pray listen, gentlemen.

In the springtime, a quarter of an hour before sundown, you
go into a wood with your gun but without your dog. You
seek out a place for yourself somewhere close by a thicket,
look around you, inspect the firing mechanism on your gun
and exchange winks with your companion. A quarter of an
hour passes. The sun sinks below the horizon, but it is still
light in the wood; the air is fresh and translucent; there is the
spirited chatter of birds; the young grass glows with a happy
emerald brilliance. You wait. The interior of the wood
gradually darkens; the crimson rays of an evening sunset
slowly slide across the roots and trunks of the trees, rise higher
and higher, moving from the lower, still almost bare,
branches to the motionless tips of the sleep-enfolded trees.
Then the very tips grow faint; the pink sky becomes a dark
blue. The woodland scent increases, accompanied by slight
wafts of a warm dampness; the breeze that has flown into the
wood around you begins to die down. The birds fall asleep –
not all at once, but by types: first the finches fall silent, a few
instants later the robins, after them the yellow buntings. The
wood grows darker and darker. The trees fuse into large
blackening masses; the first small stars emerge diffidently in
the blue sky. The birds are all asleep. Only the redstarts and
little woodpeckers continue to make an occasional sleepy
whistling. . . . Then they are quiet as well. Once again the
ringing voice of the chiff-chaff resounds overhead; somewhere
or other an oriole gives a sad cry and a nightingale offers the
first trills of its song. Your heart is heavy with anticipation,

and suddenly – but only hunters will know what I mean – suddenly the deep quiet is broken by a special kind of croaking and hissing, there is a measured beat of rapidly flapping wings – and a woodcock, beautifully inclining its long beak, flies out from behind a dark birch into your line of fire.

That is what is meant by 'standing in cover'.

In such a fashion Yermolay and I set off for 'cover'; but forgive me, gentlemen: I must first of all acquaint you with Yermolay.

Imagine to yourself a man of about forty-five, tall and lean, with a long delicate nose, a narrow forehead, little grey eyes, dishevelled hair and wide, scornful lips. This man used to go about winter and summer in a yellowish nankeen coat of German cut, but belted with a sash; he wore wide blue trousers and a cap edged with astrakhan which had been given him, on a jovial occasion, by a bankrupt landowner. Two bags were fixed to the sash, one in front, which had been artfully twisted into two halves for powder and bird-shot, and the other behind – for game; his cotton wadding Yermolay used to extract from his own, seemingly inexhaustible cap. With the money earned by him from selling his game he could easily have purchased a cartridge belt and pouch, but the thought of making such a purchase never even so much as entered his head and he continued to load his gun in his customary fashion, arousing astonishment in onlookers by the skill with which he avoided the danger of overpouring or mixing the shot and the powder. His gun had a single barrel, with a flintlock, endowed, moreover, with the awful habit of 'kicking' brutally, as a result of which Yermolay's right cheek was always more swollen than his left. How he managed to hit anything with this gun even a wiseacre might be at a loss to explain, but hit he did.

He also had a setter, a most remarkable creature named Valetka. Yermolay never fed him. 'Likely I'd start feeding a

36

dog,' he would argue, 'since a dog's a clever animal and'll find his food on his own.' And so it was, in fact: although Valetka astonished even indifferent passers-by with his unusual thinness, he lived and lived a long time; despite his miserable condition, he never even once got lost and displayed no desire to abandon his master. Once, when he was young, he disappeared for a day or two, carried away by love; but that foolishness soon took leave of him. Valetka's most remarkable characteristic was an incomprehensible indifference to everything under the sun. If I had not been talking about a dog, I would have used the word 'disillusionment'. He usually sat with his short tail tucked underneath him, frowning, shuddering from time to time and never smiling. (It is well known that dogs are capable of smiling, and even of smiling very charmingly.) He was extremely ugly, and there was not a single idle house-serf who let pass an opportunity of laughing venomously at his appearance; but Valetka endured all these taunts, and even blows, with astonishing composure. He provided particular satisfaction for cooks, who immediately dropped whatever they were doing and dashed after him with shouts and swearing whenever, through a weakness common not only to dogs, he used to stick his famished muzzle through the half-open door of the enticingly warm and sweet-smelling kitchen. Out hunting, he distinguished himself by his tirelessness and possessed a good scent; but if he happened to catch up with a wounded hare, he at once gobbled the whole lot down with pleasure, right to the last little bone, in some cool, shady place under a leafy bush and at a respectful distance from Yermolay who swore at him in any and every dialect, known and unknown.

Yermolay belonged to one of my neighbours, a landowner of the old school. Landowners of the old school dislike 'wildfowl' and stick to domestic poultry. It is only on unusual occasions, such as birthdays, name-days and elections, that the cooks of old-time landowners embark on preparing

long-beaked birds and, succumbing to a high state of excitement, as do all Russians when they have no clear idea of what
they are doing, they invent such fancy accompaniments for
the birds that guests for the most part study the dishes set in
front of them with attentiveness and curiosity, but can in no
wise resolve to taste them. Yermolay was under orders to
supply the master's kitchen once a month with a couple of
brace of grouse and partridge, but he was otherwise permitted
to live where and how he wanted. He had been rejected as a
man unfit for any kind of real work – a 'no-good', as we say
in the Oryol region. Naturally, he was given no powder and
shot, following precisely the same principles as he adopted in
not feeding his dog. Yermolay was a man of the most unusual
kind: free and easy as a bird, garrulous to a fair extent, to all
appearances scatter-brained and awkward; he had a strong
liking for drink, could never settle in one place, when on the
move he ambled and swayed from side to side – and, ambling
and swaying, he would polish off between thirty and forty
miles a day. He had been involved in a most extraordinary
variety of adventures, spending nights in marshes, up trees, on
roofs, beneath bridges, more than once under lock and key in
attics, cellars and barns, relieved of his gun, his dog, his most
essential clothing, receiving forceful and prolonged beatings –
and yet after a short time he would return home clothed, with
his gun and with his dog. One could not call him a happy
man, although he was almost always in a reasonably good
humour; generally, he looked a trifle eccentric.

Yermolay enjoyed passing the time of day with any con-
genial character, especially over a drink, but never for very
long: he would soon get up and be on his way. 'And where
are you off to, you devil? It's night outside.' 'I'm for Chaplino.' 'What's the good of you traipsin' off to Chaplino,
more'n seven miles away?' 'I'm for spending the night there
with the peasant Sofron.' 'Spend the night here.' 'No, that's
impossible.' And Yermolay would be off with his Valetka

into the dark night, through bushes and ditches, and the peasant Sofron would most likely not let him into his yard – what's more, might bash him one on the neck 'for being such a disturbance to honest folk'.

Yet no one could compare with Yermolay in skill at catching fish in the springtime flood-water or in grabbing crayfish with his bare hands, in scenting out game, luring quail, training hawks, capturing nightingales with 'woodsprite pipe' song or 'cuckoo's fly-by'.* Of one thing he was incapable: training dogs. He lacked the patience for it.

He also had a wife. He would visit her once a week. She lived in a scrappy, partly collapsed little hut, managed somehow or other, never knew from one day to the next whether she would have enough to eat and, in general, endured a bitter fate. Yermolay, that carefree and good-natured fellow, treated her roughly and coarsely, assumed a threatening and severe air in his own home – and his poor wife had no idea of how to indulge him, shuddered at his glance, bought drink for him with her last copeck and dutifully covered him with her own sheepskin coat when he, collapsing majestically on the stove, fell into a Herculean sleep. I myself had occasion more than once to notice in him involuntary signs of a certain morose ferocity. I disliked the expression on his face when he used to kill a winged bird by biting into it. But Yermolay never remained at home longer than a day: and once outside his home territory he again turned into 'Yermolka', as he was known by nickname for a good sixty odd miles around and as he used to call himself on occasion. The meanest house-serf felt himself superior to this tramp – and perhaps precisely for this reason always treated him in a friendly fashion; while peasants at first took pleasure in driving him away and trapping him like a hare in the field, but later they

* These terms are familiar to nightingale lovers: they denote the best 'figures' in a nightingale's singing.

let him go with a blessing and, once they were acquainted with this eccentric fellow, kept their hands off him, even giving him bread and striking up a conversation with him. . . . This was the fellow I chose as my hunting companion, and it was with him that I set off for 'cover' in a large birch wood on the bank of the Ista.

Many Russian rivers, after the pattern of the Volga, have one hilly bank and the other of meadowland; the Ista also. This small river winds in an exceedingly capricious fashion, crawling like a snake, never flowing straight for five hundred yards at a time, and in certain places, from the top of a steep hill, one can see six or seven miles of dams, ponds, watermills and kitchen gardens surrounded by willows and flocks of geese. There is a multitude of fish in the Ista, especially bullyheads (in hot weather peasants lift them out by hand from beneath the overhanging bushes). Little sandpipers whistle and flit to and fro along the stony banks which are dotted with outlets for cold, sparkling spring water; wild ducks swim out into the centre of ponds and look guardedly about them; herons stand up stiffly in the shade, in the inlets and below the river's steep sides.

We stood in cover for about an hour, shot a couple of brace of woodcock and, wishing to try our luck again before sunrise (one can go out for cover in the morning as well), decided to spend the night at the nearest mill. We made our way out of the wood and went down the hill. The river was rolling along, its surface dark-blue waves; the air thickened under the pressure of the night-time moisture. We knocked at the mill gates. Dogs began to yelp in the yard.

'Who's there?' called a husky and sleepy voice.

'Hunters. Let us in for the night.'

There was no answer.

'We'll pay.'

'I'll go and tell the master. . . . Aw, damn you dogs! Nothing awful's happenin' to you!'

We heard the workman enter the hut; soon he returned to the gates.

'No, the master says, he won't give orders to let you in.'

'Why won't he?'

'He's frightened. You're hunters – soon as you're in here you'll likely set fire to the mill. Just look at them firing-pieces you got there!'

'What nonsense!'

'The year afore last this mill of ours burned down. Cattle-dealers spent the night here and some way or another, you know, they set fire to it.'

'Anyway, friend, we're not spending the night outside!'

'Spend it anyway you know. . . .' He went off with a clattering of boots.

Yermolay dispatched after him a variety of unpleasant expressions. 'Let's go into the village,' he said, finally, with a sigh. But it was more than a mile to the village.

'We'll spend the night here,' I said. 'It's warm outside, and the miller'll let us have some straw if we pay him.'

Yermolay tacitly agreed. We began knocking on the gates again.

'What d'you need now?' the workman's voice called again. 'I've told you – you can't come in.'

We explained to him what we wanted. He went off to consult his master and came back with him. The wicket-gate creaked. The miller appeared, a tall man with a plump face, bull-necked, and large and round of stomach. He agreed to my suggestion.

A hundred paces from the mill stood a structure with a roof, but open on all four sides. Straw and hay were brought out to us there; the workman set up a samovar on the grass beside the river and, squatting on his haunches, began blowing busily up the samovar's chimney. The charcoal flared up and brightly illumined his youthful face. The miller ran off to waken his wife and eventually proposed that I should spend the night in the hut; but I preferred to remain out in the open air. The miller's wife brought us some milk, eggs, potatoes and bread. Soon the samovar was bubbling and we set about having some tea. It was windless and mists were rising from the river; corncrakes were crying in the vicinity; from the direction of the mill-wheels came such faint noises as the drip-drip of water from the paddles and the seepage of water through the cross-beams of the dam. We built a small fire. While Yermolay baked potatoes in the ashes, I managed to doze off.

A light-voiced, suppressed whispering awoke me. I raised my head: before the fire, on an upturned tub, the miller's wife was sitting and conversing with my hunting companion. Earlier I had recognized, by her dress, movements and way of speaking, that she was a former house-serf – not from among the peasantry or the bourgeoisie; but it was only now that I could take a good look at her features. She appeared to be about thirty; her thin, pale face still contained traces of a remarkable beauty; I was particularly taken by her eyes, so large and melancholy. She leaned her elbows on her knees and placed her face in her hands. Yermolay sat with his back to me and was engaged in laying sticks on the fire.

'There's sickness again among the cattle in Zheltukhina,' the miller's wife was saying. 'Both of father Ivan's cows have died . . . Lord have mercy on us!'

'And what about your pigs?' asked Yermolay after a short silence.

'They're alive.'

'You ought to give me a little porker, you ought.'

The miller's wife said nothing and after a while gave a sigh.

'Who are you with?' she asked.

'With the squire – the Kostomarov squire.'

Yermolay threw a few fir fronds on the fire; at once they broke into a universal crackling and thick white smoke poured straight into his face.

'Why didn't your husband let us into the hut?'

'He was frightened.'

'There's a fat old pot-belly for you . . . Arina Timofeyevna, be a dear and bring me a wee glass of some of the good stuff!'

The miller's wife rose and disappeared into the gloom. Yermolay began singing softly:

> A-walking to my sweetheart
> Wore the shoes off of my feet . . .

Arina returned with a small carafe and a glass. Yermolay straightened up, crossed himself and gulped down the drink at one go. 'That's lovely!' he added.

The miller's wife again seated herself on the tub.

'So, Arina Timofeyevna, tell me, are you still feeling poorly?'

'I'm still poorly.'

'How so?'

'The coughing at night hurts me so.'

'It seems the master's gone to sleep,' said Yermolay after a brief silence. 'Don't you go to no doctor, Arina, or it'll get worse.'

'I won't be going in any case.'

'You come and be my guest.'

Arina lowered her head.

'I'll drive my own – my wife, that's to say – I'll drive her away for that occasion,' Yermolay continued. 'Sure an' all I will!'

'You'd do better to wake up your master, Yermolay Petrovich. See, the potatoes are done.'

'Let him go on snoozing,' my faithful servant remarked with indifference. 'He's run about so much it's right he should sleep.'

I turned over in the hay. Yermolay rose and approached me.

'Come and eat, sir – the potatoes are ready.'

I emerged from beneath my roofed structure and the

miller's wife got up from her place on the tub, wishing to leave us. I started talking to her.

'Have you been at this mill long?'

'Two years come Whitsun.'

'And where is your husband from?'

Arina did not catch the drift of my question.

'Whereabouts is your husband from?' Yermolay repeated, raising his voice.

'From Belev. He's a townsman from Belev.'

'And you're also from Belev?'

'No, I'm a serf . . . I was one, that is.'

'Whose?'

'Mr Zverkov's. Now I'm free.'

'What Zverkov?'

'Alexander Silych.'

'Were you by any chance his wife's chambermaid?'

'How d'you know that? Yes, I was.'

I looked now with renewed curiosity and sympathy at Arina.

'I know your master,' I continued.

'You do?' she answered softly, and lowered her eyes.

It is fitting that I should tell the reader why I looked at Arina with such sympathy. During my period of residence in St Petersburg I happened to become acquainted with Mr Zverkov. He occupied a fairly important position and passed as a capable and well-informed man. He had a wife, plump, emotional, given to floods of tears and bad temper – a vulgar and burdensome creature; there was also a runt of a son, a real little milord, spoiled and witless. Mr Zverkov's own appearance did little in his favour: out of a broad, almost square face, mousey little eyes peered cunningly and his nose protruded, large and sharp, with wide-open nostrils; grey close-cropped hair rose in bristles above his wrinkled fore-head and his thin lips were ceaselessly quivering and shaping themselves into sickly smiles. Mr Zverkov's habitual stance was with his little legs set wide apart and his fat little hands thrust in his pockets. On one occasion it somehow came about that I shared a carriage with him on a trip out of town. We struck up a conversation. As a man of experience and business acumen, Mr Zverkov began to instruct me concerning 'the path of truth'.

'Permit me to remark to you,' he squeaked eventually, 'that all of you, you young people, judge and explain every single matter in a random fashion; you know little about your own country; Russia, my good sirs, is a closed book to you, that's what! All you read are German books. For example, you've just been saying this and that to me on this question of – well, that's to say, on this question of house-serfs. . . . Fine, I don't dispute it, that's all very fine; but you don't know them, you don't know what sort of people they are.'

Mr Zverkov loudly blew his nose and took a pinch of snuff.

'Permit me to tell, for example, one little tiny anecdote, which could be of interest to you.' Mr Zverkov cleared his throat with a cough. 'You certainly know what kind of a wife I have; it would seem hard to find anyone kinder than her, you will yourself agree. Her chambermaids don't just have food and lodging, but a veritable paradise on earth is created before their very eyes. . . . But my wife has laid down a rule for herself: that she will not employ married chambermaids. That sort of thing just will not do. Children come along and so on – well, a chambermaid in that case can't look after her mistress as she should, can't see to all her habits: she's not up to it, she's got something else on her mind. You must judge such things according to human nature.

'Well, sir, one day we were driving through our village, it'd be about – how can I say exactly? – about fifteen years ago. We saw that the elder had a little girl, a daughter, extremely pretty; there was even something, you know, deferential in her manner. My wife says to me: "Coco . . ." You understand me, that's what she – er – calls me ". . . we'll

45

take this little girl to St Petersburg; I like her, Coco . . ." "Take her with pleasure," I say. The elder, naturally, falls at our feet; such happiness, you understand, has been too much for him to expect. . . . Well, of course, the girl burst into tears like an idiot. It really is awful for them to start with – I mean, leaving the house where they were born; but there's nothing to be surprised at in that. Soon, however, she had grown used to us. To start with she was put in the maids' room, where they taught her what to do, of course. And what d'you think? The girl made astonishing progress; my wife simply fawned on her, and finally, passing over others, promoted her to be one of her own chambermaids. Take note of that! And one has to do her justice: my wife never had such a chambermaid, absolutely never had one like her: helpful, modest, obedient – simply everything one could ask for. As a result, I must admit, my wife even took to spoiling her a bit too much: dressed her superbly, gave her the same food as she had, gave her tea to drink – well, you just can't imagine how it was!

'So she spent about ten years in my wife's service. Suddenly, one fine morning, just think of it, Arine – Arina was her name – came unannounced into my study and flopped down at my feet. I will tell you frankly that I can't abide that sort of thing. A man should never forget his dignity, isn't that true? "What's it you want?" "Good master, Alexander Silych, I beg your indulgence." "In what?" "Allow me to get married." I confess to you I was astonished. "Don't you know, you silly girl, that the mistress hasn't got another chambermaid?" "I'll go on serving the mistress as I have done." "Nonsense! Nonsense! the mistress does not employ married chambermaids." "Malanya can take my place." "I beg you to keep your ideas to yourself." "As you wish . . ."

'I confess I was simply stunned. I will let you know that I'm the sort of man who finds nothing so insulting – I dare say even strongly insulting – as ingratitude. There's no need for me to tell you – you already know what my wife is: an angel in the very flesh, inexplicably good-natured. The blackest scoundrel, it seems, would take pity on her. I sent Arina away. I thought she'd probably come to her senses; I'm not one, you know, who likes to believe in man's black ingratitude and evil nature. Then what d'you think? Six months later she again honours me with a visit and makes the very same request. This time, I admit, I drove her away in real earnest and gave her due warning and promised to tell my wife. I was flabbergasted. . . . But imagine my astonishment when a short while later my wife came to me in tears and in such an excited state that I was even alarmed for her. "What on earth's happened?" "It's Arina . . ." You'll appreciate that I'm ashamed to say it out loud. "It simply can't be! Who was it?" "The lackey Petrushka."

'I exploded. I'm that sort of man – I just don't like half-measures! Petrushka wasn't to blame. He could be punished, but he wasn't to blame, in my opinion. Arina . . . well, what, well, I mean, what need to say anything more? It goes without saying that I at once ordered her hair to be cut off, had her dressed in her shabbiest clothes and packed off to the country. My wife was deprived of an excellent chambermaid, but I had no choice: one just cannot tolerate bad behaviour in one's own house. Better that a rotten limb should be cut off at once. . . . Well, now you judge for yourself – well, I mean, you know my wife, she's, she's, she's – she's an angel, when all's said and done! After all, she was attached to Arina – and Arina knew that and yet behaved shamelessly. . . . Eh? No, say what you like – eh? There's no point in discussing it! In any case, I had no choice. The ingratitude of this girl annoyed and hurt me personally – yes, me, myself – for a long time. I don't care what you say, but you'll not find any heart, any feeling, in these people! No matter how much you feed a wolf, it's still got its heart set on the forest. . . . Science to the fore! But I simply wanted to demonstrate to you. . . .'

And Mr Zverkov, without finishing, turned his head away and buried himself more snugly in his coat, manfully suppressing an unwanted agitation.

The reader no doubt understands now why I looked at Arina with sympathy.

'Have you been married long to the miller?' I asked her at last.

'Two years.'

'Do you mean that your master actually allowed you?'

'Someone bought me off.'

'Who?'

'Savely Alekseyevich.'

'Who's he?'

'My husband.' (Yermolay smiled to himself.)

'But did my master talk to you about me?' Arina added after a short pause.

I had no idea how to answer her question.

'Arina!' the miller shouted from a distance. She rose and walked away.

'Is her husband a good man?' I asked Yermolay.

'Not bad.'

'Do they have any children?'

'There was one, but it died.'

'The miller must've liked her, didn't he? Did he give a lot of money to buy her off?'

'I don't know. She knows how to read and write. In their business that's worth . . . that's a good thing. Reckon he must've liked her.'

'Have you known her long?'

'A good while. Formerly I used to go to her master's. Their estate's round about these parts.'

'And did you know the lackey Petrushka?'

'Pyotr Vasilyevich? Sure I did.'

'Where is he now?'

'Went off to be a soldier.'

48

We fell silent.

'It seems she's not well, is that so?' I asked Yermolay finally.

'Some health she has! . . . Tomorrow, you'll see, they'll be flying well from cover. It'd be a good idea for you to get some sleep now.'

A flock of wild ducks raced whistling over our heads and we heard them alight on the river not far away. It was already quite dark and beginning to grow cold; in the wood a nightingale was resonantly pouring out its song. We burrowed down in the hay and went to sleep.

Bezhin Lea

I T was a beautiful July day, one of those days which occur only when the weather has been unchanged for a long time. From early morning the sky is clear and the sunrise does not so much flare up like a fire as spread like a mild pinkness. The sun – not fiery, not molten, as it is during a period of torrid drought, not murkily crimson as it is before a storm, but bright and invitingly radiant – peacefully drifts up beneath a long, thin cloud, sends fresh gleams through it and is immersed in its lilac haze. The delicate upper edge of the long line of cloud erupts in snakey glints of light: their gleam resembles the gleam of beaten silver. But then again the playful rays break out – and as if taking wing the mighty sun rises gaily and magnificently. About midday a mass of high round clouds appear, golden-grey, with soft white edges. They move hardly at all, like islands cast down on the infinite expanses of a flooding river which flows round them in deeply pellucid streams of level blue; away towards the horizon they cluster together and merge so that there is no blue sky to be seen between them; but they have themselves become as azure-coloured as the sky and are pervaded through and through with light and warmth. The light, pale-lilac colour of the heavens remains the same throughout the day and in all parts of the sky; there is no darkening anywhere, no thickening as for a storm, though here and there pale-blue columns may stretch downwards, bringing a hardly noticeable sprinkling of rain. Towards evening these clouds disappear. The last of them, darkling and vague as smoke, lie down in rosy mistiness before the sinking sun. At the point where the sun has set just as calmly as it rose into the sky, a crimson glow lingers for a short time over the darkened earth, and, softly winking, the evening star burns upon the glow like a carefully carried candle. On such days all the colours are softened; they are bright without being gaudy; everything bears the mark of some poignant timidity. On such days the heat is sometimes very strong and occasionally even 'simmers' along the slopes of the fields. But the wind drives away and disperses the accumulated heat, and whirling dust storms – a sure sign of settled weather – travel in tall white columns along roads through the ploughland. The dry pure air is scented with wormwood, harvested rye and buckwheat. Even an hour before nightfall you can feel no dampness. It is just such weather that the farmer wants for harvesting his grain.

It was on precisely such a day that I once went out grouse-shooting in Chernsk county in the province of Tula. I found, and bagged, a fair number of birds. My full game-pouch cut mercilessly at my shoulder. But I did not finally decide to make my way home until the evening glow had already died away and chill shadows began to thicken and proliferate in air that was still bright, though no longer illumined by the rays of the sunset. With brisk steps I crossed a long 'plaza' of bushy undergrowth, clambered up a hillock and, instead of the expected familiar moor with a little oak wood to the right of it and a low-walled white church in the distance, I saw completely different places which were unknown to me. At my feet there stretched a narrow valley; directly ahead of me rose, like a steep wall, a dense aspen wood. I stopped in bewilderment and looked around. 'Ah-ha!' I thought. 'I'm certainly not where I should be: I've swerved too much to the right' – and, surprised at my mistake, I quickly descended from the hillock. I was at once surrounded by an unpleasant, motionless damp, just as if I had entered a cellar. The tall, thick grass on the floor of the valley was all wet and shone white like a smooth tablecloth; it felt clammy and horrible to walk through. As quickly as possible I scrambled across to the other side and, keeping to the left, made my way along beside the aspen wood. Bats already flitted above its sleeping treetops, mysteriously circling and quivering against the dull paleness of the sky; a young hawk, out late, flew by high up, taking a direct, keen course in hurrying back to its nest. 'Now then, as soon as I reach that corner,' I said to myself, 'that's where the road'll be so what I've done is to make a detour of about three-quarters of a mile!'

I made my way finally to the corner of the wood, but there was no road there, only some low, unkempt bushes spread out widely in front of me and beyond them, in the far distance, an expanse of deserted field. Again I stopped. 'What's all this about? Where am I?' I tried to recall where I had been during the day. 'Ah, these must be the Parakhin bushes!' I exclaimed eventually. 'That's it! And that must be the Sindeyev wood. . . . How on earth did I get as far as this? It's very odd! Now I must go to the right again.'

I turned to the right, through the bushes. Meanwhile, night was approaching and rose around me like a thunder cloud; it was as if, in company with the evening mists, darkness rose on every side and even poured down from the sky. I discovered a rough, overgrown track and followed it, carefully peering ahead of me. Everything quickly grew silent and dark; only quail gave occasional cries. A small night bird, which hurried low and soundlessly along on its soft wings, almost collided with me and plunged off in terror. I emerged from the bushes and wandered along the boundary of a field. It was only with difficulty that I could make out distant objects. All around me the field glimmered faintly; beyond it, coming closer each moment, the sullen murk loomed in huge clouds. My footsteps sounded muffled in the thickening air. The sky which had earlier grown pale once again began to shine blue, but it was the blue of the night. Tiny stars began to flicker and shimmer.

What I thought was a wood had turned out to be a dark, round knoll. 'Where on earth am I?' I repeated again out loud, stopping for a third time and looking questioningly at my yellow English piebald, Diana, who was by far the most intelligent of all four-legged creatures. But this most intelligent of four-legged creatures only wagged her small tail, dejectedly blinked her tired little eyes and offered me no practical help. I felt ill at ease in front of her and strode wildly forward, as if I had suddenly realized which way to go, circled the knoll and found myself in a shallow hollow which had been ploughed over. A strange feeling took possession of me. The hollow had the almost exact appearance of a cauldron with sloping sides. Several large upright stones stood in the floor of the hollow – it seemed as if they had crept down to that spot for some mysterious consultation – and the hollow itself was so still and silent, the sky above it so flat and dismal that my heart shrank within me. A small animal of some kind or other squeaked weakly and piteously among the stones. I hurried to climb back on to the knoll. Up to that point I had not given up hope of finding a way home, but now I was at last convinced that I had completely lost my way and, no longer making any effort to recognize my surroundings, which were almost totally obliterated by the darkness, I walked straight ahead of me, following the stars and hoping for the best. . . . For about half an hour I walked on in this way, with difficulty, dragging one foot after another. Never in my life, it seemed, had I been in such waste places: not a single light burned anywhere, not a single sound could be heard: one low hillock followed another, field stretched after endless field and bushes suddenly rose out of the earth under my very nose. I went on walking and was on the point of finding a place to lie down until morning, when suddenly I reached the edge of a fearful abyss.

I hastily drew back my outstretched leg and, through the barely transparent night-time murk, saw far below me an enormous plain. A broad river skirted it, curving away from me in a semicircle; steely gleams of water, sparkling with occasional faint flashes, denoted its course. The hill on which I was standing fell away sharply like an almost vertical precipice. Its vast outlines could be distinguished by their blackness from the blue emptiness of the air and directly below me, in the angle formed by the precipice and the plain, beside the river, which at that point was a dark, unmoving mirror, under the steep rise of the hill, two fires smoked and flared redly side by side. Figures clustered round them, shadows flickered and now and then the front half of a small curly head would appear in the bright light.

At last I knew the place I had reached. This meadowland is known in our region as Bezhin Lea. There was now no chance of returning home, especially at night; moreover, my legs were collapsing under me from fatigue. I decided to make my way down to the fires and to await the dawn in the company of the people below me, whom I took to be drovers. I made my descent safely, but had hardly let go of my last handhold when suddenly two large, ragged, white dogs hurled themselves at me with angry barks. Shrill childish voices came from the fires and two or three boys jumped up. I answered their shouted questions. They ran towards me, at once calling off the dogs who had been astonished by the appearance of my Diana, and I walked towards them.

I had been mistaken in assuming that the people sitting round the fires were drovers. They were simply peasant boys from the neighbouring villages keeping guard over the horses. During hot summer weather it is customary in our region to drive the horses out at night to graze in the field, for by day the flies would give them no peace. Driving the horses out before nightfall and back again at first light is a great treat for the peasant boys. Bareheaded, dressed in tattered sheepskin jackets and riding the friskiest ponies, they race out with gay whoops and shouts, their arms and legs flapping as they bob up and down on the horses' backs and roar with laughter. Clouds of fine sandy dust are churned up along the roadway; a steady beating of hooves spreads far and wide as the horses prick up their ears and start running; and in front of them all, with tail high and continuously changing his pace, gallops a shaggy chestnut stallion with burrs in his untidy mane.

I told the boys that I had lost my way and sat down among them. They asked me where I was from and fell silent for a while in awe of me. We talked a little about this and that. I lay down beside a bush from which all the foliage had been nibbled and looked around me. It was a marvellous sight: a reddish circular reflection throbbed round the fires and seemed to fade as it leaned against the darkness; a flame, in flaring up, would occasionally cast rapid flashes of light beyond the limit of the reflection; a fine tongue of light would lick the bare boughs of the willows and instantly vanish; and long sharp shadows, momentarily breaking in, would rush right up to the fires as if the darkness were at war with the light. Sometimes, when the flames grew weaker and the circle of light contracted, there would suddenly emerge from the encroaching dark the head of a horse, reddish brown, with sinuous markings, or completely white, and regard us attentively and gravely, while rapidly chewing some long grass and then, when again lowered, would at once disappear. All that was left was the sound as it continued to chew and snort. From the area of the light it was difficult to discern what was happening in the outer darkness, and therefore at close quarters, everything seemed to be screened from view by an almost totally black curtain; but off towards the horizon hills and woods were faintly visible, like long blurs. The immaculate dark sky rose solemnly and endlessly high above us in all its mysterious magnificence. My lungs melted with the sweet pleasure of inhaling that special, languorous and fresh perfume which is the scent of a Russian summer night. Hardly a sound was audible around us. . . . Now and then a large fish would make a resounding splash in the nearby river and the reeds by the bank would faintly echo the noise as they were stirred by the outspreading waves. . . . Now and then the fires would emit a soft crackling.

Around the fires sat the boys, as did the two dogs who had been so keen to eat me. They were still unreconciled to my presence and, while sleepily narrowing their eyes and glancing towards the fire, would sometimes growl with a special sense of their personal dignity; to start with these were only growls, but later they became faint yelps, as if the dogs regretted their inability to satisfy their appetite for me. There were five boys in all: Fedya, Pavlusha, Ilyusha, Kostya and Vanya. (I learned their names from their conversation and I now intend to acquaint the reader with each of them.)

The first of them, Fedya, the eldest, would probably have been fourteen. He was a sturdy boy, with handsome and delicate, slightly shallow features, curly fair hair, bright eyes and a permanent smile which was a mixture of gaiety and absent-mindedness. To judge from his appearance, he belonged to a well-off family and had ridden out into the fields not from necessity but simply for the fun of it. He was dressed in a colourful cotton shirt with yellow edging; a small cloth overcoat, recently made, hung open somewhat precariously on his small narrow shoulders and a comb hung from his pale-blue belt. His ankle-high boots were his own, not his father's. The second boy, Pavlusha, had dishevelled black hair, grey eyes, broad cheekbones, a pale, pock-marked complexion, a large but well-formed mouth, an enormous head – as big as a barrel, as they say – and a thick-set, ungainly body. Hardly a prepossessing figure – there's no denying that! – but I nonetheless took a liking to him: he had direct, very intelligent eyes and a voice with the ring of strength in it. His clothes gave him no chance of showing off: they consisted of no more than a simple linen shirt and much-patched trousers. The face of the third boy, Ilyusha, was not very striking: hook-nosed, long, myopic, it wore an expression of obtuse, morbid anxiety. His tightly closed lips never moved, his frowning brows never relaxed; all the while he screwed up his eyes at the fire. His yellow, almost white, hair stuck out in sharp little tufts from under the small felt cap which he was continually pressing down about his ears with both hands. He had new bast shoes and foot cloths; a thick rope wound three times round his waist drew smartly tight his neat black top-coat. Both he and Pavlusha appeared to be no more than twelve years old. The fourth, Kostya, a boy of about ten, aroused my curiosity by his sad and meditative gaze. His face was small, thin and freckled, and pointed like a squirrel's; one could hardly see his lips. His large, dark, moistly glittering eyes produced a strange impression, as if they wanted to convey something which no tongue – at least not his tongue – had the power to express. He was small in stature, of puny build and rather badly dressed. The last boy, Vanya, I hardly noticed at first: he lay on the ground quietly curled up under some angular matting and only rarely poked out from under it his head of curly brown hair. This boy was only seven.

So it was that I lay down apart from them, beside the bush, and from time to time looked in their direction. A small pot hung over one of the fires, in which 'taters' were being cooked. Pavlusha looked after them and, kneeling down, poked the bubbling water with a small sliver of wood. Fedya lay, leaning on one elbow, his sheepskin spread round him. Ilyusha sat next to Kostya and continually, in his tense way, screwed up his eyes. Kostya, with his head slightly lowered, stared off somewhere into the distance. Vanya did not stir beneath his matting. I pretended to be asleep. After a short while the boys renewed their talk.

To start with, they gossiped about this and that – tomorrow's work or the horses. But suddenly Fedya turned to

Ilyusha and, as if taking up from where they had left off their interrupted conversation, asked him:

'So you actually did see one of them little people, did you?'

'No, I didn't see him, and you can't really see him at all,' answered Ilyusha in a weak, croaky voice which exactly suited the expression on his face, 'but I heard him, I did. And I wasn't the only one.'

'Then where does he live around your parts?' asked Pavlusha.

'In the old rolling-room.'*

'D'you mean you work in the factory?'

'Of course we do. Me and Avdyushka, my brother, we work as glazers.'

'Cor! So you're factory workers!'

'Well, so how did you hear him?' asked Fedya.

'It was this way. My brother, see, Avdyushka, and Fyodor Mikheyevsky, and Ivashka Kosoy, and the other Ivashka from Redwold, and Ivashka Sukhorukov as well, and there were some other kids as well, about ten of us in all, the whole shift, see – well, so we had to spend the whole night in the rolling-room, or it wasn't that we had to, but that Nazarov, the overseer, he wouldn't let us off, he said: "Seeing as you've got a lot of work here tomorrow, my lads, you'd best stay here; there's no point in the lot o'you traipsing off home." Well, so we stayed and all lay down together, and then Avdyushka started up saying something about "Well, boys, suppose that goblin comes?" and he didn't have a chance, Avdey didn't, to go on saying anything when all of a sudden over our heads someone comes in, but we were lying down below, see, and he was up there, by the wheel. We listen, and there he goes walking about, and the floorboards really bending under him and really creaking. Then he walked right over

---

* 'Rolling-rooms' or 'dipping-rooms' are terms used in paper factories to describe the place where the papers are baled out in the vats. It is situated right by the mill, under the mill-wheel.

our heads and the water all of a sudden starts rushing, rushing through the wheel, and the wheel goes clatter, clatter and starts turning, but them gates of the Keep★ are all lowered. So we start wondering who'd raised them so as to let the water through. Yet the wheel turned and turned, and then stopped. Whoever he was, he went back to the door up-stairs and began coming down the stairway, and down he came, taking his time about it, and the stairs under him really groaning from his weight. . . . Well, so he came right up to our door, and then waited, and then waited a bit more – and then that door suddenly burst open, it did. Our eyes were poppin' out of our heads, and we watch – and there's nothing there. . . . And suddenly at one of the tubs the form† started moving, rose, dipped itself and went to and fro just like that in the air like someone was using it for swilling, and then back again it went to its place. Then at another tub the hook was lifted from its nail and put back on the nail again. Then it was as if someone moved to the door and started to cough all sudden-like, like he'd got a tickle, and it sounded just like a sheep bleating. . . . We all fell flat on the floor at that and tried to climb under each other – bloody terrified we were at that moment!'

'Cor!' said Pavlusha. 'And why did he cough like that?'

'Search me. Maybe it was the damp.'

They all fell silent.

'Are them 'taters done yet?' Fedya asked.

Pavlusha felt them.

'Nope, they're not done yet. . . . Cor, that one splashed,' he added, turning his face towards the river, 'likely it was a pike. . . . And see that little falling star up there.'

'No, mates, I've really got something to tell you,' Kostya

★ 'The Keep' is the name used in our region for the place where the water runs over the wheel.

† The net with which the paper is scooped out.

began in a reedy voice. 'Just you listen to what my dad was talkin' about when I was there.'

'Well, so we're listening,' said Fedya with a condescending air.

'You know that Gavrila, the carpenter in the settlement?'

'Sure we know him.'

'But d'you know why he's always so gloomy, why he never says nothing, d'you know that? Well, here's why. He went out once, my dad said – he went out, mates, into the forest to find some nuts. So he'd gone into the forest after nuts and he lost his way. He got somewhere, but God knows where it was. He'd been walkin', mates, and no! he couldn't find a road of any kind, and already it was night all around. So he sat down under a tree and said to himself he'd wait there till mornin' – and he sat down and started to snooze. So he was snoozin' and suddenly he hears someone callin' him. He looks around – there's no one there. Again he snoozes off – and again they're callin' him. So he looks and looks, and then he sees right in front of him a water-fairy sittin' on a branch, swingin' on it she is and callin' to him, and she's just killin' herself laughin'. . . . Then that moon shines real strong, so strong and obvious the moon shines it shows up everythin', mates. So there she is callin' his name, and she herself's all shiny, sittin' there all white on the branch, like she was some little minnow or gudgeon, or maybe like a carp that's all whitish all over, all silver. . . . And Gavrila the carpenter was just frightened to death, mates, and she went on laughin' at him, you know, and wavin' to him to come closer. Gavrila was just goin' to get up and obey the water-fairy, when, mates, the Lord God gave him the idea to cross hisself. . . . An' it was terrible difficult, mates, he said it was terrible difficult to make the sign of the cross 'cos his arm was like stone, he said, and wouldn't move, the darned thing wouldn't! But soon as he'd managed to cross hisself, mates, that water-fairy stopped laughin' and started in to cry. . . . An' she cried, mates, an' wiped her eyes with her hair that was green and heavy as hemp. So Gavrila kept on lookin' and lookin' at her, and then he started askin' her, "What's it you're cryin' for, you forest hussy, you?" And that water-fairy starts sayin' to him, "If you hadn't crossed yourself, human being that you are, you could've lived with me in joy and happiness to the end of your days, an' I'm cryin' and dyin' of grief over what that you crossed yourself, an' it isn't only me that'll be dyin' of grief, but you'll also waste away with grievin' till the end of your born days." Then, mates, she vanished, and Gavrila at once comprehended-like – how to get out of the wood, that is; but from that day on he goes around everywhere all gloomy.'

'Phew!' exclaimed Fedya after a short silence. 'But how could that evil forest spirit infect a Christian soul – you said he didn't obey her, didn't you?'

'You wouldn't believe it, but that's how it was!' said Kostya. 'Gavrila claimed she had a tiny, tiny, voice, thin and croaky like a toad's.'

'Your father told that himself?' Fedya continued.

'He did. I was lyin' on my bunk an' I heard it all.'

'What a fantastic business! But why's he got to be gloomy? She must've liked him, because she called to him.'

'Of course she liked him!' Ilyusha interrupted. 'Why not? She wanted to start tickling him, that's what she wanted. That's what they do, those water-fairies.'

'Surely there'll be water-fairies here,' Fedya remarked.

'No,' Kostya answered, 'this is a clean place here, it's free. 'Cept the river's close.'

They all grew quiet. Suddenly, somewhere in the distance, a protracted, resonant, almost wailing sound broke the silence – one of those incomprehensible nocturnal sounds which arise in the deep surrounding hush, fly up, hang in the air and slowly disperse at last as if dying away. You listen intently – it's as though there's nothing there, but it still goes on ringing.

This time it seemed that someone gave a series of long, loud shouts on the very horizon and someone else answered him from the forest with sharp high-pitched laughter and a thin, hissing whistle which sped across the river. The boys looked at each other and shuddered.

'The power of the holy cross be with us!' whispered Ilyusha.

'Oh, you idiots!' Pavlusha cried. 'What's got into you? Look, the 'taters are done.' (They all drew close to the little pot and began to eat the steaming potatoes; Vanya was the only one who made no move.) 'What's wrong with you?' Pavlusha asked.

But Vanya did not crawl out from beneath his matting. The little pot was soon completely empty.

'Boys, have you heard,' Ilyusha began saying, 'what happened to us in Varnavitsy just recently?'

'On that dam, you mean?' Fedya asked.

'Ay, on that dam, the one that's broken. That's a real unclean place, real nasty and empty it is. Round there is all them gullies and ravines, and in the ravines there's masses of snakes.'

'Well, what happened? Let's hear.'

'This is what happened. Maybe you don't know it, Fedya, but that's the place where one of our drowned men is buried. And he drowned a long time back when the pond was still deep. Now only his gravestone can be seen, only there's not much of it – it's just a small mound. . . . Anyhow, a day or so ago, the bailiff calls Yermil the dog-keeper and says to him: "Off with you and fetch the mail." Yermil's always the one who goes to fetch the mail 'cos he's done all his dogs in – they just don't somehow seem to live when he's around, and never did have much of a life no-how, though he's a good man with dogs and took to it in every way. Anyhow, Yermil went for the mail, and then he mucked about in the town and set off home real drunk. And it's night-time, a bright night, with the moon shining. . . . So he's riding back across the dam, 'cos that's where his route came out. And he's riding along, this dog-keeper Yermil, and he sees a little lamb on the drowned man's grave, all white and curly and pretty, and it's walking about, and Yermil thinks: "I'll pick it up, I will, 'cos there's no point in letting it get lost here," and so he gets off his horse and picks it up in his arms – and the lamb doesn't turn a hair. So Yermil walks back to the horse, but the horse backs away from him, snorts and shakes its head. So when he's quieted it, he sits on it with the lamb and starts off again holding the lamb in front of him. He looks at the lamb, he does, and the lamb looks right back at him right in the eyes. Then that Yermil the dog-keeper got frightened: "I don't recall," he thought, "no lambs looking me in the eye like that afore." Anyhow, it didn't seem nothing, so he starts stroking its wool and saying "Sssh, there, sssh!" And that lamb bares its teeth at him sudden-like and says back to him: "Sssh, there, sssh! . . .""

The narrator had hardly uttered this last sound when the dogs sprang up and with convulsive barks dashed from the fire, disappearing into the night. The boys were terrified. Vanya even jumped out from beneath his mat. Shouting, Pavlusha followed in hot pursuit of the dogs. Their barking quickly retreated into the distance. There was a noisy and restless scurrying of hooves among the startled horses. Pavlusha gave loud calls: 'Gray! Beetle!' After a few seconds the barking ceased and Pavlusha's voice sounded far away. There followed another short pause, while the boys exchanged puzzled looks as if anticipating something new. Suddenly a horse could be heard racing towards them: it stopped sharply at the very edge of the fire and Pavlusha, clutching hold by the reins, sprang agilely from its back. Both dogs also leapt into the circle of light and at once sat down, their red tongues hanging out.

'What's there? What is it?' the boys asked.

'Nothing,' Pavlusha answered waving away the horse.

'The dogs caught a scent. I thought,' he added in a casual tone of voice, his chest heaving rapidly, 'it might have been a wolf.'

I found myself full of admiration for Pavlusha. He was very fine at that moment. His very ordinary face, enlivened by the swift ride, shone with bold courageousness and a resolute firmness. Without a stick in his hand to control the horse and in total darkness, without even so much as blinking an eye, he had galloped all by himself after a wolf. . . . 'What a marvellous boy!' was my thought, as I looked at him.

'And you saw them, did you, those wolves?' asked the cowardly Kostya.

'There's plenty of them round here,' answered Pavlusha, 'but they're only on the prowl in the winter.'

He again settled himself in front of the fire. As he sat down he let a hand fall on the shaggy neck of one of the dogs and the delighted animal kept its head still for a long while as it directed sideward looks of grateful pride at Pavlusha.

Vanya once again disappeared under his mat.

'What a lot of horrible things you've been telling us, Ilyusha,' Fedya began. As the son of a rich peasant, it was incumbent upon him to play the role of leader (though for his own part he talked little, as if for fear of losing face). 'And it could've been some darned thing of the sort that started the dogs barking. . . . But it's true, so I've heard, that you've got unclean spirits where you live.'

'In Varnavitsy, you mean? That's for sure! It's a really creepy place! More than once they say they've seen there the old squire, the one who's dead. They say he goes about in a coat hanging down to his heels, and all the time he makes a groaning sound, like he's searching for something on the earth. Once grandfather Trofimych met him and asked him: "What's it you are searching for on the earth, good master Ivan Ivanych?"'

'He actually asked him that?' broke in the astonished Fedya.

'He asked him that.'

'Well, good for Trofimych after that! So what did the other say?'

'"Split-grass," he says. "That's what I'm looking for." And he talks in such a hollow, hoarse voice: "Split-grass. And what, good master Ivan Ivanych, do you want split-grass for?" "Oh, my grave weighs so heavy," he says, "weighs so heavy on me, Trofimych, and I want to get out, I want to get away . . ."'

'So that's what it was!' Fedya said. 'He'd had too short a life, that means.'

'Cor, stone me!' Kostya pronounced. 'I thought you could only see dead people on Parents' Sunday.'

'You can see dead people at any time,' Ilyusha declared with confidence. So far as I could judge, he was better versed in village lore than the others. 'But on Parents' Sunday you can also see the people who're going to die that year. All you've got to do is to sit down at night in the porch of the church and keep your eyes on the road. They'll all go past you along the road – them who're going to die that year, I mean. Last year, grandma Ulyana went to the church porch in our village.'

'Well, did she see anyone?' Kostya asked him with curiosity.

'Sure she did. To start with she just sat there a long, long time, and didn't see no one and didn't hear nothing. Only there was all the time a sound like a dog starting to bark somewhere. Then suddenly she sees there's someone coming along the road – it's a little boy in nothing but a shirt. She looked close and she saw it was Ivashka Fedoseyev walking along.'

'Is that the boy who died in the spring!' Fedya broke in.

'That's the one. He walks along and doesn't even raise his head. But Ulyana recognized him. But then she looks again and sees a woman walking along, and she peers and peers and

– God help us! – it's she herself, Ulyana herself, walking along.'

'Was it really her?' asked Fedya.

'God's truth. It was her.'

'But she hasn't died yet, has she?'

'No, but the year's not over yet either. You take a close look at her and then ask yourself what sort of a body she's got to carry her soul around in.'

Again they all grew quiet. Pavlusha threw a handful of dry sticks on the fire. They blackened in sharp outline against the instantly leaping flames, and began to crackle and smoke and bend, curling up their burned tips. The reflections from the light, shuddering convulsively, struck out in all directions, but particularly upwards. Suddenly, from God knows where, a small white pigeon flew directly into the reflections, fluttered around in terror, bathed by the fierce light, and then vanished with a clapping of its wings.

'Likely it's lost its way home,' Pavlusha remarked. 'Now it'll fly until it meets up with something, and when it finds it, that's where it'll spend the night till dawn.'

'Look, Pavlusha,' said Kostya, 'mightn't that be the soul of some good person flying up to heaven, eh?'

Pavlusha threw another handful of sticks on the fire.

'Maybe,' he said after a pause.

'Pavlusha, tell us, will you,' Fedya began, 'were you able to see that heavenly foreboding★ in Shalamavo?'

'You mean, when you couldn't see the sun that time? Sure.'

'Didn't you get frightened, then?'

'Sure, and we weren't the only ones. Our squire, tho' he lets us know beforehand that "Well, there'll be a foreboding for you," but soon as it gets dark they say he got real scared. And in the servants' hut, that old granny, the cook, well – soon as it's dark, listen, she ups and smashes all the pots in the oven with a pair of tongs. "Whose going to need to eat now it's the

★ The name given by the local peasants to an eclipse of the sun.

end of the world," she says. The cabbage soup ran out all over everywhere. And, boy! What rumours there were going about in our village, such as there'd be white wolves and birds of prey coming to eat people, and there'd be Trishka* himself for all to see.'

'What's this Trishka?' asked Kostya.

'Don't you know about Trishka?' Ilyusha started up heatedly. 'You're a dumb cluck, mate, if you don't know who Trishka is. It's just dunces you've got in your village, nothing but dunces! Trishka – he'll be a real astonishing person, who'll be coming, and he'll be coming when the last times are near. And he'll be the sort of astonishing person you won't be able to catch hold of, you won't be able to do nothing to him: that's the sort of astonishing person he'll be. The peasants, say, will want to try to catch him, and they'll go out after him with sticks and surround him, but what he'll do is lead their eyes astray – he'll lead their eyes astray so that they start beating each other. Say they put him in prison and he asks for some water in a ladle; they'll bring him the ladle and he'll jump right into it and vanish clean away, all trace of him. Say they put chains on him, he'll just clap his palms together and they'll fall right off him. So then this Trishka'll go walking through the villages and the towns; and this smart fellow, this Trishka, he'll tempt all Christian folk . . . but there won't be a thing you can do to him. . . . That's the sort of astonishing, real cunning person he'll be.'

'Yes, that's the one,' Pavlusha continued in his unhurried way. 'He was the one that we were all waiting for. The old men said that soon as the heavenly foreboding begins, Trishka'll be coming. So the foreboding began, and everyone poured out into the street and into the field to see what'll happen. As you know, our place is high up and open so you can see all around. Everyone's looking – and suddenly down

---

* The superstition about 'Trishka' probably contains an echo of the legend about Antichrist.

from the settlement on the mountain there's a man coming, strange-looking, with an astonishing big head. . . . Everyone starts shouting: "Oy, oy, it's Trishka coming! Oy, oy, it's Trishka!" and they all raced for hiding, this way and that! The elder of our village, he crawled into a ditch and his wife got stuck in a gate and let out such a howling noise that she fair terrified her own watch-dog, and it broke its chain, rushed through the fence and into the wood. And Kuzka's father, Dorofeyich, jumped in among the oats, squatted down there and began to make cries like a quail, all 'cos he thought to himself: "For sure that soul-destroying enemy of mankind'll spare a poor wee birdie!" Such a commotion they were all in! . . . But all the time that man who was coming was simply our barrel-maker Vavila, who'd bought himself a new can and was walking along with that empty can perched on his head.'

All the boys burst out laughing and then once again fell quiet for an instant, as people talking out in the open air frequently do. I looked around me: the night stood guard in solemn majesty; the raw freshness of late evening had been replaced by midnight's dry mildness, and it still had a long time to lie like a soft quilt over the dreaming fields; there was still a long time to wait until the first murmur, the first rustlings and stirrings of morning, the first dew-beads of dawn. There was no moon in the sky: at that season it rose late. Myriads of golden stars, it seemed, were all quietly flowing in glittering rivalry along the Milky Way, and in truth, while looking at them, one sensed vaguely the un-wavering, unstoppable racing of the earth beneath . . .

A strange, sharp, sickening cry resounded twice in quick succession across the river, and, after a few moments, was repeated farther off . . .

Kostya shuddered: 'What was that?'

'That was a heron's cry,' Pavlusha answered calmly.

'A heron,' Kostya repeated. 'Then what was it, Pavlusha,

I heard yesterday evening?' he added after a brief pause. 'Perhaps you know.'

'What did you hear?'

'This is what I heard. I was walkin' from Stone Ridge to Shashkino, and at first I went all the way along by our nut trees, but afterwards I went through that meadow – you know, by the place where it comes out like a narrow file,* where there's a tarn.† You know it, the one that's all over-grown with reeds. So, mates, I walked past this tarn an' suddenly someone starts makin' a groanin' sound from right inside it, so piteous, piteous, like: Oooh – oooh . . . oooh – oooh! I was terrified, mates. It was late an' that voice sounded like somebody really sick. It was like I was goin' to start cryin' myself . . . What would that have been, eh?'

'In the summer before last, thieves drowned Akim the forester in that tarn,' Pavlusha remarked. 'So it may have been his soul complaining.'

'Well, it might be that, mates,' rejoined Kostya, widening his already enormous eyes. 'I didn't know that Akim had been drowned in that tarn. If I'd known, I wouldn't have got so terrified.'

'But they do say,' continued Pavlusha, 'there's a kind of little frog makes a piteous noise like that.'

'Frogs? No, that wasn't frogs . . . what sort of . . .' (The heron again gave it's cry over the river.) 'Listen to it!' Kostya could not refrain from saying. 'It makes a noise like a wood-demon.'

'Wood-demons don't make a cry, they're dumb,' Ilyusha inserted. 'They just clap their hands and chatter . . .'

'So you've seen one of them, a wood-demon, have you?' Fedya interrupted him scornfully.

'No, I haven't, and God preserve that I should see one.

* A 'narrow file' is a sharp turn in a ravine.

† A 'tarn' is a deep hole filled with spring water remaining after the spring torrents, which does not dry up even in summer.

But other people have seen one. Just a few days ago one such overtook one of our peasants and was leading him all over the place through the wood and round and round some clearing or other. . . . He only just managed to get home before it was light.'

'Well, did he see him?'

'He saw him. Big as big he was, he said, and dark, all wrapped up, just like he was behind a tree so you couldn't see him clearly, or like he was hiding from the moon, and looking all the time, peering with his wicked eyes, and winking them, winking . . .'

'That's enough!' exclaimed Fedya, shuddering slightly and convulsively hunching his shoulders. 'Phew!'

'Why should this devilish thing be around in the world?' commented Pavlusha. 'I don't understand it at all!'

'Don't you scold it! It'll hear you, you'll see,' Ilyusha said.

Again a silence ensued.

'Look up there, look up there, all of you!' the childish voice of Vanya suddenly cried. 'Look at the little stars of God, all swarming like bees!'

He had stuck his small, fresh-complexioned face out from beneath the matting, was leaning on one little fist and slowly looking up with his large, placid eyes. The boys all raised their eyes to the sky, and did not lower them until quite a while had passed.

'Tell me, Vanya,' Fedya began to say in a gentle voice, 'is your sister Anyutka well?'

'She's well,' Vanya answered, with a faint lisp.

'You tell her she ought to come and see us. Why doesn't she?'

'I don't know.'

'Tell her that she ought to come.'

'I'll tell her.'

'Tell her that I'll give her a present.'

'And you'll give one to me, too?'

70

'I'll give one to you, too.'

Vanya sighed. 'No, there's no need to give me one. Better you give it to her, she's so good to us.'

And once more Vanya laid his head on the ground. Pavlusha rose and picked up the little pot, now empty.

'Where are you going?' Fedya asked him.

'To the river, to get some water. I'd like a drink.'

The dogs got up and followed him.

'See you don't fall in the river!' Ilyusha called after him.

'Why should he fall?' asked Fedya. 'He'll be careful.'

'All right, so he'll be careful. Anything can happen, though. Say he bends down, starting to dip up the water, but then a water-sprite grabs him by the hand and pulls him down below. They'll start saying afterwards that, poor boy, he fell in the water. . . . But what sort of a fall is that? Listen, listen, he's in the reeds,' he added, pricking up his ears.

The reeds were in fact moving, 'hushing', as they say in our parts.

'Is it true,' asked Kostya, 'that that ugly woman, Akulina, has been wrong in the head ever since she went in the water?'

'Ever since then. . . . And look at her now! They say she used to be real good-looking before. The water-sprite did for her. Likely he didn't expect they'd drag her out so soon. He corrupted her down there, down in his own place at the bottom of the water.'

(I had come across this Akulina more than once. Covered with tatters, fearsomely thin, with a face as black as coal, a vacant gaze and permanently bared teeth, she used to stamp about on the same spot for hours at a time, at some point on the road, firmly hugging her bony hands to her breast and slowly shifting her weight from one foot to the other just like a wild animal in a cage. She would give no sign of understanding, no matter what was said to her, save that from time to time she would break into convulsions of laughter.)

71

'They do say,' Kostya went on, 'that Akulina threw herself in the river because her lover deceived her.'

'Because of that very thing.'

'But do you remember Vasya?' Kostya added sadly.

'What Vasya?' asked Fedya.

'The one who drowned,' Kostya answered, 'in this very river. He was a grand lad, a really grand lad! That mother of his, Feklista, how she loved him, how she used to love Vasya! And she sort of sensed, Feklista did, that ruin would come to him on account of water. That Vasya used to come with us boys in the summer when we went down to the river to bathe – and she'd be all bothered, his mother would. The other women wouldn't care, going waddling by with their washtubs, but Feklista would put her tub down on the ground and start calling to him: "Come back, come back, light of my life! O come back, my little falcon!" And how he came to drown, God alone knows. He was playing on the bank, and his mother was there, raking hay, and suddenly she heard a sound like someone blowing bubbles in the water – she looks, and there's nothing there 'cept Vasya's little cap floating on the water. From then on, you know, Feklista's been out of her mind: she goes and lies down at that place where he drowned, and she lies down, mates, and starts singing this song – you remember the song Vasya used to sing all the time – that's the one she sings, plaintive-like, and she cries and cries, and complains bitterly to God . . .'

'Here's Pavlusha coming,' Fedya said.

Pavlusha came up to the fire with a full pot in his hand.

'Well, boys,' he began after a pause, 'things aren't good.'

'What's happened?' Kostya quickly asked.

'I heard Vasya's voice.'

They all shuddered.

'What's that you're saying? What's it all about?' Kostya babbled.

'It's God's truth. I was just bending down to the water and

suddenly I hear someone calling me in Vasya's voice, and it was just like it was coming from under the water: "Pavlusha, hey, Pavlusha!" I listen, and again it calls: "Pavlusha, come down here!" I came away. But I managed to get some water.'

'God preserve us! God preserve us!' the boys said, crossing themselves.

'It was a water-sprite for sure calling you, Pavlusha,' Fedya added. 'And we were only just talking about him, about that Vasya.'

'Oh, it's a real, bad omen,' said Ilyusha, giving due weight to each word.

'It's nothing, forget it!' Pavlusha declared resolutely and again sat down. 'Your own fate you can't escape.'

The boys grew quiet. It was clear that Pavlusha's words had made a profound impression on them. They began to lie down before the fire, as if preparing to go to sleep.

'What was that?' Kostya suddenly asked, raising his head. Pavlusha listened.

'It's some snipe in flight, whistling as they fly.'

'Where would they be flying?'

'To a place where there's never any winter, that's what they say.'

'There isn't such a land, is there?'

'There is.'

'Is it far away?'

'Far, far away, on the other side of the warm seas.'

Kostya sighed and closed his eyes.

More than three hours had already flowed by since I joined the boys. Eventually the moon rose. I failed to notice it immediately because it was so small and thin. This faintly moonlit night, it seemed, was just as magnificent as it had been previously. But many stars which had only recently stood high in the sky were beginning to tilt towards its dark edge; all around absolute quiet descended, as usually happens only just before morning: everything slept the deep, still

73

sleep of the pre-dawn hours. The air was not so strongly scented, and once again it seemed to be permeated with a raw dampness. O brief summer nights! The boys' talk died away along with the dying of the fires. Even the dogs dozed: and the horses, so far as I could make out by the vaguely glittering, feeble flux of the starlight, were also lying down with their heads bowed. A sweet oblivion descended on me and I fell into a doze.

A current of fresh air brushed my face. I opened my eyes to see that morning was beginning. As yet there was no sign of dawn's pinkness, but in the east it had begun to grow light. The surrounding scene became visible, if only dimly. The pale-grey sky shone bright and cold and tinged with blue; stars either winked their faint light or faded; the ground was damp and leaves were covered with the sweat of dew, here and there sounds of life, voices could be heard, and a faint, light wind of early morning began its wandering and fleet-footed journey across the earth. My body responded to it with a mild, joyful shivering. I got briskly to my feet and walked over to the boys. They slept the sleep of the dead about the embers of the fire; only Pavlusha raised himself half-way and glanced intently at me.

I nodded my head at him and set off to find my way home along the bank of the river, shrouded with smoky mist. I had hardly gone more than a mile when sunlight streamed all around me down the length of the wide damp lea, and ahead of me across the freshly green hills, from forest to woodland, and behind me along the far, dusty track, over the glistening blood-red bushes and across the river which now shone a modest blue under the thinning mist – flowed torrents of young, hot sunlight, crimson at first and later brilliantly red, brilliantly golden. Everything began quivering into life, awakening, singing, resounding, chattering. Everywhere, large drops of dew began to glow like radiant diamonds. There carried to me, pure and crystal-clear as if also washed clean by the freshness of the morning's atmosphere, the sound of a bell. And suddenly I was overtaken by the racing drove of horses, refreshed after the night, and chased along by my acquaintances, the boys.

I have, unfortunately, to add that in that same year Pavlusha died. He did not drown; he was killed in falling from a horse. A pity, for he was a fine lad!

Kasyan from the Beautiful Lands

I WAS returning from a hunting trip in a shaky little cart and, under the oppressive effects of an overcast summer day's stifling heat (it is notorious that on such days the heat can be even more insufferable than on clear days, especially when there is no wind), I was dozing as I rocked to and fro, in gloomy patience, allowing my skin to be eaten out by the fine white dust which rose incessantly from beneath the heat-cracked and juddering wheels on the hard earth track, when suddenly my attention was aroused by the unusual agitation and anxious body movements of my driver, who until that instant had been in an even deeper doze than I was. He pulled at the reins, fidgeted on his seat and began shouting at the horses, all the time glancing somewhere off to the side. I looked around. We were driving through a broad, flat area of ploughed land into which low hills, also ploughed up, ran down like unusually gentle, rolling undulations. My gaze encompassed in all about three miles of open, deserted country; all that broke the almost straight line of the horizon were distant, small groves of birch trees with their rounded, tooth-shaped tips. Narrow paths stretched through the fields, dipped into hollows and wound over knolls, and on one of these, which was due to cross our track about five hundred yards from us, I could distinguish a procession. It was at this that my driver had been glancing.

It was a funeral. At the front, in a cart drawn only by one small horse, the priest was riding at walking pace; the deacon sat next to him and was driving; behind the cart, four peasants with bared heads were carrying the coffin, draped in a white cloth; two women were walking behind the coffin. The fragile, plaintive voice of one of the women suddenly

reached my ears; I listened: she was singing a lament. Piti-
fully this ululant, monotonous and helplessly grieving melody
floated in the emptiness of the fields. My driver whipped up
the horses in the desire to forestall the procession. It is a bad
omen to meet up with a corpse on the road. He did, in fact,
succeed in galloping along the track just in time before the
procession reached it. But we had hardly gone a hundred
yards farther on when our cart gave a severe lurch, keeled over
and almost capsized. The driver stopped the wildly racing
horses, leaned over from his seat to see what had happened,
gave a wave of the hand and spat.

'What's wrong there?' I asked.

The driver got down without answering and with no sign
of hurry.

'Well, what is it?'

'The axle's broken . . . burned through,' he answered
gloomily, and, in a sudden fit of temper, tugged so sharply
at the breech-band of the trace-horse that the animal almost
toppled over on her side. However, she regained her balance,
snorted, shook her mane and proceeded with the utmost calmness to scratch the lower part of her front leg with her teeth.

I got down and stood for a short while on the road, re-
signing myself to a vague and unpleasant sense of bewilderment. The right wheel had almost completely turned inwards
under the cart and seemed to lift its hub in the air in dumb
resignation.

'What's to be done now?' I asked eventually.

'That's to blame!' said my driver, directing his whip
towards the procession which had by this time succeeded in
turning on to the track and was beginning to approach us.
'I've always noticed it,' he continued. 'It's always a bad omen
to meet up with a corpse, that's for sure.'

Again he took it out on the trace-horse who, seeing how
irritable and severe he was, decided to stand stock-still and
only occasionally gave a few modest flicks with her tail.

I took a few steps to and fro along the track and stopped again in front of the wheel.

In the meantime, the procession had caught up with us. Turning aside from the track on to the grass, the sad cortège passed by our cart. My driver and I removed our caps, exchanged bows with the priest and looks with the pall-bearers. They progressed with difficulty, their broad chests heaving under the weight. Of the two women who walked behind the coffin, one was extremely old and pale of face; her motionless features, cruelly contorted with grief, preserved an expression of stern and solemn dignity. She walked in silence, now and then raising a frail hand to her thin, sunken lips. The other woman, of about twenty-five, had eyes that were red and moist with tears, and her whole face had become swollen from crying. As she drew level with us, she ceased her lament and covered her face with her sleeve. Then the procession went past us, turning back on to the track once more, and her piteous, heart-rending lament was resumed. After following with his eyes the regular to-and-fro motion of the coffin without uttering a sound, my driver turned to me.

'It's Martin, the carpenter, the one from Ryabovo, that they're taking to be buried,' he said.

'How do you know that?'

'I could tell from the women. The old one's his mother and the young one's his wife.'

'Had he been ill, then?'

'Aye . . . the fever. . . . The manager sent for the doctor three days back, but the doctor wasn't home. He was a good carpenter, he was. Liked his drink a bit, but he was a real good carpenter. You see how his wife's grieving for him. It's like they say, though – a woman's tears don't cost nothin', they just flow like water, that's for sure.'

And he bent down, crawled under the rein of the trace-horse and seized hold of the shaft with both hands.

'Well,' I remarked, 'what can we do now?'

My driver first of all leaned his knees against the shoulder of the other horse and giving the shaft a couple of shakes, set the shaft-pad back in its place, crawled back once again under the rein of the trace-horse and, after giving her a shove on the nose while doing so, walked up to the wheel – walked up to it and, without taking his eyes off it, slowly extracted a snuff-box from beneath the skirt of his long tunic, slowly pulled open the lid by a little strap, slowly inserted two thick fingers (the tips of them could hardly fit into the snuff-box at once), kneaded the tobacco, wrinkled up his nose in readiness, gave several measured sniffs, accompanied at each inhalation of the snuff with prolonged snorting and grunting, and, after painfully screwing up and blinking his tear-filled eyes, settled into deep thoughtfulness.

'So, what do you think?' I asked when all this was over.

My driver carefully replaced the snuff-box in his pocket, brought his hat down over his brows without touching it, simply by a movement of his head, and climbed thoughtfully up on to the seat.

'Where are you off to?' I asked, not a little amazed.

'Please be seated,' he answered calmly and picked up the reins.

'But how are we going to go?'

'We'll go all right.'

'But the axle . . .'

'Please be seated.'

'But the axle's broken . . .'

'It's broken, yes, it's broken all right, but we'll make it to the new village – at walking pace, that is. It's over there to the right, beyond the wood, that's where the new village is, what they call the Yudin village.'

'But d'you think we'll get there?'

My driver did not even deign to answer me.

'I'd better go on foot,' I said.

'As you please . . .'

He waved his whip and the horses set off.

We did, in fact, reach the new village, even though the right front wheel hardly held in place and wobbled in a most unusual fashion. It almost flew off as we negotiated a small knoll, but my driver shouted at it angrily and we successfully descended the far slope.

Yudin village consisted of six small, low-roofed huts which had already begun to lean to one side or the other despite the fact that they had no doubt been put up quite recently, and not even all the yards had wattle fencing. As we entered the village, we did not meet a living soul; there were not even any chickens to be seen in the village street; there were not even any dogs, save for one black, stubby-tailed animal that jumped hastily from a completely dried-up ditch, where it must have been driven by thirst, only to dash headlong under a gate without so much as giving a bark. I turned into the first hut, opened the porch door and called for the owners: no one answered me. I called again: a hungry miaowing came from behind the inner door. I shoved it with my foot and an emaciated cat flashed past me, its green eyes glittering in the dark. I stuck my head into the room and looked around: it was dark, smoky and empty. I went into the backyard and there was no one there. A calf gave a plaintive moo in the enclosure, and a crippled grey goose took a few waddling steps off to one side. I crossed to the second hut – and there was no one there either. So I went out into the backyard.

In the very middle of the brilliantly lit yard, right out in the middle of the sun, as they say, there was lying, face downward and with his head covered with a cloth coat, someone I took to be a boy. A few paces from him, beside a wretched little cart, a miserable little horse, all skin and bones, stood in a tattered harness under a straw overhang. Its thick reddish-brown coat was dappled with small bright splashes of sunlight that streamed through narrow openings in the dilapidated thatch-work. There also, high up in their little bird-houses, starlings chattered, looking down upon the world with placid inquisitiveness from their airy home. I walked up to the sleeping figure and began to rouse it.

The sleeper raised his head, saw me and at once jumped to his feet.

'What is it? What's happened?' he started muttering in bewilderment.

I did not answer him at once because I was so astonished by his appearance. Imagine, if you please, a dwarf of about fifty years old, with a small, swarthy, wrinkled face, a little pointed nose, barely discernible little brown eyes and abundant curly black hair which sat upon his tiny head just as broadly as the cap sits on the stalk of a mushroom. His entire body was extraordinarily frail and thin, and it is quite impossible to convey in words how unusual and strange was the look in his eyes.

'What is it?' he asked me again.

I explained the position to him and he listened to me without lowering his slowly blinking eyes.

'Is it not possible then for us to obtain a new axle?' I asked finally. 'I would gladly pay.'

'But who are you? Are you out hunting?' he asked, encompassing me with his glance from head to foot.

'I'm out hunting.'

'You shoot the birds of the air, eh? . . . And the wild animals of the forest? . . . Isn't it sinful you are to be killing God's own wee birds and spilling innocent blood?'

The strange little old man spoke with a very pronounced dwelling on each word. The sound of his voice also astonished me. Not only was there nothing decrepit about it but it was surprisingly sweet, youthful and almost feminine in its gentleness.

'I have no axle,' he added after a short interval of silence.

'This one won't do' – he pointed to his own little cart – 'because, after all, yours is a big cart.'

'But would it be possible to find one in the village?'

'What sort of village is it we have here! Here, there's not anyone of us has a single thing. And there's no one at home – aren't they all out at work for sure. Be off with you!' he said, suddenly, and lay down again on the ground.

I had certainly not expected an outcome of this kind.

'Listen, old man,' I started to say, touching him on the shoulder, 'have a heart, help me.'

'Be off with you in the name o' God! It's tired out I am, an' me having gone into town and back,' he told me and pulled his cloth coat over his head.

'Please do me a favour,' I went on, 'I . . . I'll pay you . . .'

'I'm not needin' your money.'

'Please, old man . . .'

He raised himself half-way and sat himself upright, crossing his delicate, spindly legs.

'It's takin' you I might be to where they've been cutting down the trees. 'Tis a place where some local merchants have bought a piece o' woodland, the Lord be the judge of 'em, an' they're getting rid of all the trees and putting up an office they are, the Lord judge 'em for it. That's where you might order an axle from 'em or buy one ready-made.'

'Excellent!' I exclaimed delightedly. 'Excellent! Let's go.'

'An oak axle, mind you, a good one,' he continued without rising from where he was sitting.

'Is it far to where they're cutting down the trees?'

'A couple o' miles.'

'Well, then, we can get there on your little cart.'

'Oh, but wait a moment. . . .'

'Now come along,' I said. 'Come on, old man! My driver's waiting for us in the street.'

The old man got up reluctantly and followed me out into the street. My driver was in a thoroughly vexed state of mind:

he had wanted to water the horses, but it had turned out that there was very little water in the well and what there was had an unpleasant taste; and that was putting first things first, as drivers are accustomed to say. . . . However, as soon as he saw the old man he grinned broadly, nodded his head and cried out:

'If it's not little Kasyan! Good to see you!'

''Tis good to see you, Yerofey, righteous man that you are!' answered Kasyan in a despondent voice.

I at once told my driver about the old man's suggestion; Yerofey expressed his assent and drove into the yard. While Yerofey was quite deliberately making a great display of briskness in unharnessing the horses, the old man stood with one shoulder leaning against the gates and glanced unhappily either at him or at me. He appeared to be at a loss and, so far as I could see, he was not unduly delighted by our sudden visit.

'Have they resettled you as well?' Yerofey suddenly asked him as he removed the shaft-bow.

'Me as well.'

'Yuck!' said my driver through his teeth. 'You know Martin, the carpenter . . . Martin of Ryabovo, don't you?'

'That I do.'

'Well, he's dead. We just met up with his coffin.'

Kasyan gave a shudder.

'Dead?' he muttered, and stared at the ground.

'Yes, he's dead. Why didn't you cure him, eh? People say you do cures, that you've got the power of healing.'

My driver was obviously taunting and making fun of the old man.

'And that's your cart, is it?' he added, shrugging a shoulder in its direction.

''Tis mine.'

'A cart, is it, a cart!' he repeated and, taking it by the shafts, almost turned it upside down. 'A cart, indeed! But what'll you be using to get to the clearings? You won't be able to harness our horse into those shafts. Our horses are big, but what's this meant to be?'

'I wouldn't be knowing,' answered Kasyan, 'what you'll be using. For sure there's that poor creature,' he added with a sigh.

'D'you mean this?' asked Yerofey, seizing on what Kasyan had been saying, and, going up to Kasyan's miserable little horse, contemptuously stuck the third finger of his right hand in its neck. 'See,' he added reproachfully, 'gone to sleep, it has, the useless thing!'

I asked Yerofey to harness it up as quickly as possible. I wanted to go myself with Kasyan to the place where they were clearing the woodland, for those are the places where grouse are often found. When the little cart was finally ready, I somehow or other settled myself along with my dog on its warped, bast floor, and Kasyan, hunching himself up into a ball, also sat on the front support with the same despondent expression on his face – then it was that Yerofey approached me and, giving me a mysterious look, whispered:

'And it's a good thing, sir, that you're going with him. He's one of those holy men, you know, sir, and he's nicknamed The Flea. I don't know how you were able to understand him. . . .'

I was about to comment to Yerofey that so far Kasyan had seemed to me to be a man of very good sense, but my driver at once continued in the same tone of voice:

'You just watch out and see that he takes you where he should. And make sure you yourself choose the axle, the stouter the better. . . . What about it, Flea,' he added loudly, 'is there anywhere here to find a bite to eat?'

'Seek and it shall be found,' answered Kasyan, giving the reins a jerk, and we rolled away.

His little horse, to my genuine surprise, went far from badly. Throughout the entire journey Kasyan maintained a stubborn silence and answered all my questions peremptorily and unwillingly. We quickly reached the clearings, and once there we made our way to the office, a tall hut standing by itself above a small ravine which had been haphazardly dammed and turned into a pond. I found in this office two young clerks working for the merchants, both of them with teeth as white as snow, sugary sweet eyes, sugary sweet, boisterous chatter and sugary sweet, clever little smiles, did a deal with them for an axle and set off for the clearings. I thought that Kasyan would stay by the horse and wait, but he suddenly approached me.

'And is it that you're after shooting the wee birds?' he ventured. 'Is that it?'

'Yes, if I find them.'

'I'll go along with you. D'you mind?'

'Please do, please do.'

And we walked off. The area of felled trees extended for less than a mile. I confess that I looked at Kasyan more than at my dog. He had been aptly nicknamed the Flea. His black and hatless little head (his hair, by the way, was a substitute for any cap) bobbed up and down among the bushes. He walked with an extraordinarily sprightly step and literally took little jumps as he went, ceaselessly bending down, plucking herbs, stuffing them under his shirt, muttering words through his nose and shooting glances at me and my dog, giving us such keen and unusual looks. In the low bushes, the 'underbrush' and in the clearings there are often little grey birds which all the time switch from sapling to sapling and emit short whistling sounds as they dive suddenly in their flight. Kasyan used to tease them, exchanging calls with them; a young quail would fly up shrilly from under his feet and he would call shrilly after it; a lark might start rising above him, fluttering its wings and pouring out its song – Kasyan would at once catch up its refrain. But to me he said not a word.

The weather was beautiful, still more beautiful than it had

been before; yet there was still no lessening of the heat. Across the clear sky drifted, with scarcely a movement, a few distant clouds, yellowish-white, the colour of a late snowfall in the spring, flat in shape and elongated like furled sails. Their feathered edges, light and wispy as cotton, altered slowly but obviously with each passing instant; they were as if melting, these clouds were, and they cast no shadow. For a long while Kasyan and I wandered through the clearings. Young shoots which had not yet succeeded in growing more than a couple of feet high spread their thin, smooth stems round the blackened and squat stumps of trees; round, spongy fungoid growths with grey edges, the kind which they boil down to make tinder, adhered to these tree-stumps; wild strawberries spread their wispy pink runners over them; mushrooms were also esconced there in tight family clusters. One's feet were continually becoming entangled and caught by the tall grass, drenched in the sun's heat; in all directions one's eyes were dazzled by the sharp, metallic flashes of light from the young, reddish leaves on the saplings; everywhere in gay abundance appeared sky-blue clusters of vetch, the little golden chalices of buttercups, the partly mauve, partly yellow flowers of St John and Mary daisies; here and there, beside overgrown tracks, in which the traces of cart-wheels were marked by strips of short-stemmed red grass rose piles of firewood, stacked in six-foot lengths and darkened by wind and rain; slight shadows extended from them in slanting rectangles – otherwise there was no shade of any kind. A light breeze sprang up occasionally and then died. It would blow suddenly straight into one's face and caper around, as it were, setting everything happily rustling, nodding and swaying about, making the supple tips of the fern bow gracefully, so that one was delighted at it; but then it would again fade away, and everything would once more be still. Only the grasshoppers made a combined whirring, as if infuriated – such an oppressive, unceasing, insipid, dry sound. It was appropriate to the unabating, midday heat, as if literally engendered by it, literally summoned by it out of the sun-smelted earth.

Without coming across a single covey, we finally reached some new clearings. Here, recently felled aspens were stretched sadly on the ground, pressing down both grass and undergrowth beneath their weight; on some of them the leaves, still green but already dead, hung feebly from the stiff branches; on others they had already withered and curled up. A special, extraordinarily pleasant acrid scent came from the fresh, golden-white chips of wood which lay in heaps about the moistly bright tree-stumps. Far off, closer to the wood, there could be heard the faint clatter of axes and from time to time, solemnly and quietly, as if in the act of bowing and spreading out its arms, a curly-headed tree would fall.

For a long while I could find no game; finally, a landrail flew out of an extensive oak thicket which was completely overgrown with wormwood. I fired: the bird turned over in the air and fell. Hearing the shot, Kasyan quickly covered his face with his hand and remained stock-still until I had reloaded my gun and picked up the shot bird. Just as I was preparing to move farther on, he came up to the place where the bird had fallen, bent down to the grass which had been sprinkled with several drops of blood, gave a shake of the head and looked at me in fright. Afterwards I heard him whispering: 'A sin! 'Tis a sin, it is, a sin!'

Eventually the heat forced us to find shelter in the wood. I threw myself down beneath a tall hazel bush, above which a young and graceful maple had made a beautiful spread of its airy branches. Kasyan seated himself on the thick end of a felled birch. I looked at him. Leaves fluttered slightly high above, and their liquid, greenish shadows glided calmly to and fro over his puny figure, clad somehow or other in a dark cloth coat, and over his small face. He did not raise his head. Bored by his silence, I lay down on my back and began admiringly to watch the peaceful play of the entwined leaves

against the high, clear sky. It is a remarkably pleasant occupation, to lie on one's back in a forest and look upwards! It seems
that you are looking into a bottomless sea, that it is stretching
out far and wide *below* you, that the trees are not rising from
the earth but, as if they were the roots of enormous plants,
are descending or falling steeply into those lucid, glassy waves,
while the leaves on the trees glimmer like emeralds or thicken
into a gold-tinted, almost jet-black greenery. Somewhere high,
high up, at the very end of a delicate branch, a single leaf
stands out motionless against a blue patch of translucent sky,
and, beside it, another sways, resembling in its movement the
ripplings upon the surface of a fishing reach, as if the movement
were of its own making and not caused by the wind. Like
magical underwater islands, round white clouds gently float
into view and pass by, and then suddenly the whole of this
sea, this radiant air, these branches and leaves suffused with
sunlight, all of it suddenly begins to stream in the wind,
shimmers with a fugitive brilliance, and a fresh, tremulous
murmuration arises which is like the endless shallow splashing
of oncoming ripples. You lie still and you go on watching:
words cannot express the delight and quiet, and how sweet is
the feeling that creeps over your heart. You go on watching,
and that deep, clear azure brings a smile to your lips as innocent as the azure itself, as innocent as the clouds passing across
it, and as if in company with them there passes through your
mind a slow cavalcade of happy recollections, and it seems
to you that all the while your gaze is travelling farther and
farther away and drawing all of you with it into that calm,
shining infinity, making it impossible for you to tear yourself
away from those distant heights, from those distant depths. . . .

'Master, eh, master!' Kasyan suddenly said in his resonant
voice.

I raised myself up in surprise; until that moment he had
hardly answered any of my questions and now he had suddenly started talking of his own accord.

'What do you want?' I asked.

'Why is it now that you should be killing that wee bird?' he began, looking me directly in the face.

'How do you mean: why? A landrail is a game bird. You can eat it.'

'No, it wasn't for that you were killing it, master. You won't be eating it! You were killing it for your own pleasure.'

'But surely you yourself are used to eating a goose or a chicken, for example, aren't you?'

'Such birds are ordained by God for man to eat, but a landrail – that's a bird of the free air, a forest bird. And he's not the only one; aren't there many of them, every kind of beast of the forest and of the field, and river creature, and creature of the marsh and meadow and the heights and the depths – and a sin it is to be killing such a one, it should be let to live on the earth until its natural end. . . . But for man there is another food laid down; another food and another drink; bread is God's gift to man, and the waters from the heavens, and the tame creatures handed down from our fathers of old.'

I looked at Kasyan in astonishment. His words flowed freely; he did not cast around for them, but spoke with quiet animation and a modest dignity, occasionally closing his eyes.

'So according to you it's also sinful to be killing fish?' I asked.

'A fish has cold blood,' he protested with certainty, 'it's a dumb creature. A fish doesn't know fear, doesn't know happiness: a fish is a creature without a tongue. A fish doesn't have feelings, it has no living blood in it. . . . 'Blood,' he continued after a pause, 'blood is holy! Blood does not see the light of God's sun, blood is hidden from the light. . . . And a great sin it is to show blood to the light of day, a great sin and cause to be fearful, oh, a great one it is!'

He gave a sigh and lowered his eyes. I must admit that I looked at the strange old man in complete amazement. His speech did not sound like the speech of a peasant: simple people did not talk like this, nor did ranters. This language, thoughtfully solemn and unusual as it was, I had never heard before.

'Tell me, please, Kasyan,' I began, without lowering my eyes from his slightly flushed face, 'what is your occupation?'

He did not answer my question immediately. His gaze shifted uneasily for a moment.

'I live as the Lord ordains I should,' he said eventually, 'but as for an occupation, no, I don't have an occupation of any kind. 'Tis a poor mentality I have, right from when I was small. I work so long as I can, but it's a poor worker I'm being. There's nothing for me to do! My health's gone and my hands're all foolish. In the springtime, though, I catch nightingales.'

'You catch nightingales? Then why were you talking about not touching the beast of the forest and the field and other creatures?'

'Not to be killing 'em, that's the point; death will take what's due to it. Now there's Martin the carpenter: he lived his life, Martin the carpenter did, and he didn't live long and he died; and now his wife's grieving over her husband and her little ones. . . . It's not for man nor beast to get the better of death. Death doesn't come running, but you can't run away from it, neither; nor must you be helping it along. I don't kill the nightingales, Good Lord preserve us! I don't catch them to cause them pain, nor to put their lives in any peril, but for man's enjoyment, for his consolation and happiness.'

'Do you go into the Kursk region to catch them?'

'I go into Kursk and I go farther, depending how things are. I sleep in the swamplands, and also I sleep in the woodlands, and I sleep all alone in the fields and in the wild places: that's where snipe do their whistling, where you can hear the hares crying, where the drakes go hissing. . . . At eventide I take note where they are, and come morning I listen out for them, at dawn I spread my net over the bushes. There's a kind of nightingale sings real piteously, sweetly and piteously, it does . . .'

'Do you sell them?'

'I give 'em away to good people.'

'What d'you do apart from this?'

'What do I do?'

'What keeps you busy?'

The old man was silent for a moment.

'Nothing keeps me busy. 'Tis a poor worker I am. But I understand how to read and write.'

'So you're literate?'

'I understand how to read and write. The Lord God helped me, and some kind people'

'Are you a family man?'

'No, I've got no family.'

'Why's that? They've all died, have they?'

'No, it's just like it wasn't my task in life, that's all. Everything's according to the will of God, we all live our lives according to the will of God; but a man's got to be righteous – that's what! That means he must live a fitting life in God's eyes.'

'And you haven't any relatives?'

'I have. . . . I have, yes.' The old man became confused.

'Tell me, please,' I began, 'I heard my driver asking you, so to speak, why you hadn't cured Martin the carpenter? Is it true you can heal people?'

'Your driver's a just man,' Kasyan answered me thoughtfully, 'but he's also not without sin. He says I have the power of healing. What power have I got! And who is there has such power? It all comes from God. But there . . . there are herbs, there are flowers: they help, it's true. There's marigold, that's one, a kindly herb for curing human beings; there's the plantains, too; there's nothing to be ashamed of in talking about them – good clean herbs are of God's making. But others aren't. Maybe they help, but they're a sin and it's a sin to talk about them. Perhaps they might be used with the help of prayer. . . . Well, of course, there are special words. . . . But only he who has faith shall be saved,' he added, lowering his voice.

'Did you give anything to Martin?' I asked.

'I learned about him too late,' answered the old man. 'And what would've been the good! It is all ordained for man from his birth. He was not a dweller, was Martin the carpenter, not a dweller on this earth: and that's how it turned out. No, when a man's not ordained to live on this earth, the sweet sunlight doesn't warm him like it warms the others, and the produce of the earth profits him nothing, as if all the time he's being called away. . . . Aye, God rest his soul!'

'Have you been resettled here among us for long?' I asked after a short silence.

Kasyan stirred.

'No, not long: 'bout four years. Under the old master we lived all the time where we were, but it was the custodians of the estate who resettled us. The old master we had was a meek soul, a humble man he was – God grant he enter the Kingdom of Heaven! But the custodians, of course, decided justly. It looks like this is how it was meant to be.'

'But where did you live before this?'

'We came from the Beautiful Lands.'[1]

'Is that far from here?'

''Bout sixty miles.'

'Was it better there?'

'It was better . . . much better. The land's free and open there, with plenty of rivers, a real home for us; but here it's all enclosed and dried up. We've become orphans here. There where we were, on the Beautiful Lands, I mean, you'd go up a hill, you'd go up – and, Good Lord, what wouldn't you see from there? Eh? There'd be a river there, a meadow there and there a forest, and then there'd be a church, and again more meadows going far, far off, as far as anything. Just as far as far, that's how you'd go on looking and looking and wonderin' at it, that's for sure! As for here, true – the land's better: loamy soil it is, real good loam, so the peasants say. But so far as I'm concerned, there's sufficient food everywhere to keep me going.'

'But if you were to tell the truth, old fellow, you'd want to be where you were born, wouldn't you?'

'For sure I'd like to take a look at it. Still, it doesn't matter where I am. I'm not a family man, not tied to anywhere. And what would I be doing sittin' at home a lot? It's when I'm off on my way, off on my travels,' he began saying in a louder voice, 'that everything's surely easier. Then the sweet sunlight shines on you, and you're clearer to God, and you sing in better tune. Then you look-see what herbs is growing there, and you take note of 'em and collect the ones you want. Maybe there's water runnin' there, water from a spring, so you have a drink of it and take note of that as well. The birds of the air'll be singing. . . . And then on t'other side of Kursk there'll be the steppes, O such steppelands, there's a wonder for you, a real joy to mankind they are, such wide expanses, a sign of God's bounty. And they go on and on, people do say, right to the warm seas where Gamayun[2] lives, the bird of the sweet voice, to the place where no leaves fall from the trees in winter, nor in the autumn neither, and golden apples do grow on silver branches and each man lives in contentment and justice with another. . . . That's where I'd like to be going. . . . Though I've been about a bit in my time! I've been in Romyon and in Sinbirsk, that fine city, and in Moscow herself, dressed in her golden crowns. And to Oka, river of mother's milk, I've been, and to Tsna, fair as a dove, and to our mother, the Volga, and many's the people I've seen, good Chrestians all, and many's the honest towns I've been in. . . . But I'd still like to be going to that place . . . and that's it . . . and soon-like. . . . And it's not only I, sinner that I am, but many other Chrestians that go walking and wandering

93

through the wide world with nothin' but bast on their feet and seekin' for the truth' . . . Sure there are! . . . But as for what's at home, eh? There's no justice in the way men live – that's what. . . .'

Kasyan uttered these last words with great speed and almost inaudibly: afterwards he said something else, which I was unable even to hear, and his face took on such a strange expression that I was spontaneously reminded of the title 'holy man' which Yerofey had given him. He stared down at the ground, gave a phlegmy cough and appeared to collect his senses.

'O the sweet sun!' he uttered almost under his breath. 'O such a blessing, Good Lord! O such warmth here in the forest!'

He shrugged his shoulders, fell silent; glanced round distractedly and started singing in a quiet voice. I could not catch all the words of his protracted little song, but I heard the following words:

> But Kasyan's what they call me,
> And by nickname I'm the Flea . . .

'Ha!' I thought, 'he's making it up. . . .'

Suddenly he shuddered and stopped his singing, gazing intently into the forest thicket. I turned and saw a little peasant girl of about eight years of age, dressed in a little blue coat, with a chequered handkerchief tied over her head and a small wattle basket on her bare, sunburned arm. She had obviously not expected to come across us here at all; she had stumbled on us, as they say, and now stood stock-still on a shady patch of grass in a green thicket of nut trees, glancing fearfully at me out of her jet-black eyes. I had scarcely had time to notice her when she at once plunged out of sight behind a tree.

'Annushka! Annushka! Come here, don't be frightened,' the old man called to her in a gentle voice.

'I'm frightened,' a thin little voice answered.

'Don't be frightened, don't be frightened, come to me.'

Annushka silently left her hiding-place, quietly made her way round – her child's feet scarcely made any noise in the thick grass – and emerged from the thicket beside the old man. She was not a girl of about eight years of age, as it had seemed to me at first judging by her lack of inches, but of thirteen or fourteen. Her whole body was small and thin, but very well-made and supple, and her beautiful little face was strikingly similar to Kasyan's, although Kasyan was no beauty. The same sharp features, the same unusual look, which was both cunning and trustful, meditative and penetrating, and exactly the same gestures. . . . Kasyan took her in at a glance as she stood sideways to him.

'You've been out picking mushrooms, have you?' he asked.

'Yes,' she answered with a shy smile.

'Did you find many?'

'Yes.' (She directed a quick glance at him and again smiled.)

'Are there any white ones?'

'There are white ones as well.'

'Come on, show them. . . .' (She lowered the basket from her arm and partly raised the broad dock leaf with which the mushrooms were covered.) 'Ah!' said Kasyan, bending over the basket, 'They're real beauties! That's really something, Annushka!'

'Is she your daughter, Kasyan?' I asked. (Annushka's face crimsoned faintly.)

'No, she's just a relative,' Kasyan said with pretended indifference. 'Well, Annushka, you be off,' he added at once, 'and God be with you! Watch where you go. . . .'

'But why should she go on foot?' I interrupted. 'We could take her home in the cart.'

Annushka blushed red as a poppy, seized hold of the basket by its string handle and glanced at the old man in alarm.

'No, she'll walk home,' he objected in the same indifferent

tone of voice. 'Why shouldn't she? She'll get home all right. . . . Off with you now!'

Annushka walked off briskly into the forest. Kasyan followed her with his eyes, then looked down at the ground and grinned to himself. In this protracted grin, in the few words which he had spoken to Annushka and in the sound of his voice as he was talking to her there had been ineffable, passionate love and tenderness. He again glanced in the direction that she had gone, again smiled and, wiping his face, gave several nods of the head.

'Why did you send her away so soon?' I asked him. 'I would have bought some mushrooms from her. . . .'

'You can buy them there at home whenever you like, it's no matter,' he answered, addressing me with the formal 'You' for the first time.

'She's very pretty, that girl of yours.'

'No . . . how so? . . . she's just as they come,' he answered with apparent unwillingness, and from that very moment dropped back into his former taciturnity.

Seeing that all my efforts to make him start talking again were fruitless, I set off for the clearings. The heat had meanwhile dissipated a little; but my bad luck or, as they say in our parts, my 'nothing doing' continued the same and I returned to the village with no more than a single landrail and a new axle. As we were driving up to the yard, Kasyan suddenly turned to me.

'Master, sir,' he began, 'sure I'm the one you should blame, sure it was I who drove all the game away from you.'

'How so?'

'It's just something I know. There's that dog of yours, a good dog and trained to hunt, but he couldn't do anything. When you think of it, people are people, aren't they? Then there's this animal here, but what've they been able to make out of him?'

It would have been useless for me to start persuading Kasyan that it was impossible to 'cast a spell' over game and therefore I did not answer him. At that moment we turned in through the gates of the yard.

Annushka was not in the hut; she had already arrived and left behind her basket of mushrooms.

Yerofey fixed the new axle, having first subjected it to a severe and biased evaluation; and an hour later I drove away, leaving Kasyan a little money, which at first he did not wish to accept but which later, having thought about it and having held it in the palm of his hand, he placed inside the front of his shirt. During this whole hour he hardly uttered a single word; as previously, he stood leaning against the gates, made no response to my driver's reproachful remarks and was extremely cold to me in saying good-bye.

As soon as I had returned I had noticed that my Yerofey was once again sunk in gloom. And in fact he had found nothing edible in the village and the water for the horses had been of poor quality. So we drove out. With a dissatisfaction that expressed itself even in the nape of his neck, he sat on the box and dearly longed to strike up a conversation with me, but in anticipation of my initial question he limited himself to faint grumblings under his breath and edifying, occasionally caustic, speeches directed at the horses.

'A village!' he muttered. 'Call it a village! I asked for some *kvas* and they didn't even have any *kvas*.... Good God! And as for water, it was simply muck!' (He spat loudly.) 'No cucumbers, no *kvas*, not a bloody thing. As for you,' he added thunderously, turning to the right-hand horse, 'I know you, you dissemblin' female, you! You're a right one for pretendin', you are....' (And he struck her with the whip.) 'That horse has gone dead cunnin', she has, and before it was a nice, easy creature.... Gee-up there, look-see about it.'

'Tell me, please, Yerofey,' I began, 'what sort of a person is that Kasyan?'

Yerofey did not reply immediately: in general he was

thoughtful and slow in his ways, but I could guess at once that my question had cheered and calmed him.

'The Flea, you mean?' he said eventually, jerking at the reins. 'A strange and wonderful man he is, truly a holy man, and you'd not find another one like him all that quick. He's, so to speak, as like as like our grey horse there: he's got out of hand just the same ... that's to say, he's got out of the way of workin'. Well, of course, he's no worker. Just keeps himself going, but still ... For sure he's always been like that. To start with he used to be a carrier along with his uncles: there were three of 'em; but after a time, well, you know, he got bored and gave it up. Started living at home, he did, but couldn't feel settled – he's restless as a flea. Thanks be to God, it happened he had a kind master who didn't force him to work. So from that time on he's been wanderin' here, there and everywhere, like a roaming sheep. And God knows, he's remarkable enough, with his being silent as a tree-stump one moment and then talking away all of a sudden the next – and as for what he says, God alone knows what that is. Maybe you think it's his manner? It's not his manner, because he's too ungainly. But he sings well – a bit pompous-like, but not too bad really.'

'Is it true he has the power of healing?'

'A power of healing! What would he be doing with that? Just ordinary he is. But he did cure me of scrofula. . . . A lot of good it does him! He's just as stupid as they come, he is,' he added, after a pause.

'Have you known him long?'

'Long enough. We were neighbours of his in Sychovka, on the Beautiful Lands.'

'And that girl we came across in the wood – Annushka – is she a blood relation of his?'

Yeofrey glanced at me over his shoulder and bared his teeth in a wide grin.

'Huh . . . Yes, they're relations. She's an orphan, got no

mother and nobody knows who her mother was. But it's likely she's related to him: she's the spittin' image of him. . . . And she lives with him. A smart girl, she is, no denying that; and a good girl, and the old man, he dotes on her: she's a good girl. And likely he'll – you may not believe it – but likely he'll take it into his head to teach his Annushka readin' and writin'. You never know, it's just the sort of thing he'd start: he's as extrardin'ry as that, changeable-like he is, even untellable. . . . Hey, hey, hey!' My driver suddenly interrupted himself and, bringing the horses to a stop, leaned over the side and started sniffing. 'Isn't there a smell of burning? There is an' all! These new axles'll be the end of me. It seemed I'd put enough grease on. I'll have to get some water. There's a little pond over there.'

And Yerofey got down slowly from the box, untied a bucket, walked to the pond and, when he returned, listened with considerable pleasure to the way the axle-hole hissed as it was suddenly doused with water. About six times in the course of seven or so miles he had to douse the overheated axle, and evening had long since fallen by the time we returned home.

Bailiff

TEN miles or so from my estate there lives a certain acquaintance of mine, a young landowner and retired guards officer, Arkady Pavlych Penochkin. His lands are rich in game, his house designed by a French architect, his servants dressed in the English fashion, he provides excellent dinners and extends a cordial welcome to his guests; yet it is only with reluctance that one visits him. He is a man of intelligence and substance, educated according to the best standards, has done his service in a guards regiment and gone the rounds of high society, and now looks after his estate with much success. To use his own words, Arkady Pavlych is stern but just, busies himself with the welfare of his menials and metes out punishments always for their own good. 'One must treat them like children,' he says on such occasions. 'It's due to ignorance, *mon cher; il faut prendre cela en considération.*' He himself, when there is occasion for so-called unfortunate strictness, avoids sharp and abrupt gestures and prefers not to raise his voice, but rather sticks his hand out directly in front of him, saying quietly: 'Surely I asked you, my dear chap,' or 'What's the matter with you, my friend? Pull yourself together' – all the while slightly gritting his teeth and giving his mouth a slight twist. He is not tall, dapper in build, not at all bad-looking and he keeps his hands and nails admirably groomed; his rosy lips and cheeks exude good health. He has a resonant and carefree laugh and a jovial way of screwing up his bright hazel eyes. He dresses excellently and with taste; he orders French books, pictures and newspapers, but he is no book-worm: he hardly managed to finish *The Wandering Jew.*[1] He is an expert card-player. Generally speaking, Arkady Pavlych is considered to be one of the most cultured members of the gentry and the most sought-after prospective husband in our province; women are quite out of their minds about him and are particularly fulsome in their praise of his manners. He is amazingly good at conducting himself properly, is as cautious as a cat and has never for the life of him let himself be touched by a breath of scandal, although he occasionally permits the world to know what sort of man he is by taking a delight in teasing some shy wretch and snapping his head off. He stoutly avoids bad company for fear of compromising himself; though at a time of celebration he is fond of proclaiming himself a devotee of Epicurus, despite his generally poor opinion of philosophy which he calls the misty nourishment of German intellects or sometimes, quite simply, a lot of nonsense. He is also fond of music; while playing cards he sings through his teeth, but he does it with feeling; he knows parts of *Lucia*[2] and *Les Somnambules*[3] though he pitches his voice too high. During the winter he goes to St Petersburg. He keeps his house in exceptionally good order; even his coachmen have succumbed to his influence and not only give daily washings to the horse-collars and their own peasant coats, but also wash their own faces. Arkady Pavlych's house-serfs, it's true, have a habit of looking at you from under their brows – but then in Russia, it's no easy matter to tell a gloomy face from a sleepy one. Arkady Pavlych speaks in a soft and pleasant voice, lending his speech due measure and deriving enjoyment, as it were, from permitting each word to pass through his splendid, perfumed whiskers; he also makes use of many French turns of phrase, such as *'Mais c'est impayable!' 'Mais comment donc!'* and so on. Regardless of this, I at least visit him with the utmost reluctance, and if it had not been for the grouse and the partridges I would long ago no doubt have put an end to our acquaintanceship. A strange kind of unease seizes hold of you in his house; even the comforts of it evoke no pleasure, and each evening, when the frizzle-haired lackey appears before you in his sky-blue livery with its crested buttons and proceeds deferentially to pull off your boots, you feel that if only in place of his lean and hungry figure there were suddenly presented to you the strikingly wide cheekbones and impossibly blunt nose of a strapping lad just brought in from the plough by the master of the house, who had already succeeded in bursting through the seams of his newly loaned nankeen tunic in a dozen places – you would be indescribably pleased and would willingly submit to the danger of losing, along with your boot, the whole of your leg right up to the thigh . . .

Notwithstanding my dislike of Arkady Pavlych, I once had to spend a night at his house. Early the next morning I ordered my carriage to be harnessed, but he was unwilling to let me go without offering me an English breakfast and led me into his study. Tea was served together with cutlets, soft-boiled eggs, butter, honey, cheese and so on. Two menservants in peerless white gloves swiftly and silently anticipated our least wish. We were seated on a Persian divan. Arkady Pavlych was arrayed in wide silken trousers, a black velvet jacket, a fine fez with a blue tassel and yellow Chinese slippers without heels. He sipped his tea, laughed, studied his fingernails, smoked, stuffed cushions on either side of him and generally accounted himself to be in the best of moods. Having breakfasted substantially and with evident pleasure, Arkady Pavlych poured himself a glass of red wine, raised it to his lips and suddenly frowned.

'Why has the wine not been warmed?' he inquired of one of the menservants in a fairly sharp voice.

The man was confused, stood rooted to the spot and turned pale.

'Well, I am asking you, my dear chap,' Arkady Pavlych continued quietly, without taking his eyes off him.

The wretched man fidgeted, twisted his napkin and did not utter a word. Arkady Pavlych bent his head forward and meditated upon him from beneath his brows.

'*Pardon, mon cher,*' he said with a pleasant smile, giving me a friendly pat on the knee, and once again directed a stare at his manservant. 'Well, you may leave,' he added after a short silence, raised his brows and rang the bell.

There appeared a fat, dark-featured, black-haired man with a low forehead and eyes completely buried in his face.

'See about Fyodor,' said Arkady Pavlych in a low voice and with perfect self-control.

'Certainly, sir,' the fat man answered and went out.

'*Voilà, mon cher, les désagréments de la campagne,*' Arkady Pavlych gaily remarked. 'And where are you off to? Stay here and sit a while longer.'

'No,' I answered, 'it's time for me to go.'

'Always off hunting! You hunters'll be the death of me! Where are you off to today?'

'To Ryabovo, about twenty-five miles from here.'

'To Ryabovo, are you? Good Lord, in that case I'll come with you. Ryabovo is only about three miles from my own Shipilovka, and I haven't been in Shipilovka for ages – I haven't been able to find the time for it. See how things have worked out: you'll go hunting in Ryabovo today and this evening you'll be my guest. *Ce sera charmant.* We'll have dinner together – we can take my cook with us – and then you'll spend the night with me. Excellent! Excellent!' he added without waiting for my answer. '*C'est arrangé.* . . . Hey, is there anyone there? Order them to get the carriage ready, and be quick about it! You've never been in Shipilovka, have you? I would hesitate to suggest that you spend the night in my bailiff's hut except that I know you're not averse to it and would probably spend the night in Ryabovo in a hay barn. . . . Let's be off, let's be off!'

And Arkady Pavlych began singing some French love-song.

'Of course you very likely don't know,' he continued, rocking on his heels, 'that my peasants there are paying quit rent. That's the Constitution for you – what else can one do? However, they pay me their rent correctly. I would long ago, I admit, have had them working for me directly, but there's not much land there to work: it surprises me really how they make ends meet. However, *c'est leur affaire*. The bailiff I've got there is a good chap, *une forte tête*, statesman-like! You'll see how well it's all worked out, that's for sure!'

I had no choice. Instead of leaving at nine in the morning we left at two in the afternoon. Hunters will understand my impatience. Arkady Pavlych liked, as he expressed it, 'to look after himself' on such an occasion and took with him such a fantastic amount of linen, supplies, clothes, scents, cushions and different cases that any economical and self-disciplined German would have found such an abundance of things sufficient to last him a whole year. At each downgrade Arkady Pavlych delivered a short but strongly worded speech to his driver, from which I was able to conclude that my acquaintance was unmistakably a coward. However, the journey was accomplished very satisfactorily; save that during the crossing of a small, recently repaired bridge, the cart carrying the cook broke down and his stomach was crushed by a rear wheel.

Arkady Pavlych, upon seeing the fall sustained by his home-bred Carême,[4] considered it no joking matter and, in a fright, at once sent word to know whether the man's hands were unhurt. Having received an affirmative answer, he quickly regained his composure. All in all, we took a fairly long time travelling; I sat in the same carriage as Arkady Pavlych and towards the end of the journey became bored to death, the more so because in the course of several hours my acquaintance had become quite worn out and began pretending to be a liberal. Eventually we arrived, though not at Ryabovo but directly in Shipilovka; somehow or other that's how it had worked out. That day, regardless, I could not go out hunting, and with a heavy heart I submitted to my fate.

The cook had arrived a few minutes ahead of us and had evidently succeeded in giving orders and warning the people concerned, because upon entering the outskirts of the village we were met by the village elder (the Bailiff's son), a hefty, red-haired peasant a good couple of metres high, on horseback and hatless, with a new coat unbuttoned at the front.

'But where's Sofron?' Arkady Pavlych asked him.

The elder first of all jumped briskly off the horse, bowed low in his master's direction, declared: 'Good day to you, good master, Arkady Pavlych,' then raised his head, gave himself a shake and announced that Sofron had set off for Perov, but that someone had been sent after him.

'Well, then, follow behind us,' said Arkady Pavlych.

Out of politeness the elder led his horse to one side, tumbled on to it and set off at a trot behind the carriage, holding his cap in his hand. We drove through the village. We came across several peasants in empty carts on the way; they were driving from the threshing and singing songs, being bounced up and down by their carts with their legs swinging in the air; but at the sight of our carriage and the elder they suddenly grew quiet, took off their winter caps (it was summer at the time) and raised themselves as if expecting to be given orders. Arkady Pavlych bowed graciously to them. An alarmed excitement was clearly spreading through the village. Women in woollen checked skirts flung bits of wood at unappreciative or unduly noisy dogs; a lame old man with a beard that started below his very eyes pulled a horse that had not finished drinking away from the well, struck it for some unknown reason on the flank and then bowed low. Little boys in long shirts ran howling towards the huts, placed their tummies over the high doorsteps, hung their heads down, kicked up their legs behind them and in this way rolled themselves very briskly through the doors and into the dark entrance-ways, from which they did not reappear. Even chickens streamed at a hurried trot through the spaces below the gates; one lively cock, with a black breast like a satin waistcoat and a red tail that twirled right round to its comb, would have remained on the road and was just on the point of crowing, but suddenly took fright and ran off like the others.

The Bailiff's hut stood on its own amid an allotment of thick green hemp. We stopped in front of the gates. Mr Penochkin stood up, picturesquely threw off his travelling cloak and stepped out of the carriage, looking affably around him. The Bailiff's wife greeted us with low bows and approached her master's small hand. Arkady Pavlych permitted her to kiss it to her heart's content and stepped on to the porch. In the entrance-way to the hut, in a dark corner, stood the elder's wife, who also bowed, but she did not dare to approach the master's hand. In the so-called cold room, to the right of the entrance, two other women were already busy; they were carrying out all manner of rubbish, such as empty jugs, sheepskin coats of lath-like stiffness, butter jars, a cradle containing a pile of rags and a child arrayed in a motley of garments, and they were sweeping up the dirt with bath-house twigs. Arkady Pavlych sent them packing and set himself down on a bench under the icons. The drivers began to bring in trunks, boxes and other items for their master's comfort, endeavouring in every possible way to moderate the clattering made by their heavy boots.

Meanwhile, Arkady Pavlych was questioning the elder about the harvest, the sowing and other economic matters. The elder gave satisfactory answers, but somehow flabbily and awkwardly, as if he were doing up the buttons of his coat with frozen fingers. He stood by the door and all the time shrank back and glanced over his shoulder to make way for the bustling valet. Beyond his enormous shoulders I succeeded in catching sight of the Bailiff's wife quietly pummelling some other woman in the entrance-way. Suddenly a cart clattered up and stopped in front of the porch. The Bailiff came in.

This statesman-like man, as Arkady Pavlych had described him, was small in stature, broad-shouldered, grey and thick-set, with a red nose, little pale-blue eyes and a beard shaped like a fan. Let me remark in this regard that, ever since Russia has existed, there has never as yet been an example of a man gaining riches and corpulence who has not possessed a thoroughgoing beard; a man may all his life have worn nothing but a wispy goatee of a beard and suddenly, lo and behold, he's sprouted all over as if bathed in radiant light – and the wonder is where all the hairs came from! The Bailiff had assuredly been having a drop in Perov: his face had become thoroughly puffy and he dispensed around him strong whiffs of drink.

'Oh, our veritable father, our benefactor,' he began in a singsong voice and with such a look of exaltation on his face that it seemed he would instantly burst into tears, 'you've obliged yourself to visit us! Permit me your hand, your hand,' he added, stretching out his lips in anticipation. Arkady Pavlych satisfied his wish.

'Well, Sofron, my friend, how are your affairs going?' he asked in an unctuous voice.

'Oh, our veritable father,' Sofron exclaimed, 'how could they indeed go badly – our affairs, that is! You, our veritable father, our benefactor, you've most surely allowed light to shine into the life of our little village by your visit and you've given us pleasure to last the rest of our days! Glory be to thee, O Lord, Arkady Pavlych, glory be to thee, O Lord! Through your gracious kindness everything's in perfect order.'

At this point Sofron stopped a moment, looked at his master and, as though again carried away by an uncontrollable surge of emotion (the drink, mind you, had a part to play in this), once more asked for a hand and broke out in a singsong worse than before:

'Oh, our veritable father, our benefactor ... and ... See what's happened! My God, I've become a complete fool from the joy of it. . . . My God, I look at you and I can't believe it. . . . Oh, our veritable father!'

Arkady Pavlych glanced at me, smirked and asked: '*N'est-ce pas que c'est touchant?*'

'Indeed, good master, Arkady Pavlych,' the indefatigable Bailiff went on, 'how could you do such a thing? You have crushed me completely by not letting me know of your coming. After all, where'll you be spending the night? For sure, it's all filthy dirty here . . .'

'It's nothing, Sofron, nothing,' Arkady Pavlych answered with a smile. 'It's all right here.'

'But father of us all – who is it really all right for? It may be all right for our peasant friends, but surely you, my father and benefactor, oh, you, my own veritable father, how can you . . .? Forgive me, fool that I am, I've gone quite out of my wits, my God! I've lost all my senses!'

Supper was meanwhile served; Arkady Pavlych began to eat. The old man drove out his son, explaining that he wanted to make the room less stuffy.

'Well, me old dear, have you marked off the boundaries?' asked Mr Penochkin, who clearly wanted to give the impression of knowing peasant speech and kept on winking at me.

'''Tis done, good master, all of it done through your kindness. The day afore yesterday documents an' all were signed. Them Khlynov people at first were for makin' difficulties, that they were . . . difficulties, father, an' no mistake. Such demands they made . . . demands . . . God alone knows what they weren't demanding, but it was all a lot of foolishness, good master, stupid people they are. But we, good master, by your kindness did give thanks and did what was right by Mikolay Mikolayich, the one as was mediatin', an' everything was done accordin' to your orders, good master. Just as you saw fit to order it, that is how it was done, and 'twas all done with the knowledge of Yegor Dmitrich.'

'So Yegor has informed me,' Arkady Pavlych remarked importantly.

'Aye, good master, Yegor Dmitrich.'

'Well, you ought to be satisfied now, eh?'

Sofron had been waiting for just this.

'Oh, our veritable father, our benefactor!' he commenced his singsong again. 'Have mercy on me, for isn't it, our veritable father, day in and day out, night in and night out, that we're all prayin' to God for ye? . . . Of course, the land's on the short side, smallish . . .'

Penochkin interrupted him:

'Well, all right, all right, Sofron, I know you serve me conscientiously. . . . Now what about the threshing?'

Sofron sighed.

'Well, father to us all that you are, the threshin's not goin' awful well. An' there's something, good master, Arkady Pavlych, let me inform you, some little matter as 'as cropped up.' (At this point he drew closer to Mr Penochkin with outspread arms, bent forward and screwed up one eye.) 'A dead body did 'appen to be on our land.'

'How so?'

'Can't apply my mind to understandin' it, good master, father of us all – likely an enemy, it was, 'as done some devilish work. The blessin' was that it was by someone else's hand, and yet – there's no good concealin' it – it was right on our land. So I straightaway ordered it to be dragged on t'other land, so long as we had chance of doin' it, and set a guard by it and told our people: "Don't no one breathe a word" – that's what I says. But in any event I explained it to the constable, I did. I said: "It's how things are" – that's what I says, an' I give him a bit o' tea and somethin' what'd make him grateful. . . . An' so what d'you think, good master? It stayed over on t'others' land, hangin' round their necks. An' after all a dead body's likely to cost us two hundred roubles – no tup-pence-worth o' bread that isn't.'

Mr Penochkin laughed a great deal at his Bailiff's ruse and remarked to me several times, nodding in the old man's direction: '*Quel gaillard, hein?*'

In the meantime it had become quite dark outside. Arkady Pavlych ordered the table cleared and hay brought in. The valet laid out sheets for us and set out pillows; we lay down. Sofron retired to his quarters, having received the orders for the following day. Arkady Pavlych, on the point of going to sleep, persisted in chatting a little about the splendid qualities of the Russian peasant and remarked to me *à propos* of this that since Sofron had taken charge of the Shipilovka peasants there had been not so much as a farthing's-worth of quit-rent arrears. . . . The night-watchman gave a rat-tat on his board; a child, who had evidently not yet succeeded in becoming imbued with the requisite spirit of self-denial, started whimpering somewhere in the hut. We fell asleep.

The next morning we rose fairly early. I had wanted to set off for Ryabovo, but Arkady Pavlych wanted to show me his estate and begged me to stay. For my own part, I was not exactly averse to convincing myself in practice of the splendid qualities of that statesman-like man, Sofron. He appeared. He wore a blue peasant coat tied with a red sash. He was a good deal less talkative than he had been the previous day, directed keen, steady looks into his master's eyes and gave cogent, business-like answers to questions.

Together with him we set off for the threshing-floor. Sofron's son, the seven-foot-tall elder, to all appearances a man of extreme stupidity, walked along behind us, and we were also joined by the Bailiff's clerk, Fedoseyich, an ex-soldier with enormous whiskers and a most unusual expression on his face which suggested that he had been extraordinarily startled by something a very long time ago and had not yet come to his senses. We looked around the threshing-floor, the barn, the store-houses, the outbuildings, the windmill, the cattle-shed, the vegetable allotments and land planted to hemp: everything was undoubtedly in splendid order and it was only the despondent faces of the peasants that gave me cause to feel slightly puzzled. Apart from practical matters, Sofron also concerned himself with making the place pretty: all the banks of the ditches had been planted with broom, paths had been made between the ricks on the threshing-floor and spread with sand, a weathervane had been fixed to the windmill in the shape of a bear with an open maw and red tongue, a kind of Grecian pediment had been stuck on the brick-built cattle-shed and beneath the pediment was written in white paint: 'Puilt in Shipilofka vilage in year one thousand aight hunted farty. This Cattle Shet.'

Arkady Pavlych was completely overwhelmed and embarked for my benefit on a dissertation in French about the benefits of the quit-rent system, although he remarked by the way that the system of direct work was more profitable for landowners – but what of it, anyhow! He began giving his Bailiff advice on how to plant potatoes, how to prepare fodder for the cattle and so forth. Sofron listened attentively to his master's words, occasionally making his own comments, but no longer endowing Arkady Pavlych with such grandiose titles as 'our veritable father' or 'our benefactor', and insisting all the time that the land, after all, was on the small side and that it would do no harm to buy some more.

'Buy it, then,' said Arkady Pavlych, 'in my name. I'm not against that.'

To which Sofron said nothing in return, simply stroked his beard.

'Now, however, there'd be no harm in riding into the forest,' remarked Mr Penochkin. At once horses were brought for us and we rode into the forest or 'reserve', as we are accustomed to call forest areas. In this 'reserve' we found a terrific abundance of thickets and wild life, for which Arkady Pavlych praised Sofron and patted him on the back. Mr Penochkin upheld Russian notions about forestry and recounted to me on the spot a highly diverting – in his view – instance of how a certain landowner, who was fond of joking, had enlightened his woodsman by pulling out practically half the man's beard as proof of the fact that felling trees does not make a forest grow any thicker. . . . Nevertheless, in other respects, Sofron and Arkady Pavlych did not fight shy of innovations. On returning to the village, the Bailiff took us to see the winnowing machine which he had recently ordered from Moscow. The winnowing machine, it is true, worked well, but if Sofron had known the unpleasantness that awaited both him and his master on this final walk, he would no doubt have stayed at home with us.

This is what happened. As we left the outbuilding, we were confronted with the following spectacle. A few steps from the door, beside a muddy pool of water in which three ducks were carelessly splashing about, two peasants were kneeling: one was an old man of about sixty, the other a young fellow of about twenty, both barefoot, in patched shirts made of coarse hemp with rope belts at the waist. The clerk, Fedoseyich, was zealously fussing round them and would probably have succeeded in persuading them to go away, if we had stayed longer in the outbuilding, but on catching sight of us, he straightened up taut as a violin string and froze on the spot. The elder also stood there with wide-open mouth and fists clenched in bewilderment. Arkady Pavlych frowned, bit his lip and approached the petitioners. Both of them bowed silently at his feet.

'What's up with you? What are you petitioning about?' he asked in a stern voice and slightly through the nose. (The peasants looked at each other and said not a word, simply screwed up their eyes, just as if the sun were blinding them, and began to breathe faster.)

'Well, what is it?' continued Arkady Pavlych and at once turned to Sofron. 'From which family?'

'From the Toboleyev family,' the Bailiff answered slowly.

'Well, what's it you're after?' Mr Penochkin started asking again. 'Haven't you got tongues, eh? Can't you tell me what it is?' he added, giving a nod towards the old man. 'Don't be afraid, you fool.'

The old man stretched out his dark, coal-brown wrinkled neck, crookedly drew apart lips that had grown blue with age and uttered in a husky voice, 'Help us, lord and master!' and again struck the earth with his forehead. The young peasant also made an obeisance. Arkady Pavlych looked with dignity at the napes of their necks, threw back his head and placed his feet slightly apart.

'What is it? Who are you complaining about?'

'Have mercy on us, lord and master! Give us a chance to catch our breath. . . . Completely done in we are!' (The old man spoke with difficulty.)

'Who's done you in?'

'Sofron Yakovlich, it is, good master.'

Arkady Pavlych was silent for a moment.

'What's your name?'

'Antip, good master.'

'And who's this?'

'My boy, good master.'

Arkady Pavlych was again silent for a moment and twitched his whiskers.

'Well, and how has he done you in?' he asked, looking at the old man over his moustache.

'Good master, ruined us he has, utterly. Two sons, good master, he's sent off out of turn to be recruits, and now he's taking away my third son. . . . Yesterday, good master, he led away the last little cow from my yard and gave my wife a beating – that's his worship over there what done it.' (He pointed to the elder.)

'Hmmm!' pronounced Arkady Pavlych.

'Don't leave us to be completely ruined, bountiful master.'

Mr Penochkin frowned. 'What does this all mean?' he asked the Bailiff under his breath with a look of dissatisfaction.

'A drunkard, sir,' the Bailiff answered, using the formal 'sir' for the first time. 'Doesn't do any work. It's already the fifth year, sir, that he's behind with his payments.'

'Sofron Yakovlich's paid the arrears in for me,' continued the old man. 'It's the fifth year's gone by and he's paid in, and paid in he has so as I'm in bondage to him, good master, that's how it is. . . .'

'And why did you get into arrears?' Mr Penochkin asked threateningly. (The old man bowed his head.) 'Suppose it's because you like getting drunk, like roaming about from tavern to tavern?' (The old man was on the point of opening his mouth.) 'I know your sort,' Arkady Pavlych continued vehemently, 'all you do is drink and lie on the stove and let good peasants answer for you.'

'And insolent as well,' the Bailiff inserted into his master's speech.

'Well, that goes without saying. That's always the way of it – I've noticed that more than once. He'll spend the whole year lazing about and being insolent and now he flops down on his knees at your feet!'

'Good master, Arkady Pavlych,' the old man started saying desperately, 'be merciful, help me – how am I insolent? As I speak now before the Lord God, I'm being made helpless by it all, I am. He's taken a dislike to me, Sofron Yakovlich has, and why he's done so only the Lord can judge! He's ruining me utterly, good master. . . . Here's my last son – and now he's to go, too. . . .' (Teardrops glittered in the old man's yellow and wrinkled eyes.) 'Be merciful, my lord and master, help me. . . .'

'Aye, and it's not only us . . .' the young peasant was on the point of beginning.

Arkady Pavlych suddenly flared up:

'And who's asking you, eh? Nobody's asking you, so you be quiet. . . . What is this? Be quiet, I'm telling you! Be quiet! Oh, my God, this is quite simply rebellion. No, my friend, I don't advise you to try being rebellious on my property . . . on my property. . . .' (Arkady Pavlych took a step forward and then, no doubt, remembered my presence, turned away and placed his hands in his pockets.) '*Je vous demande bien pardon, mon cher,*' he said with a forced smile, lowering his voice meaningfully. '*C'est le mauvais côté de la médaille.* . . . Well, all right, all right,' he continued without looking at the peasants, 'I'll issue an order . . . all right, be off with you.' (The peasants did not rise.) 'Well, didn't I say to you . . . all right. Be off with you, I'll issue an order, I'm telling you that.'

Arkady Pavlych turned his back on them. 'No end of un-pleasantnesses,' he uttered through his teeth and made for home with big strides. Sofron followed in his wake. The clerk's eyes almost popped out of his head, just as if he was preparing himself for a very high jump. The elder drove the ducks out of the pool. The petitioners remained for a short while where they were, looked at each other and then plodded off without looking back.

Two hours later I was already in Ryabovo, and together with Anpadist, a peasant acquaintance of mine, I was preparing to go hunting. Right up to my very departure Penoch-kin had been huffy towards Sofron. I struck up a conversation with Anpadist about the Shipilovka peasants and Mr Penochkin, and I asked whether he knew the Bailiff in that village.

'Sofron Yakovlich, you mean? Sure!'

'What sort of man is he?'

'He's a dog, not a man. You won't find another dog like him this side of Kursk.'

'What do you mean?'

'It's like this. Shipilovka's no more'n registered in the name of – what's he called? – that Penkin. He doesn't really own it. It's Sofron who owns it.'

'Do you really mean that?'

'He owns it like it's his own property. The peasants all around are owing him money. They work for him like they were in bondage to him. One he'll send off with a string of carts, another he'll send off somewhere else . . . bled them white he has.'

'It seems they haven't got much land?'

'Not much? He rents two hundred and sixteen acres just from the Khlynov peasants and three hundred and twenty-four from our peasants – that's a good five hundred acres for you. And he isn't only trading in land: he does trade in horses, too, and cattle, and tar, and butter, and hemp, and this and that. . . . Clever, awful clever, he is, and rich, too, the varmint! What's bad about him is – he's always knocking someone about. A wild beast, not a man. I tell you he's a dog, a cur, a real cur if ever there was one.'

'Then why don't they complain against him?'

'Phew! The master doesn't need to bother! There aren't any arrears, so what's it got to do with him? And just you try it,' he added after a short pause, 'try complaining. No, he'll get you . . . yes, you just try it. No, he'll just get you, just like that he will. . . .'

I remembered about Antip and told him what I had seen.

'Well,' declared Anpadist, 'he'll eat him up now, eat him good and proper, he will. The elder'll start beating him up now. What bad luck he's had, the poor wretch, when you think of it! And what he's going through it for? . . . It was just that at a meeting he got cross with him, with the Bailiff, couldn't stand any more, you know. . . . Mighty big matter, that! So he began pecking at him, at Antip. Now he'll eat him right up. He's just that kind of a cur, a dog – the Lord forgive me for my sins – that he knows who to get his teeth into. The old men what are richer and with bigger families, them he doesn't touch, the bald-headed devil – but in this case he's lost his control! After all, he sent off Antip's sons out of turn to become recruits, the unpardonable rogue, the cur – the Lord forgive me for my sins!'

We went off hunting.

Salzbrunn, in Silesia
July 1847

Two Landowners

I HAVE already had the honour, kind readers, of acquainting you with some of my neighbouring landowners; please permit me now, appropriately (for the likes of us writers everything is appropriate), to acquaint you with two further landowners, on whose lands I have frequently hunted, men who are highly esteemed and well-intentioned, and who enjoy universal respect in several counties.

To begin with, I will describe to you the retired Major-General Vyacheslav Illarionovich Khvalynsky. Imagine a tall man, at one time possessing a graceful build, though now a little flabby, but by no means decrepit, not even really old – a man of mature age, in his prime, as they say. True, the formerly straight – even so, still pleasing – features of his face have changed a little, his cheeks have sagged, frequent wrinkles form ray-like surrounds to his eyes, here and there a tooth is gone, as Saadi[1] was reputed to have said, according to Pushkin; the auburn hair – at least, what has remained of it – has turned a lilac grey, thanks to a preparation bought at the Romen horse fair from a Jew who passed himself off as an Armenian; but Vyacheslav Illarionovich has a lively manner of speaking, laughs boisterously, jingles his spurs, twirls his moustache and – to cap it all – speaks of himself as an old cavalry officer, whereas it is common knowledge that real oldsters never speak of themselves as old. He usually wears a coat buttoned up to the neck, a tall cravat with starched collar and wide grey speckled trousers of military cut; his cap he wears pulled straight down over his forehead, leaving the back of his head completely bare.

He is a man of great kindness, but with some fairly strange notions and habits. For example: he can never treat impoverished noblemen or those with no rank as people who are his equals. Conversing with them, he usually looks at them sideways, leaning his cheek strongly against his firm, white collar, or he suddenly ups and glowers at them with a lucid and unwavering stare, stops talking and starts twitching the skin all over his scalp; he even takes to pronouncing words differently and does not say, for instance: 'Thank you, Pavel Vasilych', or 'Please approach, Mikhaylo Ivanych', but: 'Sonk you, Pall Asilich', or 'Pl-laase apprarch, Mikhal Vanych'. He deals even more oddly with those who occupy the lowest rungs of society: he does not look at them at all and, prior to explaining to them what he wants or giving an order, he has a way of repeating, several times in a row and with a perplexed and dreamy look on his face: 'What's your name? . . . What's your name?', placing unusually sharp emphasis on the first word 'what' and uttering the rest very rapidly, which gives his manner of speaking a fairly close resemblance to the cry of a male quail. He is a terrible one for fussing and frightfully grasping, but he is poor at managing his own affairs, having taken on as administrator of his estate a retired sergeant-major who is a Little Russian and an extraordinarily stupid man.

In the matter of estate-management, by the way, not one of us has yet out-done a certain important St Petersburg official who, having observed from the reports of his steward that the store-barns on his estate were frequently catching fire (as a result of which a great deal of his grain was being lost), issued the strictest edict to the effect that corn sheaves should not be placed in the barns until all fires were completely extinguished. This very same personage took it into his head to sow all his fields with poppies on the evidently very simple principle, so he claimed, that poppy-seed was dearer than rye, consequently poppies were more profitable. It was he who also ordered all his peasant women to wear tall head-dresses designed according to a pattern sent from St Petersburg and in fact, right up to the present day, the womenfolk on his estates still wear such head-dresses – except that the tall tops have been folded down ... But we must return to Vyacheslav Illarionovich.

Vyacheslav Illarionovich is terribly keen on the fair sex and he no sooner catches sight of some pretty girl or other on the street of his local town than he at once sets off in hot pursuit, only to develop a sudden limp – which is a remarkable state of affairs. He likes to play cards, but only with people of lower rank, so that they will address him as 'Your Excellency' while he can huff and puff at them and abuse them as much as he wishes. Whenever he happens to be playing with the Governor or some high-ranking official, a surprising change comes over him: he even smiles and nods his head and looks them intently in the eyes – he positively exudes honey and sweetness. . . . He even loses without grumbling.

Vyacheslav Illarionovich reads little and, when he does, he continuously moves his moustache and eyebrows – first his moustache, then his eyebrows, just as if a wave was passing upwards across his face. This wave-like movement on the face of Vyacheslav Illarionovich is particularly noteworthy when he happens – in the presence of guests, naturally – to be reading through the columns of the *Journal des Debats*. At the elections of marshals of nobility he plays a fairly important role, but out of meanness he always refuses the honourable title of marshal. 'Gentlemen,' he says to the members of the nobility who usually approach him on the subject, and he says it in a voice redolent with condescension and self-confidence, 'I am much obliged for the honour; but I have resolved to devote my leisure hours to solitude.' And, having once uttered these words, he will jerk his head several times to right and left, and then, with dignity, let the flesh of his chin and cheeks lap over his cravat.

In the days of his youth he was adjutant to some important personage, whom he never addressed otherwise than by his name and patronymic. They say that he assumed rather more than the duties of an adjutant, that decked out, for example, in full parade uniform, with everything buttoned-up and in place, he used to attend to his master's needs in the bath-house – but one can't believe everything one hears. Besides, General Khvalynsky is himself by no means fond of mentioning his service career, which is in general a somewhat odd circumstance; he also, it seems, has no experience of war. He lives, does General Khvalynsky, in a small house, by himself; he has had no experience of married happiness in his life, and consequently is regarded as an eligible bachelor even now – indeed, an advantageous match. Yet he has a housekeeper, a woman of about thirty-five, black-eyed and black-browed, buxom, fresh-faced and bewhiskered, who walks about on week-days in starched dresses, adding muslin sleeves on Sundays.

Splendid is Vyacheslav Illarionovich's behaviour at large banquets given by landowners in honour of Governors and other persons in authority: on such occasions, it might be said, he is truly in his element. It is usual for him on such occasions to sit, if not directly to the Governor's right, then not far from him; at the beginning of the banquet he is concerned more than anything with preserving a sense of his own dignity and, leaning back, though without turning his head, directs his eyes sideways at the stand-up collars of the guests and the round napes of their necks; then, towards the end of the sitting, he grows expansively gay, smiles in all directions (he had smiled in the Governor's direction from the beginning of the meal) and even occasionally proposes a toast in honour of the fair sex – an ornament to our planet, as he puts it. Likewise, General Khvalynsky makes a good showing on all solemn and public occasions, at inquiries, assemblies and exhibitions; masterly, also, is his fashion of receiving a blessing from a priest. At the end of theatrical performances, at river-crossings and other such places, Vyacheslav Illarionovich's servants never make a noise or shout; on the contrary, making a path for him through a crowd or summoning a carriage, they always say in pleasant, throaty baritones: 'If you please, if you please, make way for General Khvalynsky' or 'General Khvalynsky's carriage. . . .' His carriage, if the truth be told, is of fairly ancient design; his footmen wear fairly tattered livery (it is hardly worth mentioning that it is grey with red piping); his horses are also fairly antiquated and have given service in their time; but Vyacheslav Illarionovich makes no pretensions to dandyishness and does not even consider it proper for a man of his rank to throw dust in people's eyes.

Khvalynsky has no particular gift for words, or it may be that he has no chance of displaying his eloquence since he cannot tolerate either disputes or rebuttals and studiously avoids all lengthy conversations, particularly with young people. Indeed, this is the proper way to handle things; any other way would be disastrous with the people as they are today: in no time at all they'd stop being servile and start losing respect for you. In the presence of those of higher rank Khvalynsky is mostly taciturn, but to those of lower rank, whom he evidently despises but who are the only ones he knows, he delivers sharp, abrupt speeches, endlessly using such expressions as: 'You are, however, talking rubbish', or 'At last I find it necessary, my good fellah, to put you in your place', or 'Now, damn it all, you surely ought to know who you're talking to,' and so on. Postmasters, committee chairmen and station-masters are especially awed by him. He never receives guests at home and lives, so rumour has it, like a regular Scrooge. Despite all this, he is an excellent landowner. Neighbours refer to him as 'an old fellow who's done his service, a man who's quite selfless, with principles, *vieux grognard*, old grouser that he is'. The public prosecutor of the province is the only man to permit himself a smile when mention is made in his presence of General Khvalynsky's splendid and solid qualities – but, then, such is the power of envy!

Let me pass now to another landowner.

Mardary Apollonych Stegunov bore no resemblance at all to Khvalynsky; he was hardly likely to have served anywhere and was never accounted handsome. Mardary Apollonych is a squat little old man, roly-poly and bald, with a double chin, soft little hands and a thoroughgoing paunch. He is a great one for entertaining and has a fondness for pranks; he lives, as they say, in clover; and winter and summer he walks about in a striped quilted dressing-gown. In only one respect is he similar to General Khvalynsky: he is also a bachelor. He has five hundred serfs. Mardary Apollonych takes a fairly superficial interest in his estate; ten years ago, so as not to be too far behind the times, he bought from the Butenops in Moscow a threshing machine, locked it in his barn and then rested content. On a fine summer day he may indeed order his racing buggy to be harnessed and then ride out into the field to see how the grain is ripening and to pick cornflowers.

He lives, does Mardary Apollonych, completely in the old style. Even his house is of antiquated construction: the entrance hall, as one might expect, smells of *kvas*, tallow candles and leather; on the right stands a sideboard with pipes and hand-towels; the dining-room contains family portraits, flies, a large pot of geraniums and a down-in-the-mouth piano; the drawing-room has three divans, three tables, two mirrors and a wheezy clock of blackened enamel with fretted, bronze hands; the study has a table piled with papers, a bluish draught-screen pasted with pictures cut from various works of the last century, cupboards full of stinking books, spiders and thick black dust, a stuffed arm-chair and an Italian window and a door into the garden that has been nailed up. . . . In a word, everything is quite appropriate. Mardary Apollonych has a mass of servants, and they are all dressed in old-fashioned style: long blue coats with high collars, trousers of some muddy colouring and short yellowish waistcoats. They use the old-fashioned address 'good master' in speaking to guests.

His estate is managed by a bailiff drawn from among his peasants, a man with a beard as long as his sheepskin coat; his house is run by an old woman, wrinkled and tight-fisted, with a brown kerchief wound round her head. His stables contain thirty horses of various sizes; he rides out in a home-made carriage weighing well over two and a half tons. He receives guests with the utmost warmth and entertains them lavishly – that is to say, thanks to the stupefying characteristics of Russian cookery, he deprives them, until right up to the evening, of any opportunity of doing anything apart from playing preference. He himself never occupies himself with anything and has even given up reading his dream-book. But we still have a good many such landowners in Russia. It may be asked: what's led me to mention him and why? In place of a straight answer, let me tell you about one of my visits to Mardary Apollonych.

I went over to his place one summer, about seven o'clock in the evening. Evening prayers had just concluded, and the priest, a young man, evidently very shy and only recently graduated from his seminary, was sitting in the drawing-room beside the door, perched on the very edge of a chair. Mardary Apollonych, as was his custom, received me exceptionally fondly: he was genuinely delighted to receive guests and, by and large, he was the kindest of men. The priest rose and picked up his hat.

'One moment, one moment, my good fellow,' said Mardary Apollonych without leaving hold of my arm. 'You mustn't be going. I've ordered them to bring you some vodka.'

'I don't drink, sir,' the priest mumbled in confusion and reddened up to his ears.

'What rubbish! You say you're a priest and you don't drink!' Mardary Apollonych retorted. 'Mishka! Yushka! Vodka for the gentleman!'

Yushka, a tall and emaciated old man of about eighty, came

in with a glass of vodka on a dark-painted tray covered with a variety of flesh-coloured splodges.

The priest proceeded to refuse.

'Drink, my good fellow, and no fussing, it's not proper,' the landowner remarked in a reproachful tone.

The poor young man acquiesced.

'Well now, my good fellow, you can go.'

The priest started bowing.

'All right, all right, be off with you. . . . An excellent fellow,' Mardary Apollonych continued, watching him depart, 'and I'm very satisfied with him. The only thing is – he's still young. Preaches sermons all the time, and he doesn't drink. But how are you, my good fellow? What're you doing, how're things? Let's go out on to the balcony – you see what a fine evening it is.'

We went out on to the balcony, sat down and began to talk. Mardary Apollonych glanced downwards and suddenly became frightfully excited.

'Whose are these chickens? Whose are these chickens?' he started shouting. 'Whose are these chickens walking about the garden? Yushka! Yushka! Off with you and find out at once whose are these chickens walking about the garden. Whose are these chickens? How many times I've forbidden this, how many times I've said so!'

Yushka ran off.

'What disorders there are!' repeated Mardary Apollonych. 'It's terrible!'

The unfortunate chickens – as I recall it now, there were two speckled and one white one with a crest – continued walking under the apple trees with the utmost lack of concern, occasionally expressing their feelings by making prolonged cluckings, when suddenly Yushka, hatless and armed with a stick, and three other house-serfs who were well on in years made a combined attack on them. A riot followed. The chickens squawked, flapped their wings, leapt about and cackled deafeningly; the house-serfs ran to and fro, stumbling and falling; and their master shouted from the balcony like one possessed: 'Catch them, catch them! Catch them, catch them! Catch them, catch them, catch them! Whose are these chickens, whose are these chickens?' Finally, one of the house-serfs succeeded in catching the crested chicken by forcing its breast to the ground, and at that very moment a girl of about eleven years of age, thoroughly dishevelled and with a switch in her hand, jumped over the garden fence from the street.

'So that's who the chickens belong to!' the landowner exclaimed triumphantly. 'They're Yermila the coachman's! See, he's sent his little Natalya to drive them back! It's not likely he'd send Parasha,' the landowner interjected under his breath and grinned meaningfully. 'Hey, Yushka! Forget the chickens and bring little Natalya here.'

But before the puffing Yushka could reach the terrified little girl, she was grabbed by the housekeeper, who had appeared from nowhere, and given several slaps on her behind.

'That's right, that's right,' the landowner said, accompanying the slaps. 'Yes, yes, yes! Yes, yes, yes! And mind you take the chickens off, Avdotya,' he added in a loud voice and turned to me with a shining face: 'Quite a chase, my good fellow, what? I've even worked myself into a sweat – just look at me!'

And Mardary Apollonych rattled off into thunderous laughter.

We remained on the balcony. The evening was really unusually beautiful. Tea was served to us.

'Tell me,' I began, 'Mardary Apollonych, are they yours, those settlements out there on the road, beyond the ravine?'

'They're mine. What of it?'

'How could you allow such a thing, Mardary Apollonych? It's quite wrong. The tiny huts allotted to the peasants are horrible, cramped things; there's not a tree to be seen anywhere; there's nothing in the way of a pond; there's only one

well, and that's no use. Surely you could have found somewhere else? And rumour has it that you've even taken away
their old hemp-fields.'

'But what's one to do about these redistributions of the
land?' Mardary Apollonych asked me in turn. 'This redistri-
bution's got me right here.' He pointed to the back of his
neck. 'And I don't foresee any good coming from it. And as
to whether I took away their hemp-fields and didn't dig out a
pond for them there – about such matters, my good fellow, I
haven't the foggiest. I'm just a simple man and I have old-
fashioned ways. In my way of thinking, if you're the master,
you're the master, and if you're a peasant, you're a peasant.
And that's that.'

It goes without saying that such a lucid and convincing
argument was unanswerable.

'What's more,' he continued, 'those peasants are a bad sort,
not in my good books. Particularly two families over there.
Even my late father, God rest his soul in the Kingdom of
Heaven, even he wasn't fond of them, not at all fond of them.
And I'll tell you something I've noticed: if the father's a thief,
then the son'll be a thief, it doesn't matter how much you
want things to be otherwise. . . . Oh, blood-ties, blood-ties –
they're the big thing! I tell you quite frankly that I've sent
men from those two families to be recruits out of their turn
and shoved them around here, there and everywhere. But
what's one to do? They won't give up breeding. They're so
fertile, damn them!'

In the meantime, the air grew completely quiet. Only
occasionally a light breeze eddied around us and, on the last
occasion, as it died down around the house it brought to our
ears the sound of frequent and regular blows which resounded
from the direction of the stables. Mardary Apollonych had
only just raised a full saucer to his lips and was already on the
point of distending his nostrils, without which, as everyone
knows, no true Russian can imbibe his tea, when he stopped,

pricked up his ears, nodded his head, drank and, setting the saucer down on the table, uttered with the kindest of smiles and as if unconsciously in time with the blows: 'Chooky-chooky-chook! Chooky-chook! Chooky-chook!'

'What on earth is that?' I asked in astonishment.

'It's a little rascal being punished on my orders. Do you by any chance know Vasya the butler?'

'Which Vasya?'

'The one who's just been waiting on us at dinner. He's the one who sports those large side-whiskers.'

The fiercest sense of outrage could not have withstood Mardary Apollonych's meek and untrammeled gaze.

'What's bothering you, young man, eh?' he said, shaking his head. 'You think I'm wicked, is that why you're staring at me like that? Spare the rod and spoil the child, you know that as well as I do.'

A quarter of an hour later I said good-bye to Mardary Apollonych. On my way through the village I saw Vasya the butler. He was walking along the street and chewing nuts. I ordered my driver to stop the horses and called to him.

'Did they give you a beating today, my friend?' I asked him.

'How do you know about it?' Vasya answered.

'Your master told me.'

'The master did?'

'Why did he order you to be beaten?'

'It served me right, good master, it served me right. You don't get beaten for nothing here. That's not how things are arranged here – oh, no. Our master's not like that, our master's ... you won't find another master like ours anywhere else in the province.'

'Let's go!' I told my driver. *Well, that's old-style Russia for you!* I thought as I travelled home.

Death

I HAVE a neighbour, a youthful squire and youthful hunter. One beautiful July morning I rode over to his place with a proposal that he should join me on a grouse shoot. He agreed. 'Only,' he said, 'let's go by way of some small property of mine in the Zusha[1] direction. I'd like to have a look at Chaplygino, my oak wood, d'you know it? They're cutting it down.'

'Let's be off, then.'

He ordered a horse to be saddled and dressed himself in a short green jacket with bronze buttons bearing the image of a boar's head, pulled on a worsted game-bag and silver flask, and having thrown a new French sports-gun over his shoulder, disported himself before the mirror, not without some approbation, and shouted for his dog, Esperance, a gift from a cousin, an elderly maiden lady with a warm heart but without a hair on her head.

We set off. My neighbour took with him the local guardian of the peace, Arkhip, a stout and thick-set peasant with a square-shaped face and cheekbones of positively antediluvian dimensions, and a young man of about nineteen, lean, fair-haired and shortsighted, with sloping shoulders and a long neck, Mr Gottlieb von der Kock, recently engaged as a manager from the Baltic provinces. My neighbour had not long before inherited his estate. It had come to him as an inheritance from his aunt, Kardon-Katayeva, the widow of a state's counsellor, a woman of unusual obesity who, even when lying in bed, had a habit of emitting protracted and piteous groans. We reached his small property and Ardalion Mikhaylich (my neighbour)

129

said, addressing his companions: 'Wait for me out here in the clearing.'

The German bowed, slid from his horse, extracted a small book from his pocket – a novel, it appeared, by Johanna Schopenhauer[2] – and seated himself in the shade of a bush, while Arkhip remained out in the sun for a solid hour without budging an inch. Ardalion Mikhaylich and I made a round of the undergrowth, but were unable to find a single bird. My friend announced that he was determined to set off for his wood. I was also far from convinced that our hunting would be successful on such a day and trailed along behind him. We returned to the clearing. The German made a note of his page, stood up, placed his book in his pocket and, not without some difficulty, mounted his short-tailed reject of a mare which neighed and kicked at the slightest touch. Arkhip sprang to life, gave a sharp tug at both reins, clapped his legs against the animal's flanks and eventually managed to set off on his cowed and shaken little steed. Off we went.

Ardalion Mikhaylich's wood had been known to me since my childhood. I had often gone to Chaplygino in the company of my French tutor, Monsieur Désiré Fleury, an excellent chap (who, however, only just avoided ruining my health irretrievably by forcing me to take the medicines of Leroy every evening). The entire wood consisted of some two or three hundred enormous oaks and ash trees. Their stately, powerful trunks used to stand out in magnificent dark relief against the golden transparency of the green-leaved rowans and nut trees; rising on high they composed their fine proportions against the lucid blue sky and there spread out the domes of their far-reaching, angular branches; hawks, merlins, kestrels, all whistled and hovered above their motionless crests and colourful woodpeckers tapped away loudly at their thick bark; the resonant song of the blackbird suddenly rang out amid the thick foliage in the wake of the lilting call of the oriole; below, in the undergrowth, robins, siskins and chiffchaffs chirruped and sang; finches darted to and fro across the paths; white hares ran along the edge of the wood in cautious stops and starts, and nut-brown squirrels leapt friskily from tree to tree, suddenly stopping with tails raised above their heads. In the grass, around tall ant-hills and in the mild shadiness offered by the beautiful fretwork of ferns, violets used to flower, and lilies of the valley, and reddish mushrooms grew, russula, emetic agaric, milk agaric, fairy clubs and red fly agaric; and in the meadows, among the widespread bushes, wild strawberries would glow crimson. . . . . And what deep shade there was in the wood! At noon, when the heat was greatest, it would be dark as night: peaceful, fragrant, moist. . . . Time would pass for me so gaily at Chaplygino that it was, I admit, not without a feeling of sadness that I now rode into this all-too-familiar wood. The bitter, snowless winter of 1840 had not spared my old friends, the oaks and ash trees. Desiccated and naked, covered here and there with diseased leaf, they rose sadly above the young trees which 'had supplanted them but not replaced them'. . . .*[3] Some, well covered with foliage on their lower boughs, raised on high, as if in reproach and desperation, their lifeless, broken upper branches; from other trees amidst foliage which was still quite thick, although not as abundant or overflowing as it was formerly, there stuck out fat, dry limbs of dead wood; from others, the bark had already fallen away; and there were some that had fallen down completely and lay rotting on the ground like corpses. Who could have foreseen that there would have been shadows in Chaplygino, where once there wasn't a single shadow to be found! As I looked at the dying trees, I thought: Surely you

* In 1840 there were most cruel frosts and snow did not fall before the end of December; all the foliage was frozen to death, and many fine oak forests were destroyed by this merciless winter. It is difficult to replace them; the fertility of the earth is obviously declining; on waste lands that have been 're-served' (that is to say, which have had icons carried round them) birches and aspens are growing up of their own accord in place of the noble trees which used to grow there; for we know no other way of propagating our woodlands.

must know shame and bitterness? And I recalled the lines from Koltsov: [4]

> Where have you gone to
> Speech high and mighty,
> Strength so haughty,
> Courage so kingly?
> Where is it now
> The green sap and the power?

'Why was it, Ardalion Mikhaylich,' I began, 'that these trees weren't cut down the year afterwards? They won't give you a tenth of what they were worth before.'

He simply shrugged his shoulders.

'You should have asked my aunt – merchants came to her, brought money, badgered her.'

'*Mein Gott! Mein Gott!*' von der Kock exclaimed at every step. 'Such a sham! Such a sham!'

'What sham?' my neighbour remarked with a smile.

'This eez a shame, what I wishes to te*ll*.' (It is well known that all Germans, once they have finally mastered our Russian letter 'l', dwell on it amazingly.)

His compassion was particularly aroused by the oaks which lay on the ground – and no wonder, for many a miller would have paid a high price for them. But our guardian of the peace, Arkhip, maintained an imperturbable composure and showed not the least sign of regret; on the contrary, it was even with a certain pleasure that he jumped over them and lashed at them with his riding crop.

We made our way to the place where the felling was going on, when suddenly, after the sound of a falling tree, there resounded cries and talk, and a few seconds later a young peasant, pale and dishevelled, raced towards us out of a thicket.

'What's the matter? Where are you running?' Ardalion Mikhaylich asked him.

He stopped at once.

'Ardalion Mikhaylich, sir, there's been an accident.'

'What's the matter?'

'Maxim, sir, has been knocked down by a tree.'

'How did it happen? Do you mean Maxim the contractor?'

'Yes, sir, the contractor. We started cutting down an ash tree, and he stood and watched. . . . He was standing there a long time, and then he went to the well to get water, like he wanted to have a drink, see. Then all of a sudden the ash tree starts creaking and falling right down on him. We shout to him: Run, run, run. . . . He could've thrown himself to one side, but instead he decides to run straight on . . . he got scared, you know. The ash tree's top boughs fell right on him and covered him. God only knows why it fell so quickly. Probably it was all rotten inside.'

'So it struck Maxim, did it?'

'It struck him, sir.'

'Did it kill him?'

'No, sir, he's still alive, but it's no good: his legs and arms are broken. I was just running to get Seliverstych, the doctor.'

Ardalion Mikhaylich ordered the guardian of the peace to gallop into the village for Seliverstych and himself set off at a brisk trot for the site of the felling. I followed him.

We found the wretched Maxim on the ground. Ten or so peasants were gathered round him. We alighted from our horses. He was hardly groaning at all, though occasionally he opened wide his eyes, as if looking around him with surprise, and bit his blue lips. His chin quivered, his hair was stuck to his temples and his chest rose irregularly: he was clearly dying. The faint shadow of a young lime tree ran calmly aslant his face. We bent down to him, and he recognized Ardalion Mikhaylich.

'Sir,' he began to say in a scarcely audible voice, 'the priest . . . send for him . . . order to send . . . God has . . . has punished me . . . my legs, arms, all broken . . . today . . . Sunday . . . but I . . . but I . . . you see . . . I didn't let the lads off.'

He fell silent. His breath came in short gasps.

'My money ... the wife ... give it to the wife ... after what's owing ... Onisim knows ... who I ... owe what ...'

'We've sent for the doctor, Maxim,' my neighbour said. 'Perhaps you won't die after all.'

He wanted to open wide his eyes and with an effort raised his brows and eyelids.

'No, I'll die. See ... see, there she's coming, there she is, there. ... Forgive me, lads, if I've in any way ...'

'God'll forgive you, Maxim Andreyich,' the peasants said in husky unison and removed their caps. 'And you forgive us.'

He gave a sudden desperate shake of the head, lifted his chest regretfully and again sank back.

'He shouldn't have to die here,' Ardalion Mikhaylich exclaimed. 'Lads, get the mat from the cart over there and let's carry him to the hospital.'

A couple of men rushed to the cart.

'Off of Efim ... Sychovsky,' the dying man began to babble, 'I bought a horse yesterday. ... I put money down. ... So the horse is mine ... see the wife gets that as well ...'

They began to lay him on the mat. He started trembling all over, like a shot bird, and straightened up.

'He's dead,' the peasants said.

Silently, we mounted our horses and rode off.

The death of the wretched Maxim put me in a reflective mood. What an astonishing thing is the death of a Russian peasant! His state of mind before death could be called neither one of indifference, nor one of stupidity; he dies as if he is performing a ritual act, coldly and simply.

A few years ago a peasant belonging to another country neighbour of mine was burned in a barn. (He would, in fact, have remained in the barn had not a visitor from town pulled him out half dead: he doused himself in a pitcher of water and at a run broke down the door under the overhang which was already alight.) I visited him in his hut. It was dark inside, the atmosphere stuffy and smoky. 'Where is the sick man?' I inquired.

'Over there, sir, above the stove,' answered the singsong voice of an old woman weighed down by her burden of grief.

I approached and found a peasant covered in a sheepskin, breathing painfully.

'Well, how are you feeling?'

The sick man grew restless, wanted to raise himself, but he was covered in wounds and close to death.

'Lie down, lie down. Well? How is it?'

'I'm poorly, that's for sure,' he said.

'Does it hurt you?'

No answer.

'Is there anything you need?'

Silence.

'Shall I order some tea to be sent to you, eh?'

'There's no need.'

I left him and sat down on a bench. I sat for a quarter of an hour, half an hour, and all the while the silence of the grave reigned in the hut. In one corner, by a table under the icons, a five-year-old girl was hiding, eating bread. From time to time her mother warned her to be quiet. Out on the porch people walked about, clattered and talked and a sister-in-law of the dying man was chopping cabbage.

'Ha, Aksinya!' he mumbled eventually.

'What is it?'

'Give me a little *kvas*.'

Aksinya gave him some. The silence once more returned. I asked in a whisper: 'Have they given him the last rites?'

'Yes.'

In that case, everything was in order: he was simply awaiting death, nothing else. I could not stand it any more and left.

On another occasion, I remember, I called in at the hospital in Red Hills village to see the assistant-doctor, Kapiton, an acquaintance of mine and a devoted hunter.

The hospital occupied what had formerly been the wing of the manor. The lady of the manor had herself established it – that is, she had ordered to be placed over the door a blue sign with letters in white reading: 'Red Hills hospital', and she had herself entrusted to Kapiton a beautiful album for noting down the names of the sick. On the first page of this album one of the benevolent lady's sycophants and time-servers had inscribed the following trite verses:

> *Dans ces beaux lieux, où règne l'allégresse,*
> *Ce temple fut ouvert par la Beauté;*
> *De vos seigneurs admirez la tendresse,*
> *Bons habitants de Krasnogorié!**

And another gentleman had added below:

> *Et moi aussi j'aime la nature!*
> Jean Kobyliatnikoff

The assistant-doctor had purchased six beds out of his own money and, after calling down a blessing on his work, had set about caring for all God's people. Apart from himself, the hospital had a staff of two; Pavel, a wood-carver, given to fits of madness, and a woman with a withered arm, Melikitrisa, who was the hospital cook. Both of them made up medicines, dried herbs and concocted herbal infusions; they also used to subdue patients if they became delirious. The mad wood-carver was sullen in appearance and a man of few words: by night he used to sing a ditty concerning 'a beautiful Venus' and he would importune every visitor to the hospital with the request that he be allowed to marry a certain Malanya, a girl long since dead. The woman with the withered arm used to beat him and made him look after the turkeys.

One day I was sitting with Kapiton. We had just begun to chat about our most recent hunting expedition when suddenly a cart drove into the yard with an unusually fat grey horse in

* Krasnogorié = Red Hills.

harness (of the dray-horse variety only used by millers). In the cart sat a solid-looking peasant, in a new coat, sporting a mottled beard.

'Hey there, Vasily Dmitrich,' Kapiton shouted out of the window, 'you're welcome to come in. . . . It's the Lybovshinsky miller,' he whispered to me.

The peasant climbed down from the cart, groaning as he did so, and entered Kapiton's room, where he glanced round for the icon and crossed himself.

'Well, Vasily Dmitrich, what's new? You're ill, that's obvious: your face looks pasty.'

'Yes, Kapiton Timofeyich, something's wrong.'

'What's the trouble?'

'It's like this, Kapiton Timofeyich. Not long ago I bought mill-stones in the town. Well, I brought them home, but when I started unloading them from the cart, I put too much into it, you know, and something went pop in my stomach, just as if it'd got torn. And from then on I've felt bad all the time. Today it hurts real bad.'

'Hmmm,' murmured Kapiton and sniffed some tobacco, 'that means a hernia. How long ago did this happen to you?'

'It's ten days ago, now.'

'Ten?' Kapiton drew in breath through his teeth and shook his head. 'Let me feel. Well, Vasily Dmitrich,' he said at last, 'I'm sorry for you, because I like you, but that condition of yours is not at all good. You're ill right enough, and no joking. Stay here with me, and I'll do all I can for you, but I don't promise anything.'

'You really mean it's that bad?' muttered the astonished miller.

'Yes, Vasily Dmitrich, it's that bad. If you'd come to me a couple of days earlier, I'd have been able to put you right with a flick of the wrist. But now you've got an inflammation here, that's what it is, and before long it'll turn into St Anthony's fire.'

137

'But it's just not possible, Kapiton Timofeyich.'

'And I'm telling you it is.'

'But how can it be!' (In response Kapiton shrugged his shoulders.) 'Am I going to die because of this silly business?'

'I'm not saying that. I'm simply telling you to stay here.'

The peasant thought about this a bit, looked at the floor, then glanced up at us, scratched the nape of his neck and was ready to put his cap on.

'Where are you off to, Vasily Dmitrich?'

'Where to? It's obvious where to – home, if things are that bad. If things are like that, there's a lot to be put in order.'

'But you'll do yourself real harm, Vasily Dmitrich. I'm surprised that you even got here at all. Stay here, I beg you.'

'No, Brother Kapiton Timofeyich, if I'm going to die, I'll die at home. If I died here, God knows what a mess there'd be at home.'

'It's still not certain, Vasily Dmitrich, how it's going to turn out. . . . Of course, it's dangerous, very dangerous, there's no doubt about that, and that's why you ought to stay here.'

The peasant shook his head. 'No, Kapiton Timofeyich, I won't stay. Just you write out a prescription for a little medicine.'

'Medicine by itself won't help.'

'I'm not staying, I'm telling you that.'

'Well, as you wish. . . . Mind you, you've only yourself to blame afterwards!'

Kapiton tore a little page out of the album and, after writing out a prescription, gave some advice on what still had to be done. The peasant took the sheet of paper, gave Kapiton a half-rouble piece, walked out of the room and sat in his cart.

'Good-bye, then, Kapiton Timofeyich. Think kindly of me and don't forget the little orphans, if it should happen. . . .'

'Stay here, Vasily, stay here!'

The peasant merely gave a shake of the head, struck the horse with the reins and rode out of the yard. I went out on to the street and looked after him. The road was muddy and pot-holed. The miller drove carefully, without hurrying, skilfully guiding the horse and bowing to those he met on the way. . . . Four days later he was dead.

In general, Russians surprise one when it comes to dying. I can recall to mind now many who have died. You I recall, my friend of old, the student who never completed his education, Avenir Sorokoumov, fine and most noble person! I see again your consumptive, greenish face, your thin, russet-coloured hair, your timid smile, your fascinated gaze and long-limbed body; I hear your weak, kindly voice. You lived at the house of the Great Russian landowner, Gur Krupyanikov, taught Russian grammar, geography and history to his children, Fofa and Zyoza, and patiently endured the heavy-handed humour of Gur himself, the crude familiarity of his butler, the tasteless pranks of his wicked little boys and not without a bitter smile, but also without complaint, fulfilled all the capricious demands made upon you by his bored wife; despite this, how you used to enjoy your leisure, how filled with beatitude were your evenings, after supper, when, finally rid of all obligations and duties, you would sit by the window, thoughtfully smoking your pipe or greedily thumbing through some mutilated and much-fingered copy of a thick journal which had been brought from town by a surveyor who was just as homeless a wretch as you were! How you used to enjoy in those days all kinds of verses and stories, how easily tears would be brought to your eyes, with what pleasure you used to laugh, how rich was your childishly pure soul in sincere love for mankind and in high-minded compassion for all that was good and beautiful! True, you were not remarkable for undue wit: nature had endowed you neither with a good memory, nor with diligence; at the university you were considered one of the worst students; you used to sleep during lectures and preserved a solemn silence at examinations. But whose eyes lit up with joy, who used to catch his breath at the successes and accomplishments of a fellow-student? You did, Avenir. . . . Who believed blindly in the high calling of his friends, who took such pride in extolling them, who was so fierce in their defence? Who knew neither envy nor ambition, who selflessly sacrificed his own interests, who gladly deferred to people who were unworthy so much as to unlatch the buckle of his shoes? . . . You did, you did, my good Avenir! I remember how you said goodbye to your comrades with a heavy heart when you went off to your 'temporary employment'; evil forebodings tormented you. . . . And for good reason: in the country things were bad for you; there was no one in the country at whose feet you could sit in reverent attentiveness, no one to wonder at, no one to love. . . . Both the provincials and the educated landowners treated you simply as a schoolteacher, some displaying rudeness, others indifference. And you, for your own part, cut a poor figure with your shyness, and blushing, and sweatiness, and your stammer. . . . Even your health was not improved by the country air; you melted away, poor fellow, like a wax candle! True, your little room looked out on to the garden; cherry trees, apple trees and limes sprinkled their delicate blossoms on your table, your ink-pot and your books; on the wall hung a little pale-blue silk cushion for a watch, given to you as a parting gift by a warm-hearted and sensitive little German governess with fair curls and sweet blue eyes; and sometimes an old friend from your Moscow days would visit and put you in an ecstasy of excitement over his own or another's verses; but your loneliness, the unbearable grind of your vocation as a teacher, the impossibility of freeing yourself, but the endless autumns, the endless winters, the relentless advance of disease. . . . Wretched, wretched Avenir!

I visited Sorokoumov shortly before his death. He was almost unable to walk. The landowner, Gur Krupyanikov, had not driven him from his house, but had ceased to pay him and had hired another teacher for Zyoza. Fofa had been put in the cadet corps. Avenir was sitting beside the window in an ancient Voltairean arm-chair. The weather was wonderful. A bright autumn sky shone a gay blue above a dark-brown row of naked limes; here and there on their boughs the last, radiantly golden leaves fluttered and rustled. The frost-bound earth perspired and thawed in the sunlight; its slanting, pink-tinged rays struck lengthwise across the pale grass; a faint crackling seemed to dwell in the air, and in the garden the voices of workmen had a clear, sharp resonance.

Avenir wore an antiquated Bokhara dressing-gown; a green neckerchief cast a deathly hue upon his terribly wasted face. He was extremely delighted to see me, stretched out his hand, began to say something and started coughing. I gave him time to compose himself and took a seat near him. On Avenir's knees lay an exercise book into which the poems of Koltsov had been painstakingly copied. Giving a smile, he tapped the book with his hand.

'That's a poet,' he managed to say, with an effort holding back his cough, and embarked on declaiming some of the verse in a scarcely audible voice:

> What if a falcon's
> Wings are tied?
> What if all ways
> Are to him denied?[5]

I stopped him; the doctor had forbidden him to talk. I knew how to indulge him. Sorokoumov had never, as they say, 'followed' science, but he was always curious to know what, so to speak, the great minds of the present day had been thinking and what conclusions had been reached. There had been a time when he used to catch a fellow-student in a corner and began plying him with questions: he would listen, wonder, believe every word and afterwards repeat it all as his own. German philosophy held a particularly strong fascination for him. I began to tell him about Hegel (as you can appreciate, these matters relate to days long since gone by). Avenir gave affirmative nods of the head, raised his eyebrows, smiled, saying in a whisper, 'I understand, I understand!... Ah, that's good, that's good!' The child-like curiosity of the dying man, of this poor, neglected, homeless fellow, touched me, I confess, to the point of tears. It must be said that Avenir, in contrast to most consumptives, never deluded himself in the least about his illness. And why should he? He did not sigh over it, and was not crushed in spirit by it, nor did he once make reference to his condition.

Gathering his strength, he began to talk about Moscow, about fellow-students, about Pushkin and the theatre and Russian literature; he recalled our feastings, the heated debates which occurred in our circle and with regret he uttered the names of two or three friends who had died ...

'Do you remember Dasha?' he added finally. 'There was a soul of pure gold! A pure heart! And how she loved me!... What's happened to her now? Probably dried up, wasted away, hasn't she, poor thing?'

I did not dare to disenchant the sick man – and, indeed, there was no reason for him to be told that his Dasha was now fatter than she was tall and carrying on with merchants, the brothers Kondachkov, and powdered and rouged herself, and spoke in a squeaky voice and used bad language.

However, I thought, looking at his exhausted features: Is it impossible to drag him out of this place? Perhaps there is still a chance of curing him.... But Avenir would not let me finish what I was proposing.

'No, thank you, good friend,' he murmured, 'it doesn't matter where one dies. You can see I won't live until the winter, so why bother people unnecessarily? I'm used to this house. It's true that the people in charge here ...'

'... are bad people, do you mean?' I inserted.

'No, not bad, just rather like bits of wood. But I haven't any reason to complain about them. There are neighbours: Kasatkin, the landowner, has a daughter who is educated, kind, the sweetest of girls . . . not one of the proud kind. . . .'

Sorokoumov once again had a fit of coughing.

'It would be all right,' he continued, having got his breath back, 'if they'd just allow me to smoke a pipe. . . . No, I'm not going to die before I smoke a whole pipe!' he added, winking slyly at me. 'Good Lord, I've lived enough, and I've known some good people. . . .'

'You ought at least to write to your relatives,' I interrupted him.

'What for? To ask for help? They won't be able to help me, and they'll learn about me soon enough when I die. There's no point in talking about it. . . . Better, tell me what you saw when you were abroad.'

I began to tell him. He stared at me, drinking in my words. Towards evening, I left, and about ten days later I received the following letter from Mr Krupyanikov:

With this letter I have the honour to acquaint you, my dear sir, with the fact that your friend, the student Mr Avenir Sorokoumov, who has been residing at my house, passed away four days ago at two o'clock in the afternoon and was today given a funeral in my parish at my expense. He begged me to send you the accompanying volumes and exercise books. It transpired that he had 22 and one half roubles in his possession, which, together with his other things, will be delivered into the possession of his relatives. Your friend passed away in full command of his senses and, it may be said, with a similar degree of insensitiveness, without exhibiting the slightest signs of regret even when we were saying good-bye to him in a family group. My wife, Kleopatra Alexandrovna, sends you her respects. The death of your friend could not but have an adverse effect on her nerves; so far as I am concerned, I am well, God be praised, and I have the honour to remain –

Your most humble servant,
G. Krupyanikov.

There are many other examples that occur to me, so many that it would be impossible to tell them all. I will limit myself to one only.

An elderly lady, a landowner, was dying in my presence. The priest began to read the prayer for the dying over her, when he suddenly noticed that the sick woman was in fact passing on and hurriedly handed her the cross. The elderly lady took umbrage at this.

'Why all the hurry, sir?' she said with a tongue that was already stiffening. 'You'll be in time. . . .'

She lay back and she had just placed her hand under her pillow when she drew her last last breath. There was a rouble piece lying under the pillow: she had wanted to pay the priest for reading the prayer for her own death. . . .

Yes, Russians surprise one when it comes to dying!

Singers

THE small village of Kolotovka, which belonged at one time to a female landowner who had been nicknamed locally The Stripper on account of her fast and lively temperament (her real name remained unknown), but which now belongs to some St Petersburg German, is situated on the slope of a bare hill, split from top to bottom by an awful ravine that gapes like an abyss and winds its pitted and eroded course right down the centre of the main street, dividing the two sides of the miserable settlement more effectively than a river since a river can at least be bridged. A few emaciated willows straggle timidly down its sandy sides; on the very bottom, which is dry and yellow as copper, lie enormous slabs of clayey stone. There is no denying that its appearance is far from happy, and yet all who live in the locality are thoroughly familiar with the road to Kolotovka, travelling there gladly and often.

At the head of the ravine, a few steps from the point where it begins as a narrow crevice, there stands a small, square hut, quite by itself and apart from the others. It is roofed with straw and it has a chimney; one window is turned towards the ravine like a watchful eye, and on winter evenings, when illumined from within, may be seen far off through the faint frost-haze twinkling like a lodestar for many a passing peasant. A small blue sign has been fixed above the door of the hut, since this hut is a tavern, nicknamed The Welcome.* Drink cannot be said to be sold in this tavern below the normal price but it is patronized much more assiduously than all the other

* The Welcome is the name given to any place where people gather willingly, any kind of shelter.

establishments of this kind in the locality. The reason for this is mine host, Nikolay Ivanych.

Nikolay Ivanych – at one time a well-built, curly-headed, red-cheeked youngster, but now an extraordinarily stout, greying man with a plump face, slyly good-humoured eyes and fleshy temples criss-crossed with wrinkles as fine as threads – has lived more than twenty years in Kolotovka. He is a busy and competent man, like the majority of tavern-keepers. Though outstanding neither for unusual kindliness, nor for a gift of the gab, he possesses the knack of attracting and keeping his patrons, who are happy after their fashion to sit in front of his brew under the calm and welcoming, albeit watchful, gaze of such a phlegmatic host. He has a great deal of sound good sense; he is equally familiar with the way of life of the landowners, the peasants and the townspeople; when difficulties arise he can offer advice that is not at all stupid, but, being a man of cautious and egotistical nature, he prefers to remain on the sidelines and only by remote, as it were, hints, uttered without the least apparent intent, does he suggest to his patrons – and then only his favourite patrons – the right course to take. He has a good grasp of all the important or interesting things a Russian should know: of horses, cattle, forestry, brick-making, crockery, textiles and leatherware, singing and dancing. When he has no patrons, he usually sits like a sack on the ground outside the door of his hut, his thin little legs drawn up under him, and exchanges pleasantries with all who pass by. He has seen a great deal in his time and has survived more than his fair number of small-time gentry who have dropped in on him for 'a spot of the pure stuff'; he knows all that's going on in the entire region and yet he never gossips, never even so much as gives a sign that he knows what a policeman with the keenest nose for crime could not even suspect. He keeps what he knows to himself, occasionally chuckling and shuffling his tankards about. Neighbours show him respect: General Sherepetenko, the highest ranking of the landowners in the county, gives him a deferential bow every time he drives past his little hut. Nikolay Ivanych is a man with influence: he forced a well-known horse thief to return a horse which he had taken from the yard of one of his friends and talked persuasively to peasants from a neighbouring village who were reluctant to accept a new manager, and so on. But one mustn't imagine that he does such things out of a love of justice or community zeal – oh, no! He simply endeavours to put a stop to whatever might disturb his own peace of mind. Nikolay Ivanych is married and he has children. His wife, a brisk, sharp-nosed woman of middle-class origins, with eyes that dart to and fro, has recently grown plump, like her husband. He relies upon her for everything, and it is she who keeps the money under lock and key. Loud-mouthed drunkards are wary of her, nor is she fond of them: there is little profit to be got from them, only a lot of noise; the taciturn and serious patrons are more to her liking. Nikolay Ivanych's children are still little; the first children all died in infancy, but the surviving ones have grown to look like their parents. It is a pleasure to see the intelligent little faces of those healthy boys.

It was an intoleraby hot July day when, slowly dragging one foot after another, I and my dog climbed up the hill beside the Kolotovka ravine in the direction of The Welcome tavern. The sun blazed in the sky, as if fit to explode; it steamed and baked everything remorselessly, and the air was full of suffocating dust. Glossy-feathered rooks and crows hung their beaks and gazed miserably at those who passed by, as if literally imploring their sympathy. Only the sparrows kept their spirits up and, spreading their feathers, chirruped away more fiercely than ever, squabbled round the fences, took off in flights from the dusty roadway and soared in grey clouds above the plantations of green hemp. I was tormented by thirst. There was no water to be got close by: in Kolotovka, as in so many other steppe villages, the peasants, for want of springs and wells, are accustomed to drink a kind of liquid mud from the ponds. . . . But who would call that beastly drink water? I wanted to beg a glass of beer or *kvas* from Nikolay Ivanych.

It has to be confessed that at no time of year does Kolotovka offer a spectacle to please the eye; but it evokes an especially sad feeling when the glittering July sun pours its merciless rays down on the rust-coloured and only partly thatched roofs of the huts, and the deep ravine, and the scorched, dust-laden common ground where gaunt chickens roam about hopelessly on spindly legs, and the grey, skeletal frame of a house of aspen wood, which has holes in place of windows and is all that remains of the former manor house (now overgrown with nettles, wormwood and other weeds), and the dark-green, literally sun-smelted pond, covered with bits of goose fluff and edged with half-dried mud, and a dam knocked askew, beside which, on earth so finely trodden it resembles ash, sheep huddle miserably together, sneezing and scarcely able to draw breath from the heat, and with patient despondency hang their heads as low as possible, as if awaiting the time when the intolerable heat will finally pass.

With weary steps I drew close to Nikolay Ivanych's dwelling, arousing, quite naturally, a state of excitement in the little boys which grew into an intently senseless staring, and in the dogs a state of dissatisfaction which expressed itself in barks so shrill and malicious that it seemed their innards were being torn out of them and they were left with nothing to do but cough and catch their breaths – when suddenly there appeared in the tavern doorway a tall, hatless man in a frieze overcoat tied low down with a blue sash. To all appearances he was a house-serf; clusters of grey hair rose untidily above his dry and wrinkled face. He called to someone, making hurried motions with his arms which clearly waved about a good deal more expansively than he wished. It was obvious that he had already managed to have something to drink.

'Come on, come on now!' he burbled, with an effort raising his thick eyebrows. 'Come on, Winker, will you! You just go at a crawl, you do, mate. It's no good, it isn't. Here they're waitin' for you, and you just goin' at a crawl. . . . Come on.'

'Well, I'm coming, I'm coming,' responded a querulous voice, and there appeared from behind the hut on the right a smallish man, who was fat and lame. He wore a fairly smart cloth jacket, with his arms through one of the sleeves; a tall, pointed cap, tilted directly forward over his brows, lent his round, puffy face a sly and comic look. His little yellow eyes darted about and a strained, deferential smile never left his thin lips; while his nose, long and sharp, projected impudently in front of him like a rudder. 'I'm coming, my dear fellow,' he continued, limping in the direction of the drinking establishment. 'Why're you calling to me? Who's waiting for me?'

'Why'm I callin' to you?' the man in the frieze overcoat said reproachfully. 'Oh, you, Winker, you're a wonder, mate, you are – they're callin' you to the tavern, and you go askin' why? It's all good fellows that're waitin' for you – Yashka the Turk's there, and Gentleman Wildman, and Barrowboy from Zhizdra. Yashka's made a bet with Barrowboy – a pot of ale he's staked on whoever gets the better of whom, who sings the best, that's to say. . . . See?'

'Yashka'll be singing?' the man nicknamed Winker asked with lively interest. 'Do you really mean that, you Nit?'

'I do mean that,' the Nit answered with dignity, 'and there's no need for you to be askin' silly questions. 'Course he'll be singin' if he's made a bet, you old bumbler you, you ruddy menace, Winker!'

'Well, get going, then, you dim-wit!' Winker retorted.

'Come on, then, and give me a kiss, me old dear,' the Nit said in his prattling way, holding wide his arms.

'Look at him, gone soft in the head in his old age,' Winker

responded contemptuously, thrusting him aside with his elbow, and both of them, bending down, went in through the low door.

The conversation I had heard strongly aroused my curiosity. More than once rumours had reached me about Yashka the Turk as the best singer in the region, and now I was suddenly presented with a chance of hearing him in competition with another master. I redoubled my steps and entered the establishment.

Probably few of my readers have had a chance of seeing the inside of a rural tavern; but we hunters drop in anywhere and everywhere! They are exceedingly simply arranged. They consist usually of a dark entrance and a parlour divided in two by a partition beyond which none of the patrons has the right to go. In this partition, above a wide oak table, there is a big longitudinal opening. The drink is sold at this table, or counter. Labelled bottles of various sizes stand in rows on the shelves directly opposite the opening. In the forward part of the hut, which is given over to the patrons, there are benches, one or two empty barrels and a corner table. Rural taverns are for the most part fairly dark, and you will hardly ever see on the log walls any of those brightly coloured popular prints with which most peasant huts are adorned.

When I entered The Welcome tavern, quite a large company was already gathered there.

Behind the counter, as usual, and occupying almost the whole width of the opening, stood Nikolay Ivanych, dressed in a colourful calico shirt and, with a lazy smirk on his plump cheeks, pouring out with his large white hand two glasses of liquor for the two friends who had just entered, Winker and the Nit; while at his back, in a corner beside the window, his sharp-eyed wife could be seen. In the middle of the parlour stood Yashka the Turk, a thin, lithe man of about twenty-three dressed in a long-hemmed coat of a light shade of blue. He looked like a dare-devil factory lad and, so it seemed, could hardly boast of perfect health. His sunken cheeks, large restless grey eyes, straight nose with delicate spirited nostrils, white sloping forehead below backswept light-auburn curls, large but beautiful, expressive lips – his entire face betokened a man of sensibility and passion. He was in a state of great excitement: he blinked his eyes, breathed irregularly and his hands shook feverishly – indeed, he was in a fever, that anxious, sudden state of fever which is familiar to everyone who speaks or sings before an assembled company. Beside him stood a man of about forty, broad-shouldered, with broad cheekbones, a low forehead, narrow Mongol eyes, short flat nose, square chin and black shiny hair as hard as bristles. The expression on his dark, lead-coloured face, especially on his pale lips, could have been called savage, had it not also been so tranquilly thoughtful. He hardly stirred at all and did no more than look slowly round him from time to time, like an ox looking round from beneath a yoke. He was dressed in a kind of very worn frockcoat with smooth bronze buttons; an old black silk kerchief encased his huge neck. He was called Gentleman Wildman. Directly opposite him, on a bench beneath the icons, sat Yashka's rival, Barrowboy from Zhizdra. He was a thick-set man of about thirty, small in stature, pock-marked and curly-headed, with a blunt turned-up nose, lively brown eyes and a wispy little beard. He was glancing rapidly about him, his hands tucked under him, carelessly chattering and now and then tapping his dandified, fancifully decorated boots. His dress consisted of a new thin peasant coat of grey cloth with a velveteen collar, to which the edge of the red shirt tightly fastened round his neck stood out in sharp contrast. In the opposite corner, to the right of the door, there sat at a table some little peasant or other wearing a narrow, worn-out coat with an enormous tear in the shoulder. Sunlight streamed in a pale yellow flood through the dusty panes of the two small windows and seemed to be unable to overcome the habitual darkness of the parlour: everything was so meagrely lit that it seemed blurred. Despite this, the air was almost cool, and all sense of the suffocating and oppressive heat slipped from my shoulders like a discarded burden as soon as I stepped through the porch.

My arrival, as I could sense, somewhat confused Nikolay Ivanych's guests to start with; but seeing that he bowed to me as to someone familiar, they were put at their ease and paid no more attention to me. I asked for some beer and sat down in the corner next to the peasant in the torn coat.

'Well, what's doing?' the Nit suddenly roared, drinking back his glass at a gulp and accompanying his exclamation with the same strange waving gestures, without which he evidently never pronounced a single word. 'What're we waiting for? Begin now, if you're goin' to begin. Eh? Yashka?'

'Get started, get started,' Nikolay Ivanych added by way of encouragement.

'We'll begin, presuming it's all right,' Barrowboy announced with cold-blooded audacity and a self-confident smile. 'I'm ready.'

'And I'm ready,' Yakov declared excitedly.

'Well, get going, lads, get going,' Winker hissed squeakily.

But, despite the unanimously expressed wish, no one began; Barrowboy did not even rise from the bench. There was a general air of expectancy.

'Begin!' said Gentleman Wildman in a sharp, sullen voice.

Yakov shuddered. Barrowboy rose, gave a tug at his sash and coughed.

'An' who's to begin?' he asked in a slightly less confident voice, speaking to Gentleman Wildman who continued to stand motionlessly in the middle of the room, his stout legs set wide apart and his powerful arms thrust into the pockets of his broad trousers, almost up to the elbows.

'It's you, you, Barrowboy,' the Nit started babbling, 'you're the one, mate.'

Gentleman Wildman looked at him from beneath his brows.

The Nit gave a faint croak, got confused, glanced somewhere up towards the ceiling, shrugged his shoulders and became silent.

'Throw for it,' Gentleman Wildman announced in measured tones. 'Put the ale on the counter.'

Nikolay Ivanych bent down, lifted the pot of ale from the floor with a groan and set it on the table.

Gentleman Wildman glanced at Yakov and said: 'Well!' Yakov dug around in his pockets and produced a copper which he tested between his teeth. Barrowboy extracted from beneath the hem of his coat a new leather money-bag, slowly untied the string and, having poured a mass of small change into his hand, picked out a new copper coin. The Nit shoved his threadbare cap with its torn, battered peak down in front of them: Yakov threw his coin in it, as did Barrowboy.

'You choose,' said Gentleman Wildman, turning to Winker.

Winker gave a self-satisfied grin, seized the cap in both hands and began shaking it. Momentarily a profound silence reigned while the coins chinked faintly against each other. I looked attentively around: all the faces expressed tense expectancy; Gentleman Wildman screwed up his eyes; my neighbour, the little peasant in the torn coat, even he stretched his neck forward in curiosity. Winker put his hand into the cap and drew out Barrowboy's coin; everyone sighed with relief. Yakov reddened, and Barrowboy drew his hand through his hair.

'Didn't I say it was you!' the Nit exclaimed. 'Sure I did!'

'Now, now, none o' that squawking,' Gentleman Wildman remarked contemptuously. 'Begin!' he went on, nodding his head to Barrowboy.

'What song ought I to sing?' asked Barrowboy, becoming upset.

'Sing what you like,' answered Winker. 'Whatever comes into your head, sing that.'

'Of course, sing what you like,' added Nikolay Ivanych.

slowly folding his arms across his chest. 'Nobody's giving you any orders. Sing what you like, only sing it well. Afterwards we'll decide as our conscience dictates.'

'Nacherly, as conscience dictates,' the Nit inserted, and licked the edge of his empty glass.

'Give me time, mates, to get my throat cleared a bit,' Barrowboy started saying, passing his fingers along the collar of his coat.

'Now, now, don't start trying to get out of it – begin!' Gentleman Wildman said decisively, and lowered his eyes to the floor.

Barrowboy thought for a moment, gave a shake of the head and took a step forward. Yakov fixed his eyes on him, drinking him in . . .

But before I embark on a description of the contest itself, I consider it necessary to say a few words about each of the participants in my story. The lives of some of them were already known to me before I encountered them in The Welcome tavern; about the others I picked up information at a later date.

Let's begin with the Nit. This man's real name was Yevgraf Ivanov; but no one in the region knew him as anything save the Nit, and he prided himself on such a nickname because it suited him so well. And there is no doubt that nothing could have been more appropriate for describing his insignificant and eternally agitated countenance. He was a feckless, bachelor house-serf, long ago given up for good by his masters, who, though having no post and not receiving a penny in wages, nevertheless found means each day of making merry at other people's expense. He had a mass of acquaintances who plied him with drink and tea, they themselves not knowing why, because not only was he far from entertaining company but he even, to the contrary, bored everyone stiff with his senseless chatter, intolerable sponging, feverish body-movements and endless unnatural laughter. He did not know how to sing or dance; since birth he had never once spoken not only an intelligent, but even a sensible, word; he rattled on the whole time and talked whatever nonsense came into his head – he was a real nit, in fact! Even so, no drinking bout could occur within a twenty-five mile radius without his lanky figure milling round among the guests, to such an extent had people grown used to him and accustomed to his presence like an unavoidable evil. True, he was treated with contempt, but Gentleman Wildman was the only one who knew how to tame his witless outbursts.

Winker bore no sort of resemblance to the Nit. The title of Winker also suited him, although he did not wink his eyes more than other people; everyone knows, though, what past-masters Russians are at contriving nicknames. Despite my attempting to gain a fuller picture of this man's past, his life still contained for me – and probably for many others as well – dark spots, areas, as bookish people like to say, obscured by profound mists of uncertainty. I learned simply that he had at one time been a coachman for an elderly childless lady, that he had run off with the troika of horses left in his charge, had disappeared for a whole year and, having no doubt discovered for himself the disadvantages and perils of a vagrant's life, returned of his own accord, but already lame, threw himself at the feet of his mistress and, having erased his crime during the course of several years of exemplary behaviour, gradually regained her favour, finally earned her complete trust, became one of her bailiffs and, at her death, turned out in some mysterious way to have been given his freedom, enrolled himself among the *petit-bourgeois* stratum of the population, began renting areas of kitchen garden from his neighbours, grew rich and now lived in the pink. He was a man of experience, with a mind to his own affairs, neither malicious nor kindly, but chiefly prudent; he was a tough nut, who knew what people were like and had learned how to make use of them. He was cautious and at the same time as resourceful as a vixen; he was as garrulous as an old woman and yet he never used to say too much, but always made everyone else speak their minds; mind you, he never tried to pass himself off as a simpleton, as some rascals of that ilk do, and it would have been difficult for him to pretend because I had never seen more perspicacious and intelligent eyes than his crafty little 'peepers'.* Their gaze was never simple and straightforward – they were always looking you up and down, always investigating you. Sometimes Winker would spend whole weeks thinking over some apparently simple operation, and then in a flash he would make up his mind to launch into a desperately audacious business; it would seem that he was about to come a cropper, and yet before you'd had time to give a second look everything was a howling success, everything was going along swimmingly. He was fortunate and he believed in his good fortune, just as he believed in omens. He was in general very superstitious. He was not liked, because he did not concern himself with other people's business, but he was respected. His entire family consisted of one small son, on whom he doted, and who, being educated by such a father, would no doubt go a long way. 'Wee Willy Winker takes after his father' were the words already being spoken under their breaths by old men sitting on earthen seats and discussing this and that between themselves on summer evenings; and everybody understood what was meant by that and felt no need to add anything to it.

About Yakov the Turk and Barrowboy there is no reason to say a great deal. Yakov, nicknamed the Turk, because he was in fact the offspring of a captured Turkish girl, was by nature an artist in every sense of that word, whereas by calling he was a dipper in the paper factory of a local merchant; as for Barrowboy, whose fate, I admit, has remained unknown to me, he seemed to be a slippery and lively product of the

* People of the Orlov region refer to eyes as 'peepers', just as they call mouths 'eaters'.

small-town *bourgeoisie*. But it is worth being a little more detailed about Gentleman Wildman.

The first impression produced by the sight of this man was a sense of crude, heavy but irresistible strength. He had an awkward build, as if he had been 'knocked together', as they say, but he exuded an air of unbreakable good health and, strange though it may seem, his bear-like figure was not without its own kind of grace, which may have been due to a completely calm assurance of his own powers. At a first glance it was difficult to decide to what social stratum this Hercules belonged; he did not look like a house-serf, or one of the *petit-bourgeois*, or an impoverished retired clerk, or a bankrupt member of the minor nobility turned huntsman and strong-arm man: he was precisely himself and no more. Nobody knew where he had come from before dropping in on our county; gossip had it that he came from small-time landowning stock and was supposed to have been in the government service previously; but nothing positive was known about him and, besides, there was nobody from whom one could learn anything about him – certainly not from the man himself, because no one was more morose and taciturn. Also, no one could say for sure how he lived: he occupied himself with no special trade, never travelled off to work with anyone, had practically no acquaintances, yet he never seemed to be without money – not much, it was true, but some. It was not so much that he conducted himself modestly – there was in general nothing modest about him whatever – but he conducted himself quietly; he lived literally without taking notice of anyone around him and quite definitely without needing anyone. Gentleman Wildman (that was his nickname; his real name was Perevlesov) enjoyed enormous authority throughout the entire region; he was obeyed instantly and without question, although he not only had no right at all to order people about, but he did not even make the slightest pretence of expecting obedience from anyone he might chance to meet.

He had only to speak and they obeyed; strength will always exact its due. He hardly drank at all, did not consort with women and was passionately fond of singing. There was much that was enigmatic about this man; it seemed as if certain mighty powers sullenly lurked within him, knowing, as it were, that if they were once roused, if they once broke free, they would be sure to destroy both the man himself and everything they came in contact with; and if I am not terribly mistaken, precisely such an outburst had occurred in the life of this man, and he, schooled by the experience and barely saved from perishing, implacably held himself in check with a rod of iron. I was particularly struck by the mixture in him of a certain in-born, natural ferocity and a similarly in-born nobility of spirit – a mixture which I had not encountered before in anyone else.

Meanwhile, Barrowboy took a pace forward, half closed his eyes and began to sing in an exceptionally high falsetto. He had a fairly pleasant, sweet voice, although it was a little husky; he played with his voice, twisting it round and round like a top, ceaselessly running up and down the scale and all the time returning to the high notes, which he endeavoured particularly to hold and prolong, dropping into silence and then suddenly catching up the earlier refrain with a certain carefree, arrogant audacity. His shifts from one to the other were sometimes fairly bold, sometimes quite amusing: to an expert they would have given a good deal of pleasure; a German would have been annoyed by them. He was a Russian *tenore di grazia, ténor léger*. The song he sang was gay, for dancing, the words of which, so far as I could make them out through the endless embellishments, additional consonants and ejaculations, were as follows:

> I'll plough, my young one so pretty,
> A small patch for thee;
> I'll sow, my young one so pretty,
> Bright red flowers for thee.

He sang, and everyone listened to him with great attention. He was obviously conscious of performing in front of people experienced in the art of singing and therefore, as they say, gave it all he'd got. Certainly, in our parts people know something about singing, and it is not for nothing that the village of Sergiyevsky, on the main Orlov highway, is famed throughout Russia for its especially pleasant and harmonious melodies. Barrowboy sang for a long time without arousing any exceptionally strong sympathy in his listeners; he lacked support, a chorus; finally, after one particularly successful shift which made even Gentleman Wildman smile, the Nit could not contain himself and shouted with joy. Everyone became animated. The Nit and Winker began in low voices to catch up the refrain, joining in and occasionally shouting:

'Great, man, great! Get it, boyo! Get it, hold it, keep at it, stretch it, you snake! Stretch it, go on, and again! Make it hot again, man, you old dog, you! Oh, the devil take your soul, man!' and so on.

Behind the counter Nikolay Ivanych approvingly shook his head to right and left. The Nit eventually started tapping his feet, mincing on tiptoe and jerking one shoulder, and Yakov's eyes simply burst into flame like coals and his whole body quivered like a leaf as he smiled all over his face. Only Gentleman Wildman did not alter the look on his face and remained in his former posture without moving; but his gaze, directed at Barrowboy, softened a little, although the expression on his lips remained contemptuous. Encouraged by these signs of general enjoyment, Barrowboy completely gave himself up to a veritable whirling frenzy of sounds and began to execute such convolutions, such clickings and drummings with his tongue, began such wild throaty trills that when, finally, exhausted, pale and covered in hot perspiration, he flung back his whole body and emitted a last dying cry, a general and unanimous shout of approval greeted him in a fierce outburst.

The Nit threw himself at Barrowboy's neck and began to hug him to the point of suffocation with his long bony arms; a blush appeared on the fleshy face of Nikolay Ivanych which literally made him look younger; Yakov, like a madman, started shouting: 'O boy, O boy, O boy!' Even my neighbour, the peasant in the ragged coat, could not restrain himself, and, striking the table with his fist, gave a cry of 'Bahgum that was good, the devil take it, that was good!' and resolutely spat to one side.

'Well, mate, that was a delight!' cried the Nit without releasing the utterly exhausted Barrowboy from his embraces. 'That was a delight, no denyin'! You've won, mate, you've won! Congratulations! That pot of ale's all yours! Yashka won't come near you, I'm tellin' you he won't come near. . . . Just you remember what I've said!' (And he once more clasped Barrowboy to his chest.)

'Let him go, let him go, like a ruddy clingin' vine you are!' Winker started saying in annoyance. 'Let him sit down on the bench. You can see he's tired. A bloody idiot you are, mate, a right bloody idiot! What's the good o' stickin' to 'im like a wet leaf in a steambath, eh?'

'So all right, let him sit down, and I'll drink to his health,' said the Nit and approached the counter. 'You'll do the payin', mate,' he added, turning to Barrowboy.

The latter gave a nod of the head, sat down on the bench, took a cloth out of his cap and began wiping his face; while the Nit drank down a glass with greedy swiftness and, after the manner of heavy drinkers, grunted and assumed a sadly preoccupied look.

'You sing well, mate, real well,' Nikolay Ivanych remarked gently. 'And now it's your turn, Yashka. Don't be bashful. We'll see who's better than whom, we'll just see. . . . But Barrowboy sings awful well, my God he does!'

'Ve-ery well,' commented his wife and looked with a smile towards Yakov.

160

Singers

'Ah, that was good!' my companion repeated in a soft voice.

'Hey, you twister-Woody!'* the Nit all of a sudden started yelling and, going up to the little peasant with the tear in the shoulder of his coat, stuck his finger out at him, began jumping about and pouring out a torrent of rumbustious laughter. 'Woody! Woody! Ha, bah-gum harry-on you twister!† Waddya come here for, twister?' he shouted through his laughter.

The wretched peasant was confused and was on the point of leaving as soon as possible when suddenly there boomed out the resonant voice of Gentleman Wildman:

'What kind of bloody awful animal's making that noise?' he rasped through his teeth.

'I wasn't doin' nothin',' the Nit mumbled, 'it weren't nothin'. . . . Just like I was . . .'

'Well, then, shut up!' retorted Gentleman Wildman. 'Yakov, begin!'

Yakov seized hold of his own throat.

'Well, mate, it's . . . something's wrong. . . . Hmm. . . . Honest, I don't know what's wrong wi' it . . .'

'Enough of that, don't start being bashful. You ought to be ashamed! What's all the squirming for? Sing just the way God makes you.'

And Gentleman Wildman lowered his eyes to the floor, expecting no more fuss.

Yakov said nothing, glanced around and covered his face with his hand. Everyone drank him in with their eyes, especially Barrowboy, on whose face there appeared, through

* 'Woodies' is the name given to inhabitants of the southern forest areas (*poles'ye*), a long forest belt which originates on the boundary between Bolkhov and Zhizdra counties. They are distinguished by having many peculiarities in their way of life, habits and speech. They are called twisters owing to their suspicious and tight-fisted disposition.

† 'Woodies' add the exclamation 'Ha!' and 'Bah-gum!' to almost every word. 'Harry-on' instead of 'hurry-on'.

his normal self-assured look and look of triumph at his success, an involuntary faint uneasiness. He leaned back against the wall and again placed both hands under him, but he no longer swung his feet about. When, at last, Yakov uncovered his face, it was pale as death; his eyes scarcely gleamed through his lowered eyelashes. He drew in a deep breath and began to sing.

The first sound his voice gave was weak and uneven, seeming to emerge not from his chest but to have been carried from somewhere far away, just as if it had flown by accident into the room. This quivering, ringing sound acted strangely upon all of us; we glanced at each other, and Nikolay Ivanych's wife literally stiffened. The first sound was followed by another, much firmer and long-drawn, but still clearly sobbing like a violin string when, after being suddenly plucked by a strong finger, it wavers in one final, quickly fading *tremolo* of sound, after which there followed a third and, little by little growing in intensity and volume, the plaintive song poured forth. 'More than one path through the field wound its way' was the song he sang, and each one of us felt a wave of sweetness and shivery anticipation creeping over us. I confess that I had rarely heard such a voice: it was slightly broken and rang as if cracked; to start with it even had a suggestion of sickliness about it; but it also contained unfeigned depth of passion, and youthfulness, and strength, and sweetness, and a kind of attractively uncaring, mournful piteousness. The honest, fiery soul of Russia resounded and breathed through it and quite simply seized us by the heart, plucked directly at our Russian heart-strings. The song grew and overflowed. Yakov was obviously possessed by inspiration: all shyness gone, he was giving himself completely to his exaltation; his voice no longer quivered – it sobbed, but with that scarcely noticeable, inner tremor of passion which plunges like an arrow into the soul of the listener, and ceaselessly it grew in strength, firmness and volume.

I remember how one evening, at the ebbing of the tide, on the smooth sandy shore of a sea thundering and roaring with the breaking of heavy waves in the far distance, I saw a large white seagull; it stood motionless, its silky breast turned to the crimson brilliance of the evening, and only now and then slowly spread out its long wings in a gesture of welcome to the familiar sea and low, blood-red sun; this I recalled as I listened to Yakov. He sang, quite oblivious of his rival and all of us, yet evidently uplifted, as a spirited swimmer is borne up by the waves, by our silent, devotional participation. He sang, and in every sound his voice made there breathed something familiar as our birthright and so vast no eye could encompass it, just as if the Russian steppe were being unrolled before us, stretching away into an endless distance. I felt emotions throb in my heart and tears rose to my eyes. I was suddenly surprised by the sound of mute, suppressed crying. I glanced round – it was mine host's wife weeping, her bosom pressed to the window. Yakov cast a quick glance in her direction and began to pour out the song still more resonantly, still more sweetly than before; Nikolay Ivanych fixed his eyes on the floor and Winker turned away; the Nit, quite sodden with emotion, stood there, his mouth stupidly gaping; the colourless little peasant was quietly sobbing in his corner and rocking his head to the accompaniment of a tearful whispering; and down the iron face of Gentleman Wildman, from beneath eyebrows that had been drawn completely together, a single heavy tear slowly trickled; Barrowboy had raised a clenched fist to his forehead and was absolutely still . . .

I do not know how the universal tension would have been dispersed had not Yakov suddenly finished on a high, unusually thin note, just as if his voice had broken. Nobody shouted, nobody even stirred; they all waited, as it were, to see whether he was going to continue; but he simply opened his eyes, literally astonished at our silence, looked round at us with an inquiring gaze and recognized that he had won.

'Yasha,' said Gentleman Wildman, placed a hand on his shoulder – and stopped.

We were all motionless as if stunned. Barrowboy quietly stood up and approached Yakov. 'You ... it's yours ... you've won,' he uttered at last with difficulty and flung himself out of the room.

His quick, decisive movement seemed to break the spell: everyone suddenly burst into loud and joyful talking. The Nit jumped in the air, began babbling and waving his arms about like the vanes of a windmill; Winker walked lamely up to Yakov and kissed him on both cheeks; Nikolay Ivanych straightened himself and solemnly announced that he would provide another pot of ale on his own account; Gentleman Wildman gave a series of jovial laughs, of a kind which I had never expected to see on his face; the colourless little peasant over and over again muttered in his corner as he drew both sleeves over his eyes, cheeks, nose and beard: 'Ha, that was good, by God it was good; bah-gum I'll be a son of a bitch, but that was good!'; and Nikolay Ivanych's wife, quite red in the face, quickly stood up and withdrew. Yakov delighted in his victory like a child; his whole face was transformed; his eyes in particular glittered with happiness. They dragged him to the counter, and he summoned the tearful little peasant to join in and sent one of mine host's little sons after Barrowboy, who, however, was not to be found, and the celebrating began. 'You're goin' to sing again, you'll sing to us till it's dark,' the Nit kept on repeating, raising his arms high in the air.

I took a final look at Yakov and went out. I did not want to remain – I was frightened of spoiling my impression. But the heat was as unbearable as before. It seemed to hang over the very surface of the earth in a thick, heavy layer; against the dark-blue sky certain tiny, bright fires appeared to lick up through the very fine, almost black, dust. Everything was silent; there was something hopeless, depressed about this profound silence of exhausted nature. I made my way to a hayloft and lay down on the recently mown grass which had already dried out almost completely. For a long while I was unable to doze off; the enthralling voice of Yakov still rang in my ears. . . . Finally heat and weariness exacted their due and I fell into a dead sleep.

When I awoke, everything was already dark; the grass scattered round me had a strong scent and was ever so slightly damp; through the thin laths of the half-covered roof pale stars winked feebly. I went out. The glow of sunset had long since died away and its final traces hardly showed at all on the horizon; but in the recently white-hot air the heat could still be felt even through the night's freshness, and one's lungs still yearned for a cooling breeze. There was no wind, nor were there any clouds; the sky stood all about me, clear and transparently dark, quietly flickering with numberless but scarcely visible stars. Lights flashed in the village; from the brightly lit tavern near by there came a dissonant, vague hubbub, through which I seemed to make out the voice of Yakov. Wild laughter broke out explosively from time to time. I went up to the little window and pressed my face to the glass.

I saw an unhappy, though a motley and lively enough scene: everyone was drunk – everyone, beginning with Yakov. With bared breast he was sitting on a bench and, singing in a husky voice some dancing song of the streets, idly fingered and plucked the strings of a guitar. His damp hair hung in clusters over his terribly pale face. In the middle of the tavern the Nit, completely 'unwound' and without his coat, was dancing with skips and jumps in front of the peasant in the colourless overcoat; the little man, in his turn, was with difficulty tapping and scraping his dog-tired feet and, smiling senselessly through his dishevelled beard, gave occasional waves

of the hand, as though wishing to say: 'So what the hell!'
Nothing could have been more comic than his face; no
matter how much he jerked his brows up, his heavy eyelids
refused to rise and remained fallen over his barely visible,
bleary, though extremely syrupy little eyes. He was in the
pleasant condition of someone who is rolling drunk, to whom
every passer-by, upon glancing in his face, invariably remarks:
'You're doing fine, mate, you're doing fine!' Winker, red-
faced as a crab and with widely distended nostrils, was giving
roars of venomous laughter from one corner; only Nikolay
Ivanych maintained his unvarying composure, as befitted a
true tavern-keeper. Many new faces had gathered in the room;
but I did not see Gentleman Wildman there.

I turned away and began quickly to descend the hill on
which Kolotovka is situated. At the foot of this hill there is a
broad plain; flooded with murky waves of evening mist, it
appeared to be even vaster than it was and seemed to flow
into the darkened sky. I was taking large steps down the road
alongside the ravine, when suddenly somewhere far off in the
plain a boy's shrill voice cried out. 'Antropka! Antropka-a-a!'
he shouted with insistent and tearful desperation, prolonging
and prolonging the last syllable.

He was silent for several instants and then resumed his
shouting. His voice carried resonantly through the still,
lightly dreaming air. At least thirty times he called out
Antropka's name, when suddenly from the opposite end of
the wide field, as if from another world, came the hardly
audible answer:

'Wh-a-a-a-at?'

The boy's voice at once cried out with gleeful spite:

'Come here, you devil pip-sque-e-e-eak!'

'Why-y-y-y?' the other answered after a short time.

''Cos dad wants to be-e-eat you,' the second voice hurriedly
shouted.

The second voice made no further reply, and the boy again

started calling for Antropka. His shouts, more and more in-
frequent and faint, still reached my ears by the time it had
grown completely dark and I was skirting the edge of the
forest which surrounds my little village and lies about three
miles from Kolotovka.

'Antropka-a-a!' still seemed to resound in the air, filled with
shades of night.

Meeting

I WAS sitting in a birch wood one autumn, about the middle of September. From early morning there had been occasional drizzle, succeeded from time to time by periods of warm sunny radiance; a season of changeable weather. The sky was either covered with crumbling white clouds or suddenly clear for an instant in a few places, and then, from behind the parted clouds, blue sky would appear, lucid and smiling, like a beautiful eye. I sat and looked around me and listened. The leaves scarcely rustled above my head; by their very noise one could know what time of year it was. It was not the happy, laughing *tremolo* of spring, not the soft murmuration and long-winded talkativeness of summer, not the shy and chill babblings of late autumn, but a hardly audible dreamy chattering. A faint wind ever so slightly moved through the treetops. The interior of the wood, damp from the rain, was continually changing, depending on whether the sun was shining or whether it was covered by cloud; the interior was either flooded with light, just as if everything in it had suddenly smiled: the delicate trunks of the not-too-numerous birches would suddenly acquire the soft sheen of white silk, the wafer-thin leaves which lay on the ground would suddenly grow multi-coloured and burn with crimson and gold, while the beautiful stems of tall curly bracken, already embellished with their autumn colouring which resembles the colour of overripe grapes, would stand there shot through with light, endlessly entangling and criss-crossing before one's eyes; or suddenly one would again be surrounded by a bluish dusk: the bright colours would instantly be extinguished and the birches would all stand there white, without a gleam on them, white as snow that has only just fallen and has not yet been touched by the chilly sparkling rays of the winter sun; and secretively, slyly, thinly drizzling rain would begin to filter and whisper through the wood.

The foliage on the birches was still almost completely green, although it had noticeably faded; only here and there stood a young tree all decked out in red or gold, and one could not help watching how brightly it flared up when the sun's rays broke, gliding and scintillating, through the myriad network of fine branches only just washed by glittering rain. There was not a single bird to be heard: all had taken cover and fallen silent; only the mocking little voice of the tom-tit tinkled occasionally like a little steel bell.

Before I had stopped in this little birch wood, I had gone with my dog through a grove of tall aspens. I confess that I am not particularly fond of that tree – the aspen – with its pale-mauve trunk and grey-green, metallic foliage which it raises as high as possible and spreads out in the air like a quivering fan; nor do I like the continual flutterings of its round untidy leaves which are so awkwardly attached to their long stalks. It acquires beauty only on certain summer evenings when, rising on high in isolation among low bushy undergrowth, it meets the challenge of the ebbing rays of the sunset and gleams and trembles, suffused from its topmost branches to its roots by a uniform yellow and purple light; or when, on a clear windy day, it is all noisily streaming and babbling against the blue sky, and every leaf, seized by the wind's ardour, appears to want to tear itself free, fly away and hurry off into the distance. But in general I dislike this tree and therefore, without stopping to rest in the aspen grove, I made my way to the little birch wood, settled myself under a tree whose branches began close to the ground and were able, in consequence, to shelter me from the rain, and, having gazed admiringly at the surrounding view, fell into the kind of untroubled and mild sleep familiar only to hunters.

I cannot say how long I was asleep, but when I opened my

eyes the entire interior of the wood was filled with sunlight and in all directions through the jubilantly rustling foliage a bright blue sky peered and seemed to sparkle; the clouds had vanished, dispersed by the wind that had sprung up; the weather had cleared, and in the air could be felt that special dry freshness which, imbuing the heart with a feeling of elation, almost always means a peaceful and clear evening after a rainy day.

I was on the point of rising and again trying my luck, when suddenly my eyes lighted on a motionless human form. I looked closely and saw that it was a young peasant girl. She was sitting twenty paces from me, her head lowered in thought and both hands dropped on her knees; in the half-open palm of one of them lay a thick bunch of wild flowers and at each breath she took the bunch slipped quietly down on to her checked skirt. A clean white blouse, buttoned at the neck and at the wrists, gathered in short soft folds about her waist; two rows of large yellow beads fell from her neck on to her bosom. She was very pretty in her own way. Her thick fair hair of a beautiful ash colour was parted into two carefully styled semi-circles below a narrow crimson ribbon drawn almost down to her temples, which were white as ivory; the rest of her face was faintly sunburned to that golden hue which is only acquired by a delicate skin. I could not see her eyes because she did not raise them; but I clearly saw her fine, high eyebrows and long eyelashes, which were damp, and on one of her cheeks I saw the dried traces of a tear that had come to rest at the edge of her slightly pale lips and glittered in the sunlight. The whole appearance of her head was very charming; even the slightly thick and rounded nose did nothing to spoil it. I particularly liked the expression on her face for the way in which it was so artless and gentle, so melancholy and full of childish bewilderment at her own grief.

She was evidently waiting for someone. Something crackled faintly in the wood and she at once raised her head and looked round; in the transparent shade her large eyes, bright and frightened, flashed quickly before me like the eyes of a doe. She listened for a few moments without taking her wide-open eyes from the place where the faint sound had been made, then heaved a sigh, turned her head calmly back, bent still farther down and began slowly to finger the flowers. Her eyelids reddened, her lips gave a quiver of bitterness and another tear slipped from beneath her thick lashes, coming to rest on her cheek where it glittered radiantly. Some time passed in this way, and the poor girl did not move save to make a few regretful gestures with her hands and to go on listening and listening. Again something made a noise in the wood and she was instantly alerted. The noise continued, grew louder as it approached, and finally could be heard the noise of rapid, decisive footsteps. She straightened herself and appeared to be overcome with shyness; her attentive features began to quiver and burn with expectation. The figure of a man could be glimpsed through the thicket. She peered in that direction, blushed suddenly, gave a joyful and happy smile, got ready to stand up and once again suddenly lowered her head, growing pale and confused – and she only raised her faltering, almost imploring gaze to the newcomer when he had stopped beside her.

I examined him with curiosity from my hiding-place. I confess that he produced an unpleasant impression on me. To all appearances he was the pampered valet of some rich young master. His clothes displayed pretensions to good taste and dandified casualness: they consisted of a short, bronze-coloured top-coat buttoned up to the neck and inherited, more than likely, from his master, a little rose-tinted neck-tie with mauve tips and a black velvet cap with gold lace edging worn pulled down over the eyebrows. The rounded collar of his white shirt pressed unmercifully up against his ears and bit into his cheek, while his starched cuffs covered his hands right down to the red and crooked fingers which were embellished with gold and silver rings containing turquoise forget-me-nots. His face – ruddy, fresh-complexioned and impudent – belonged to the category of faces which, so far as I have been able to judge, almost invariably annoy men and, unfortunately, are very often pleasing to women. He clearly made an effort to endow his rather coarse features with an expression of superciliousness and boredom; he endlessly screwed up his already tiny milk-grey eyes, frowned, let his mouth droop at the edges, gave forced yawns and with a casual, though not entirely skilled, air of abandon either patted the reddish, artfully coiled hair on his temples or twiddled the little yellow hairs that stuck out on his fat upper lip – in a word, he showed off insufferably. He began to show off as soon as he saw the young peasant girl waiting for him; he slowly approached her at a lounging pace, came to a stop, shrugged his shoulders, stuck both hands into the pockets of his top-coat and, with hardly more than a fleeting and indifferent glance at the poor girl, lowered himself to the ground.

'Well,' he began, still looking away to one side, swinging his leg and yawning, 'have you been here long?'

The girl was unable to answer him immediately.

'A long time, sir, Victor Alexandrych,' she said eventually in a scarcely audible voice.

'Ah!' He removed his cap, grandly drew his hand through his thick, tightly coiled hair, which began almost at his eyebrows, and, glancing round with dignity, once more carefully covered his priceless head. 'And I'd almost completely forgotten. After all, look how it rained!' He yawned once more. 'There's a mass of things to be done, what with everything to be got ready and the master swearing as well. Tomorrow we'll be off . . .'

'Tomorrow?' the girl said and directed at him a look of fright.

'That's right – tomorrow. Now, now, now, please,' he

added hastily and with annoyance, seeing that she had begun to tremble all over and was quietly lowering her head, 'please, Akulina, no crying. You know I can't stand crying.' And he puckered up his snub nose. 'If you start, I'll leave at once. What silliness – blubbering!'

'No, I won't, I won't,' Akulina uttered hurriedly, making herself swallow her tears. 'So you're leaving tomorrow?' she added after a brief pause. 'When will God bring you back to see me again, Victor Alexandrych?'

'We'll meet again, we'll meet again. If not next year, then later. It seems the master wants to enter government service in St Petersburg,' he continued, speaking the words casually and slightly through the nose, 'and maybe we'll go abroad.'

'You'll forget me, Victor Alexandrych,' Akulina said sadly.

'No, why should I? I won't forget you. Only you've got to be sensible, not start playing up, obey your father . . . I'll not forget you – no-o-o.' And he calmly stretched himself and again yawned.

'You mustn't forget me, Victor Alexandrych,' she continued in an imploring voice. 'I've loved you so much, it seems, and it seems I've done everything for you. . . . You tell me to listen to my father, Victor Alexandrych. . . . There's no point in listening to my father . . .'

'Why not?' He uttered these words as it were from his stomach, lying on his back with his arms behind his head.

'There's no point, Victor Alexandrych. You know that yourself . . .'

She said nothing. Victor played with the steel chain of his watch.

'You're not a fool, Akulina,' he started saying at last, 'so don't talk nonsense. I want what's best for you, do you understand me? Of course, you're not stupid, you're not a complete peasant girl, so to speak; and your mother also wasn't always a peasant girl. But you're without any education, so you've got to listen when people tell you things.'

'I'm frightened, Victor Alexandrych.'

'Hey, there, that's a lot of nonsense, my dear. What's there to be frightened of! What's that you've got there,' he added, turning to her, 'flowers?'

'Flowers,' answered Akulina despondently. 'They're some field tansies I've picked,' she continued, brightening slightly, 'and they're good for calves. And these are marigolds, they help against scrofula. Just look what a lovely little flower it is! I've never seen such a lovely little flower before in all my born days. Then there are some forget-me-nots, here are some violets. But these I got for you,' she added, taking out from beneath the yellow tansies a small bunch of blue cornflowers tied together with a fine skein of grass, 'would you like them?'

Victor languidly stretched out his hand, took the bunch, casually sniffed the flowers and began to twiddle them in his fingers, gazing up in the air from time to time with thoughtful self-importance. Akulina looked at him and her sad gaze contained such tender devotion, such worshipful humility and love. Yet she was also afraid of him, and fearful of crying; and taking her own leave of him and doting on him for the last time; but he lay there in the lounging pose of a sultan and endured her worship of him with magnanimous patience and condescension. I confess that his red face vexed me with its pretentiously disdainful indifference through which could be discerned a replete and self-satisfied vanity. Akulina was so fine at that moment, for her whole heart was trustfully and passionately laid open before him, craving him and yearning to be loved, but he . . . he simply let the cornflowers drop on the grass, took a round glass in a bronze frame out of the side pocket of his top-coat and started trying to fix it in place over his eye; but no matter how hard he tried to keep it in place with a puckered brow, a raised cheek and even with his nose, the little eyeglass kept on falling out and dropping into his hand.

'What's that?' Akulina asked finally in astonishment.

'A lorgnette,' he answered self-importantly.

'What's it for?'

'So as to see better.'

'Show it me.'

Victor frowned, but he gave her the eyeglass.

'Don't break it, mind.'

'You needn't worry, I won't.' She raised it timidly to her eye. 'I don't see anything,' she said artlessly.

'It's your eye, you've got to screw up your eye,' he retorted in the voice of a dissatisfied mentor. She screwed up the eye before which she was holding the little glass. 'Not that one, not that one, idiot! The other one!' exclaimed Victor and, giving her no chance to correct her mistake, took the lorgnette from her.

Akulina reddened, gave a nervous laugh and turned away.

'It's obviously not for the likes of me,' she murmured.

'That's for sure!'

The poor girl was silent and let fall a deep sigh.

'Oh, Victor Alexandrych, what'll I do without you?' she suddenly said.

Victor wiped the lorgnette with the edge of his coat and put it back in his pocket.

'Yes, yes,' he said eventually, 'it sure will be hard for you to start with.' He gave her several condescending pats on the shoulder; she ever so quietly lifted his hand from her shoulder and timidly kissed it. 'Well, all right, all right, you're a good kid,' he went on, giving a self-satisfied smile, 'but what can I do about it? Judge for yourself! The master and I can't stay here; it'll be winter soon now and to spend the winter in the country – you know this yourself – is just horrible. But it's another matter in St Petersburg! There are simply such wonderful things there, such as you, stupid, wouldn't be able to imagine even in your wildest dreams! What houses and streets, and the sochiety, the culture – it's simply stupendous!' Akulina listened to him with greedy interest, her lips slightly parted like a child's. 'Anyhow,' he added, turning over, 'why am I telling you all this? You won't be able to understand it.'

'Why say that, Victor Alexandrych? I've understood it, I've understood everything.'

'What a bright one you are!'

Akulina lowered her head.

'You never used to talk to me like that before, Victor Alexandrych,' she said without raising her eyes.

'Didn't I before? Before! You're a one! Before indeed!' he commented, pretending to be indignant.

Both were silent for a while.

'However, it's time for me to be going,' said Victor, and was on the point of raising himself on one elbow.

'Stay a bit longer,' Akulina declared in an imploring voice.

'What's there to wait for? I've already said good-bye to you.'

'Stay a bit,' Akulina repeated.

Victor again lay back and started whistling. Akulina never took her eyes off him. I could tell that she was slowly working herself into a state of agitation: her lips were working and her pale cheeks were faintly crimsoning.

'Victor Alexandrych,' she said at last in a breaking voice, 'it's sinful of you . . . sinful of you, Victor Alexandrych, in God's name it is!'

'What's sinful?' he asked, knitting his brows, and he raised himself slightly and turned his head towards her.

'It's sinful, Victor Alexandrych. If you'd only say one kind word to me now you're leaving, just say one word to me, wretched little orphan that I am . . .'

'But what should I say to you?'

'I don't know. You should know that better than me, Victor Alexandrych. Now you're going away, and if only you'd say a word. . . . Why should I deserve this?'

'What a strange girl you are! What can I say?'

'Just say one word . . .'

'Well, you've certainly gone on and on about the same thing,' he said in disgruntlement and stood up.

'Don't be angry, Victor Alexandrych,' she added quickly, hardly restraining her tears.

'I'm not angry, it's only that you're stupid. . . . What do you want? You know I can't marry you, don't you? Surely you know I can't? So what's it you want? What is it?' He stuck his face forward in expectation of her answer and opened wide his fingers.

'I don't want anything . . . anything,' she answered, stammering and scarcely daring to stretch her trembling hands out towards him, 'only if you'd just say one word in farewell . . .'

And tears streamed from her eyes.

'Well, so there it is, you've started crying,' Victor said callously, tipping his cap forward over his eyes.

'I don't want anything,' she went on, swallowing her tears and covering her face with both hands, 'but what'll it be like for me in the family, what'll there be for me? And what's going to happen to me, what's going to become of me, wretch that I am! They'll give their orphan girl away to someone who doesn't love her . . . O poor me, poor me!'

'Moan away, moan away!' muttered Victor under his breath, shifting from one foot to the other.

'If only he'd say one little word, just one word. . . . Such as, Akulina, I . . . I . . .'

Sudden heart-rending sobs prevented her from finishing what she was saying. She flopped on her face in the grass and burst into bitter, bitter tears. Her whole body shook convulsively, the nape of her neck rising and falling. Her long-restrained grief finally poured forth in torrents. Victor stood for a moment or so above her, shrugged his shoulders, turned and walked away with big strides.

Several moments passed. She grew quiet, raised her head, jumped up, looked about her and wrung her hands; she was on the point of rushing after him, but her legs collapsed under her and she fell on her knees. I could not hold myself back and rushed towards her, but she had hardly had time to look at me before she found the strength from somewhere to raise herself with a faint cry and vanish through the trees, leaving her flowers scattered on the ground.

I stopped there a moment, picked up the bunch of cornflowers and walked out of the wood into a field. The sun was low in the pale clear sky and its rays had, as it were, lost their colour and grown cold; they did not shine so much as flow out in an even, almost watery, light. No more than half an hour remained until evening, but the sunset was only just beginning to crimson the sky. A flurrying wind raced towards me across the dry, yellow stubble; hastily spinning before it, little shrivelled leaves streamed past me across the track and along the edge of the wood; the side which faced on to the field like a wall shuddered all over and glistened with a faint sparkling, distinctly though not brightly; on the red-tinted grass, on separate blades of grass, on pieces of straw, everywhere innumerable strands of autumn cobwebs glittered and rippled. I stopped, and a feeling of melancholy stole over me, for it seemed to me that the sombre terror associated with the approaching winter was breaking through the cheerless, though fresh, smile of nature at this time of withering. High above me, ponderously and sharply sundering the air with its wings, a vigilant raven flew by, turned its head, looked sidewards at me, took wing and disappeared beyond the wood with strident cawings; a large flock of pigeons rose smartly from a place where there had been threshing and after suddenly making a huge wheeling turn in the air settled busily on to the field – a sure sign of autumn! Someone rode by on the other side of a bare hillock, his empty cart clattering noisily . . .

I returned home; but the image of the poor Akulina took a long time to fade from my mind, and her cornflowers, which have long since withered, remain with me to this day . . .

Hamlet of the Shchigrovsky District

O N one of my trips I received an invitation to dine with a wealthy landowner and hunter, Alexander Mikhailych G. His village was situated about three miles from a small group of dwellings where I was staying at that time. I dressed up in my frock-coat, without which I advise no one to leave home, even though it be only for a hunting trip, and set off for Alexander Mikhailych's place. Dinner was to begin at six; I arrived at five and found, already assembled, a large number of members of the nobility in uniforms, evening dress and other less specific types of costume. My host greeted me cordially, but at once hurried off into the servants' hall. He was awaiting the arrival of an eminent dignitary and felt a degree of excitement over it that was hardly in keeping with his independent position in the world and his wealth. Alexander Mikhailych had never been married and disliked women; his parties were attended only by men. He lived on a big scale, had enlarged and done up his ancestral home in magnificent fashion, every year ordered from Moscow wines to the tune of fifteen thousand roubles and in general enjoyed the greatest respect. He had long ago retired from service and was not seeking honours of any kind. . . . Why on earth, then, should he have fussed himself over the visit of an official guest and been so excited by it ever since the morning of his banquet? That remains obscured by the mists of uncertainty, as a notary of my acquaintance used to say when he was asked whether he took bribes from willing donors.

Parting with my host, I began to wander about the rooms. Almost all the guests were complete strangers to me; about twenty of them were already seated at the card tables. Among those playing preference were two military men with distinguished, if slightly down-at-heel, faces, and a few civilian gentlemen wearing high, tight collars and the kind of pendant, dyed whiskers affected only by resolute but well-disposed people (these well-disposed people were engaged in importantly sorting their cards and casting sideward glances at newcomers without moving their heads); also five or six district officials with round tummies, puffy, sticky little hands and modestly immobile little feet (these gentlemen spoke in soft voices, regaled everyone with timid smiles, held their cards close to their shirt-fronts and, when playing trumps, did not thump them down on the table but, on the contrary, let them drop with a floating motion on to the green cloth and, as they gathered in their winnings, produced a slight, but very decorous and polite creaking sound). Other members of the nobility were sitting on divans or clustered in groups about the doorways and windows; a no longer young, though outwardly effeminate, landowner was standing in one corner, trembling and blushing and agitatedly twisting the watch signet on his stomach, though no one was paying any attention to him; other gentlemen, adorned in rounded frock-coats and chequered trousers of Moscow workmanship tailored by the foreigner, Fiers Klyukhin, master of his guild in perpetuity, were engaged in unusually free and lively discussion, liberally turning the fat, bare napes of their necks in one direction or another; a young man of about twenty, blond and myopic, dressed from head to foot in black, was visibly embarrassed, but continued to smile venomously.

I was, however, beginning to grow a little bored when suddenly I was joined by a certain Voinitsyn, a young man who had failed to complete his education and was now living in Alexander Mikhailych's house in the capacity of . . . it would be difficult to say precisely in what capacity. He was an excellent shot and adept at training dogs. I had known him earlier in Moscow. He belonged to the run of young men who used to 'play dumb as a post' at every examination – that is to say, who never uttered a word in answer to the professor's questions. These gentlemen were also known, in stylish parlance, as 'sideburn-ites'.[1] (These matters relate to the distant past, as you can readily appreciate.) It would be arranged as follows: they would call upon Voinitsyn, for instance. Voinitsyn, who until that moment had been sitting straight and motionless on his bench, perspiring hotly from head to toe and slowly, though fatuously, rolling his eyes around – he would rise, hastily button up his uniform right to the top and saunter crabwise to the examiners' table.

'Be good enough to take a ticket,' a professor would say affably.

Voinitsyn would stretch out a hand and agitatedly finger the little pile of tickets.

'You don't have to choose one, if you don't mind,' would remark the querulous voice of some tetchy old man, a professor from another faculty, who had conceived a sudden dislike for the unfortunate 'sideburn-ite'. Voinitsyn would submit to his fate, take a ticket, show its number and walk to the window to sit down while a previous examinee answered a question. At the window Voinitsyn would not take his eyes off the ticket, save perhaps once again to roll his eyes slowly around, and would remain stock-still in every limb. Eventually, however, the previous examinee would be finished. He would be told: 'Good, you may go,' or even 'Good, sir, very good, sir,' depending upon his abilities. Then they would call upon Voinitsyn. Voinitsyn would rise and approach the table with a firm step.

'Read out the question,' they would tell him.

Holding it in both hands, Voinitsyn would raise the ticket to the tip of his nose, read out the question slowly and slowly lower his arms.

'Well, sir, be so good as to answer,' the first professor would say casually, resting back in his chair and crossing his hands on his chest.

A silence deep as the grave would fall upon the proceedings. 'What's wrong with you?'

Voinitsyn would be silent. The old man from another faculty would begin to grow annoyed.

'Come on, say something, man!'

This Voinitsyn of mine would remain silent, as if he had given up the ghost. The shaven nape of his neck would jut out still and sharp before the curious gaze of his comrades. The old man's eyes were ready to jump out of his head: he had finally begun to loathe Voinitsyn.

'Isn't it rather strange, after all,' another examiner would remark, 'that you should stand there dumb as a post? So you don't know the answer, is that it? If that's so, say so.'

'Permit me to take another ticket,' the unfortunate chap would mumble. The professors exchanged looks.

'Very well, then,' says the chief examiner with a wave of his hand.

Voinitsyn again takes a ticket, again goes to the window, again returns to the table and again is as silent as a corpse. The old fellow from another faculty is just about to eat him alive. Finally they send him packing and award him a zero mark. By now you would think he'd at least make tracks. Not at all! He returns to his place and adopts the same motionless pose until the conclusion of the examination, when he leaves, exclaiming: 'What a sweat that was! What a business!' And all day he strolls around Moscow, occasionally clutching his head and bitterly cursing his wretched fate. Never once, of course, does he so much as glance at a book, and the next day the same thing happens all over again.

It was this Voinitsyn who took his place next to me. We talked together about our Moscow days, about our hunting experiences.

'If you wish,' he suddenly whispered to me, 'I'll introduce you to our leading local wit?'

'Do me that honour.'

Voinitsyn led me up to a man of small stature, with a tall tuft of hair on the top of his head and whiskers, dressed in a brown frock-coat and a colourful neck-tie. His embittered, lively features conveyed a real air of wit and vindictiveness. A sour, fugitive smile endlessly contorted his lips; his small, dark, puckered eyes looked boldly out from beneath uneven eyelashes. Standing beside him was a landowner, broad of beam, soft, sugary – a real Lord Honeybun – and one-eyed. His laughter always anticipated the little man's witticisms and he was literally melting with pleasure. Voinitsyn introduced me to the local wit, one Pyotr Petrovich Lupikhin by name. We made our introductions and exchanged the initial words of greeting.

'And now allow me to introduce you to my best friend,' said Lupikhin suddenly in a sharp tone of voice, seizing the sugary landowner by the arm. 'Now don't you be retiring, Kirila Selifanych,' he added, 'they won't bite you. Here, my dear sirs,' he continued, while the embarrassed Kirila Selifanych gave such awkward bows that it seemed his stomach was about to collapse, 'here, sir, I recommend to you a most excellent member of the gentry. He enjoyed splendid health until he was fifty years of age, and then he suddenly took it into his head to cure his eyesight, as a result of which he lost the use of one eye. Since then he's been dispensing cures to his peasants with the same degree of success. . . . And they, it goes without saying, have shown a similar devotion. . . .'

'What a fellow,' Kirila Selifanych muttered and burst into laughter.

'Do complete what you were saying, my friend, do go on,' Lupikhin inserted. 'After all, they could well elect you to the judges' bench, and they will elect you, you'll see. Well, suppose, of course, that the court assessors do all the thinking for you, there'd still be a need in any event to express somebody else's ideas, let's say. What if the Governor should unexpectedly drop by and ask: "What's the judge stammering for?" Well, suppose they say it's an attack of paralysis, then he'll say: "Bleed him, then, bleed him!" And that in your position, you'll agree, wouldn't be right and proper.'

The sugary landowner went off into a drum-roll of laughter.

'Look at him laughing,' Lupikhin continued, gazing wickedly at the quivering stomach of Kirila Selifanych. 'And why shouldn't he laugh?' he added, turning to me. 'He's well fed, healthy, childless, his peasants aren't mort-gaged – after all, he's curing them – and his wife's a bit dotty.' (Kirila Selifanych turned slightly to one side, feigning not to catch this, and continued to roar with laughter.) 'I can laugh just the same, and my wife's run off with a land surveyor.' (He showed his teeth in a grin.) 'Perhaps you didn't know that? Yessir! She just upped and ran off and left me a letter which read: "Dear Pyotr Petrovich, forgive me, carried away by passion, I'm going off with the friend of my heart. . . ." And the land surveyor only captured her heart by not cutting his nails and wearing his pants skin-tight. You're surprised? "Such a frank fellow," you'll say. . . . And, my God! we men of the steppes know how to open up the womb of truth. However, let's go to one side. There's no need for us to go on standing next to a future judge. . . .'

He took me by the arm and we went to the window.

'I pass here for a wit,' he said to me in the course of con-versation, 'but you mustn't believe that. I'm simply an em-bittered man and I speak my mind out loud. That's why I'm so unrestrained. And why should I stand on ceremony, in fact? I don't give a damn for any opinions and I'm not out for anything for myself. I have a wicked tongue – so what of it? A man with a wicked tongue at least doesn't need to have a mind. But how refreshing it is, you wouldn't believe it. . . . Well, take a look, for example, at our host! Now I ask you, why on earth is he scurrying about like that, all the time glancing at the clock, smiling, perspiring, making himself look important and leaving us to die of hunger? A high-ranking dignitary's not so unusual a sight, after all! There he is, there he is, again running – he's even started hobbling about, look at him!'

And Lupikhin gave a screeching laugh.

'One thing wrong is that there are no ladies,' he continued with a deep sigh. 'It's a stag occasion – otherwise it would've been useful for the likes of us. Take a look, take a look,' he exclaimed suddenly, 'Prince Kozelsky's coming – there he is, that tall man with a beard and yellow gloves. You can tell at once that he's been abroad. . . . And he makes a habit of arriving so late. That man alone, I tell you, is as stupid as a couple of merchants' horses, but you just take the trouble to notice how condescendingly he addresses the likes of us, how magnanimously he permits himself to smile at the pleasantries of our famished mothers and daughters! Sometimes he even tries to be witty on his own account, although he doesn't live here permanently; and the kind of witty remarks he makes! Just like trying to saw at a tow-rope with a blunt knife! He can't stand the sight of me . . . I'll go and pay my respects to him.'

And Lupikhin ran off in the Prince's direction.

'And here comes my private enemy,' he announced, suddenly turning back to me. 'See that stout man with the tanned face and bristles on his head – there, the one who's grasping his hat in his hand and stealing along by the wall, glancing all around him like a veritable wolf? For four hundred roubles I sold him a horse that was worth a thousand, and this lowly creature now has every right to despise me; and yet he is so devoid of the capacity for understanding, especially in the morning, before he's taken his tea, or immediately after dinner, that if you say "How d'you do?" to him he'll answer: "How what, sir?" And here comes a general,' Lupikhin went on, 'a civil-service general in retirement, a general who's lost all his money. He has a daughter of sugar-beet refinement and a factory of scrofula – I'm sorry, I didn't get that right.

. . . Anyhow, you understand what I mean. Ah! and here's an architect just dropped by! A German, replete with whiskers and no idea of his business – wonders'll never cease! But as a matter of fact there's no need for him to know his business: all he has to do is take bribes and put up more columns, more pillars, that is, for the pillars of our aristocracy!'

Lupikhin again gave vent to laughter. But suddenly an anxious excitement spread through the entire house. The dignitary had arrived. Our host literally plunged into the entrance hall. Several devoted members of his staff and some eager guests rushed after him. The noisy conversation changed into soft, pleasant talk, similar to the springtime humming of bees in their native hives. Only the indefatigably waspish Lupikhin and the superb drone Kozelsky did not lower their voices. . . . And finally came the queen herself – the dignitary entered. Hearts were wafted to meet him, sitting torsoes were raised a trifle; even the landowner who had bought the horse cheaply from Lupikhin, even he thrust his chin into his chest. The dignitary maintained his dignity with the utmost aplomb: nodding his head back as though bowing, he spoke a few appreciative words, each of which began with the letter 'a' uttered protractedly through the nose, and with a disapproval amounting to ravening hunger he glanced at Prince Kozelsky's beard and offered the index finger of his left hand to the penniless civil-service general with the factory and daughter. After a few minutes, in the course of which the dignitary succeeded in remarking twice how glad he was that he had not arrived late for the dinner, the entire company proceeded into the dining-room, the bigwigs leading the way.

It is hardly necessary to tell the reader how the dignitary was given the seat of honour between the civil-service general and the provincial marshal of nobility, a man of unrestrained and dignified expression entirely in keeping with his starched shirt-front, infinitely broad waistcoat and round snuff-box full of French tobacco; how our host fussed, dashed about, busied himself importantly, urged his guests to partake of what was offered, smiled in passing at the dignitary's back and, standing in one corner like a schoolboy, hastily spooned down a plate of soup or had a bite of beef; how the butler brought in a fish more than three feet long with a floral bouquet in its mouth; how the servants, all liveried and severe of face, morosely approached each member of the gentry either with Malaga or dry Madeira and how almost all these gentlemen, especially the elderly, drank glass after glass as though submitting unwillingly to a sense of duty; how finally bottles of champagne began to pop and toasts began to be made: the reader is, no doubt, only too familiar with such matters. But particularly noteworthy, it seemed to me, was an anecdote told by the dignitary himself amid a universally joyous hush.

Someone – it may have been the penniless general, a man acquainted with the latest literary trends – remarked on the influence of women in general and particularly their influence on young men. 'Yes, indeed,' said the dignitary in amplification, 'that is true. But young men should be kept under the strictest control, otherwise they tend to go out of their minds over any and every kind of skirt.' (Childishly happy smiles sped across the faces of all the guests; one landowner's expression even lit up with gratitude.) '*Bee*-cause young men are stupid.' (The dignitary, probably for the sake of grandness, sometimes altered the accepted accentuation of words.) 'Take, for example, my son Ivan,' he continued. 'The fool's only just twenty, but he comes to me suddenly and says: "Permit me, sir, to get married." I tell him: "You're a fool, do your service first. . . ." Well, of course, despair, tears. . . . But in my view that's it. . . .' (The dignitary pronounced the words 'that's it' more with his stomach than his lips; he paused and directed a majestic glance at his neighbour, the general, at the same time raising his brows quite unexpectedly high. The civil-service general inclined his head pleasantly a little to one side and with extraordinary rapidity blinked one eye, which was turned towards the dignitary.) 'And now what d'you think,' the dignitary started up again, 'now he himself writes to me and says: "Thank you, sir, for teaching me not to be so foolish." That's how one ought to handle such matters.' All the guests, needless to say, were in full agreement with the speaker and apparently grew quite enlivened at receiving such pleasure and such injunctions. After dinner the entire company rose and moved into the drawing-room with a great deal more noisiness, though it was still within the bounds of decency and on this occasion literally justified. They all sat down to cards.

Somehow or other I passed the time until it was evening and, having ordered my driver to have my carriage ready for five o'clock the next morning, I retired to bed. But during the course of that same day it still remained for me to make the acquaintance of a certain remarkable person.

Owing to the number of guests no one slept in a room by himself. The small, greenish, dampish room, to which my host's butler led me, was already occupied by another guest, who had already undressed completely. Seeing me, he swiftly plunged under the counterpane, with which he covered himself right up to his nose, twisted and turned a little on the crumbling feather mattress and grew still, looking sharply up from beneath the rounded rim of his cotton nightcap. I went up to the other bed (there were only two of them in the room), undressed and lay down between the damp sheets. My neighbour began turning over in his bed. I wished him good night.

Half an hour passed. Despite all my efforts, I was quite unable to get to sleep: an endless succession of vague, unnecessary thoughts dragged one after another persistently and monotonously through my mind just like the buckets of a water-lifting machine.

'It seems you're not asleep?' my neighbour said.

'As you see,' I answered. 'And you're also wakeful?'

'I'm always wakeful.'

'How is that?'

'That's how it is. I go to sleep without knowing why; I lie and lie and then I'm asleep.'

'Why, then, do you get into bed before you feel like sleeping?'

'What do you suggest I should do?'

I did not reply to my neighbour's question.

'It surprises me,' he continued after a short silence, 'that there are no fleas here. Where, one wonders, have they got to?'

'You sound as if you regret not having them,' I remarked.

'No, I don't regret not having them; but I do like things to be consistent.'

Listen to the words he's using, I thought.

My neighbour again grew silent.

'Would you like to make a bet with me?' he suddenly asked fairly loudly.

'About what?' My neighbour was beginning to amuse me.

'Hmm . . . about what? About this: I feel sure that you take me for a fool.'

'If you please . . .' I mumbled in surprise.

'For a country bumpkin, an ignoramus. . . . Admit it.'

'I do not have the pleasure of knowing you,' I protested. 'How can you deduce . . .'

'How! I can deduce from the very sound of your voice: you've been answering me so casually. . . . But I'm not at all what you think.'

'Allow me . . .'

'No, *you* allow me. In the first place, I speak French no worse than you, and German even better. In the second place, I spent three years abroad: in Berlin alone I lived about eight months. I have studied Hegel, my good sir, and I know Goethe by heart. What is more, I was for quite a while in love with the daughter of a German professor and then, back here, I got married to a consumptive lady – a bald-headed but very remarkable individual. It would seem, then, that I'm of the same breed as you. I'm not a country bumpkin, as you suppose . . . I'm also consumed by introspection and there's nothing straightforward about me whatever.'

I raised my head and looked with redoubled interest at this odd fellow. In the faint illumination of the night-light I could scarcely make out his features.

'There you are now, you're looking at me,' he continued, adjusting his nightcap, 'and no doubt you're asking yourself: How is it that I didn't notice him today? I'll tell you why you didn't notice me – because I do not raise my voice; because I hide behind others, standing behind doors, talking with no one; because when the butler passes me with a tray he raises his elbow beforehand to the level of my chest. . . . And why do all these things happen? For two reasons: firstly, I am poor, and secondly, I have become reconciled. . . . Tell me the truth, you didn't notice me, did you?'

'I really did not have the pleasure . . .'

'Oh, sure, sure,' he interrupted me, 'I knew it.'

He raised himself a little and folded his arms; the long shadow of his nightcap bent round from the wall to the ceiling.

'But admit it,' he added, suddenly glancing sideways at me, 'I must seem to you to be an extremely odd fellow, an original character, as they say, or perhaps something even worse, let's suppose: perhaps you think I'm trying to make myself out to be an eccentric?'

'Again I must repeat to you that I don't know you . . .'

He lowered his head for an instant.

'Why I should've started saying these things quite out of the blue to you, someone I don't know at all – the Lord, the Lord alone knows!' (He sighed.) 'It's not due to any kinship of souls! Both you and I, we're both respectable people – we're egoists, that's to say. My business is not the slightest concern of yours, nor yours of mine, isn't that so? Yet neither of us can get to sleep. . . . So why not talk a little? I'm in my stride now, which doesn't happen to me often. I'm shy, you see, but not shy on the strength of being a provincial, a person of no rank or a pauper, but on the strength of the fact that I'm an awfully conceited fellow. But sometimes, under the influence of favourable circumstances and eventualities, which, by the way, I'm in no condition either to define or foresee, my shyness vanishes completely, as now, for instance. Set me face to face now with, say, the Dalai Lama himself and I'd ask even him for a pinch of snuff. But perhaps you'd like to go to sleep?'

'On the contrary,' I protested in haste, 'I find it very pleasant conversing with you.'

'That is, I entertain you, you mean. . . . So much the better. Well, then, sir, I'll tell you that in these parts people do me the honour of calling me original – those people, that's to say, who may casually happen to let fall my name along with the rest of the rubbish they talk. "With my fate is no one very much concerned. . . ."[2] They aim to hurt my pride. Oh, my God! If they only did but know that I'm perishing precisely because there's absolutely nothing original about me whatever, nothing except such childish pranks, for instance, as my present conversation with you; but such pranks aren't worth a jot. They're the cheapest and most despicable form of originality.'

He turned to face me and threw wide his arms.

'My dear sir!' he exclaimed. 'I am of the opinion that life on this earth is intended, generally speaking, for original people; only they have the right to live. *Mon verre n'est pas grand, mais je bois dans mon verre,*[3] someone once said. You see, don't you,' he added in a low voice, 'what pure French pronunciation I have? What's it to me if your head's leonine and roomy and you understand everything, know a great deal, keep up with the times, but you've got nothing at all that's uniquely your own, uniquely special, uniquely personal! You'll be just one more lumber-room of commonplaces with which to clutter up the world – and what sort of enjoyment is to be derived from that? No, at least be stupid, but stupid in your own way! At least have your own smell, some personal smell! And don't think my demands as regards this smell are formidable . . . God forbid! There's a bottomless pit of such kinds of original people: wherever you look you'll find one; every man alive's an original person in that sense – except that I haven't happened to be one of them!'

'Nevertheless, though,' he continued, after a short pause, 'what expectations I aroused in my youth! What an exalted opinion I had of my own person before going abroad and immediately after my return! Abroad, of course, I kept my ears pinned back, made my own way in the world, just as people of our sort should – people who know it all, see the point of everything, but, in the end, when you look at them you realize they haven't learned the first blessed thing!'

'Original, original!' he elaborated, giving a reproachful shake of the head. 'They call me original, but it turns out in fact that there's no one on earth less original than your most humble servant. I most likely was born in imitation of someone else. . . . Yes, by God! I live my life as well in imitation of a few authors whom I've studied, living by the sweat of my brow: I've done my bit of studying and falling in love and, at last, getting married, not as it were of my own free will, but just as if I was performing some duty, doing some lesson – who knows which it was?'

He tore his nightcap from his head and flung it down on the bed.

'If you like, I'll tell you the story of my life,' he asked me in an abrupt tone of voice, 'or, better, a few features of my life?'

'Do me that honour.'

'Or, no, I'd better tell you how I got married. After all, marriage is a serious affair, the touchstone of the whole man; in it is reflected, as in a mirror . . . no, that analogy's too banal. If you don't mind, I'll take a pinch of snuff.'

He extracted a snuff-box from beneath his pillow, opened it and began talking again while waving the opened snuff-box in the air.

'My good sir, you should appreciate my position. Judge for yourself what – what, if you'll be so kind – what good I might derive from the encyclopedia of Hegel?[4] What is there in common, will you tell me, between this encyclopedia and Russian life? And how would you want it applied to our circumstances – and not only it alone, the encyclopedia, but in general German philosophy – and more than that – German science?'

He jumped up and down on his bed and began muttering in a low voice, gritting his teeth maliciously:

'So that's how it is, that's how it is! So why on earth did you drag yourself abroad? Why didn't you sit at home and study the life around you on the spot? You would then have recognized its needs and future potential, and so far as your vocation, so to speak, was concerned you'd have been able to reach a clear understanding. . . . Yet, if you'll allow me,' he continued, again altering his tone of voice as if justifying himself and succumbing to shyness, 'where can people of our sort learn to study something that not a single scholar has yet set down in a book? I would have been glad to take lessons from it – from Russian life, that is; but the trouble is, the poor darling thing doesn't say a word in explanation. "Take me as I am," it seems to say. But that's beyond my powers. It ought to give me something to go on, offer me something conclusive. "Something conclusive?" they ask; "here's something conclusive: Lend your ear to our Moscow sages,[5] don't they sing as sweetly as nightingales?" But that's just the trouble: they whistle away like Kursk nightingales and don't talk like human beings. . . . So I gave the matter a good deal of thought and came to the conclusion that science was apparently the same the world over, just as truth was, and took the plunge by setting out, with God's help, for foreign lands to live among heathens. . . . What more d'you want me to say in justification? Youth and arrogance got the better of me. I didn't want, you know, to develop a premature middle-aged spread, although they say it's worth it. What's more, if nature hasn't given you much flesh on your bones to start with, you won't get much fat on your body no matter what happens!'

'However,' he added, after a moment's thought, 'I promised to tell you, it seems, how my marriage came about. Listen now. In the first place, I should tell you that my wife is no longer among the living, and in the second place . . . in the second place I see that I will have to tell you about my boyhood, otherwise you won't understand anything. . . . Surely you want to get to sleep?'

'No, not at all.'

'Excellent. Just listen to it, though – there's Mister Kantagryukhin snoring in the next room like a postillion! I was born of poor parents – I say parents because legend has it that, besides a mother, I also had a father. I don't remember him. They say he was rather dim-witted, with a large nose and freckles, light-brown hair and a habit of taking in snuff through one nostril; there was a portrait of him hanging in my mother's bedroom, in a red uniform with a black collar standing up to the ears – extraordinarily ugly. I used to be taken past it whenever I was being led in for a beating, and my mama, under such circumstances, would always point to it and declare: "He wouldn't treat you so lightly." You can imagine what an encouraging effect that had on me! I had neither brothers nor sisters – that's to say, if the truth be told, there was a little brother bedridden with rickets of the neck and he soon died. . . . And why, d'you think, should the English disease of rickets find its way into the Shchigrovsky district of Kursk Province? But that's beside the point. My mama undertook my education with all the headstrong ardour of a *grande dame* of the steppes; she undertook it right from the magnificent day of my birth until the moment I reached sixteen years of age. . . . Are you following what I'm saying?'

'Of course; do go on.'

'Very well. As soon, then, as I reached sixteen, my mama, without the slightest delay, expelled my French tutor – a German by the name of Philipovich who'd taken up residence among the Nezhin Greeks – and carted me off to Moscow, entered me for the university and then gave up her soul to the Almighty, leaving me in the hands of a blood-relation of mine, the attorney Koltun-Babura, an old bird famous not only in the Shchigrovsky district. This blood uncle of mine, the attorney Koltun-Babura, fleeced me of all I'd got, as is customary in such cases. . . . But again that's beside the point. I entered the university well enough prepared – I must give that much due to my maternal parent; but a lack of originality was even then beginning to make itself apparent in me. My boyhood had in no way differed from the boyhood of other youths: I had grown up just as stupid and flabby, precisely as if I'd lived my life under a feather-bed, just as early I'd begun repeating verses by heart and moping about on the pretext of having a dreamy disposition. . . . With what in mind? With the Beautiful in mind, and so on. I went the same way at the university: I at once joined a circle. Times were different then. . . . But perhaps you don't know what a circle is? I recall that Schiller said somewhere:

> *Gefährlich ist's den Leu zu wecken,*[6]
> *Verderblich ist des Tigers Zahn,*
> *Jedoch der schrecklichste der Schrecken –*
> *Das ist der Mensch in seinem Wahn!**

I assure you that wasn't what he wanted to say; what he wanted to say was:

> *Das ist ein "kruzhok" in der Stadt Moskau!'†*

* Fearful it is the lion to waken, And dreadful is the tiger's tooth, But most awful of all things together taken, – Is man in his madness and lack of truth!

† Is a students' circle in the city of Moscow!

'But what do you find so horrible about a students' circle?'
I asked.

My neighbour seized his nightcap and tilted it forward on to
his nose.

'What do I find so horrible?' he cried. 'This is what: a
circle – a circle's the destruction of any original development;
a circle is a ghastly substitute for social intercourse, for women,
for living; a circle. . . . Wait a minute, I'll tell you what a
circle really is! A circle is a lazy and flabby kind of communal,
side-by-side existence, to which people attribute the significance and appearance of an intelligent business; a circle re-
places conversation with discourses, inclines its members to
fruitless chatter, distracts you from isolated, beneficial work,
implants in you a literary itch; finally, it deprives you of freshness and the virginal strength of your spirit. A circle – it's
mediocrity and boredom parading under the name of brother-
hood and friendship, a whole chain of misapprehensions and
pretences parading under the pretext of frankness and consider-
ation; in a circle, thanks to the right of each friend to let his
dirty fingers touch on the inner feelings of a comrade at any
time or any hour, no one has a clean, untouched region left
in his soul; in a circle, respect is paid to empty gasbags, conceited brains, young men who've acquired old men's habits;
and rhymesters with no gifts at all but with "mysterious"
ideas are nursed like babies; in a circle, young, seventeen-year-
old boys talk saucily and craftily about women and love, but
in front of women they are either silent or they talk to them
as if they were talking to a book – and the things they talk
about! A circle is a place where underhand eloquence flour-
ishes; in a circle, the members watch one another no less
closely than do police officials. . . . Oh, students' circles!
They're not circles, they're enchanted rings in which more
than one decent fellow has perished!'

'But surely you're exaggerating, allow me to remark,' I
interrupted.

My neighbour glanced at me in silence.

'Perhaps – the Good Lord knows the sort of person I am – perhaps I am exaggerating. For people of my sort there's only one pleasure left – the pleasure of exaggerating. Anyhow, my dear sir, that's how I spent four years in Moscow. I am quite incapable of describing to you, kind sir, how quickly, how awfully quickly that time passed; it even saddens and vexes me to remember it. You would get up in the morning and, just like tobogganing downhill, you'd soon find you were rushing to the end of the day; suddenly it was evening already; your sleepy manservant'd be pulling your frock-coat on to you – you'd dress and plod off to a friend's place and light up your little pipe, drink glass after glass of watery tea and talk away about German philosophy, love, the eternal light of the spirit and other lofty matters. But here I also used to meet independent, original people: no matter how much they might try to break their spirits or bend themselves to the bow of fashion, nature would always in the end assert itself; only I, miserable fellow that I was, went on trying to mould myself like soft wax and my pitiful nature offered not the least resistance! At that time I reached the age of twenty-one. I entered into ownership of my inheritance or, more correctly, that part of my inheritance which my guardian had been good enough to leave me, entrusted the administration of my estate to a freed house-serf, Vasily Kudryashev, and left for abroad, for Berlin. Abroad I spent, as I have already had the pleasure of informing you, three years. And what of it? There also, abroad, I remained the same unoriginal being. In the first place, there's no need to tell you that I didn't acquire the first inkling of knowledge about Europe itself and European circumstances; I listened to German professors and read German books in the place of their origin – that was all the difference there was. I led a life of isolation, just as if I'd been a monk of some kind; I took up with lieutenants who'd left the service and were cursed, as I was, with a thirst for knowledge, but were very hard of understanding and not endowed with the gift of words; I was on familiar terms with dim-witted families from Penza and other grain-producing provinces; I dragged myself from coffee-house to coffee-house, read the journals and went to the theatre in the evenings. I had little intercourse with the natives, would converse with them in a somewhat strained way and never had a single one of them to visit me, with the exception of two or three importunate youngsters of Jewish origin who kept on running after me and borrowing money from me – it is a good thing *der Russe* has a trustful nature.

'A strange trick of fortune brought me finally to the home of one of my professors. This is how it happened: I came to him to sign on to his course, but he suddenly took it into his head to invite me home for an evening. This professor had two daughters, about twenty-seven years old, such dumpy things – God be with them – with such majestic noses, hair all in frizzly curls, eyes of the palest blue and red hands with white fingernails. One was called Linchen, the other Minchen. I started visiting the professor's house. I ought to tell you that this professor was not so much foolish as literally punch-drunk: when he lectured he was fairly coherent, but at home he stumbled over his words and wore his spectacles stuck up all the time on his forehead; yet he was a most learned chap. . . . And then what? Suddenly it seemed to me I'd fallen in love with Linchen – and this seemed to be the case for a whole six months. I talked with her little, it's true, mostly just looked at her; but I read aloud to her various touching works of literature, squeezed her hands in secret and in the evenings used to sit dreaming beside her, gazing fixedly at the moon or simply up in the air. At the same time, she could make excellent coffee! What more could one ask for? Only one thing bothered me: at the very moment, as they say, of inexplicable bliss there would be a sinking feeling at the pit of my stomach and my abdomen would be assailed by a melancholy, cold shivering. In the end I couldn't abide such happiness and ran away. I spent a further two years abroad even after that: I went to Italy, in Rome I stood for a while in front of the Transfiguration, and in Florence I did the same thing in front of the Venus; I became subject to sudden, exaggerated enthusiasms, just like fits of bad temper; in the evenings I would do a little writing of verses, begin keeping a diary; put in a nutshell, I did exactly what everyone else did. And, yet, look how easy it is to be original! For instance, I'm a complete philistine when it comes to painting and sculpture, but to admit such a thing out loud – no, quite impossible! So you hire a guide, dash off to see the frescoes . . .'

He again lowered his head and again flung down his nightcap.

'So I returned finally to my native country,' he continued in a tired voice, 'and came to Moscow. In Moscow I underwent a surprising change. Abroad I had mostly kept my mouth shut, but now I suddenly began talking with unexpected vigour and at the same time conceived God knows how many exalted ideas about myself. Indulgent people cropped up to whom I seemed to be almost a genius; ladies listened considerately to my blatherings; but I did not succeed in remaining at the height of my fame. One fine day gave birth to some gossip on my account (I don't know who trotted it out into the light of God's world; probably some old maid of the male sex – the number of such old maids in Moscow is infinite), it was born and started putting out shoots and runners as fast as a strawberry plant. I got entangled in them, wanted to jump free, break through the sticky threads, but there was nothing doing. So I left. That's where I showed what an empty person I was; I should have waited until it had blown over, in the way people wait for nettle-rash to pass, and those very same indulgent people would again have opened their arms to me, those very same ladies would again have smiled at my eloquence. . . . But that's just my problem:

I'm not original. A feeling of honesty, you understand, awoke in me: I became somehow ashamed of chattering ceaselessly all the time, holding forth yesterday in the Arbat, today in Truba Street, tomorrow in the Sitsevo-Vrazhok, and always about the same thing. What if that's what they expect of you? Take a look at the real old battleaxes in that line of country: it doesn't mean a thing to them; on the contrary, that's all they want; some of them have been wagging their tongues for twenty years and all the time in the same direction. That's real self-assurance, real egotistical ambition for you! I had it, too – ambition, that is – and even now it's not completely left me. But the bad part of it is that, I repeat, I'm not original. I've stopped half-way: nature should either have allowed me a great deal more ambition or have given me none at all. But in the first stages things really got very steep for me; at the same time, my journey abroad had finally exhausted my means and I had no desire to marry a merchant's daughter with a body already as flabby as jelly, even though young. So I retreated to my place in the country. I suppose,' my neighbour added, again glancing at me sideways, 'I can pass over in silence the first impressions of country life, all references to the beauties of nature, the quiet charm of a life of solitude and so on . . .'

'You can, you can,' I responded.

'So much the better,' the speaker continued, 'Since it's all nonsense, at least so far as I'm concerned. I was as bored in the country as a puppy put under lock and key, although, I admit, as I returned for the first time in springtime past a birch grove that was familiar to me my head was dizzy and my heart beat fast in vague, delightful anticipation. But such vague expectations, as you yourself know, never come to anything; on the contrary, the things that actually happen are always those one had somehow never expected: epidemics among the cattle, arrears of rent, public auctions and so on, and so forth. Making out from day to day with the help of my bailiff

Yakov, who had taken the place of the former manager and turned out subsequently to be just as much of a pilferer, if not a greater one, and who, to top it all, poisoned my existence with the smell of his tarred boots, I recalled one day a neighbouring family of my acquaintance consisting of a retired colonel's widow and two daughters, ordered my carriage to be harnessed and went to visit them. That day must always remain fixed in my memory: six months later I was married to the widow's younger daughter!'

The speaker let his head drop and raised his arms high in the air.

'Not that,' he continued heatedly, 'I'd want to give you a poor impression of my late lamented spouse! God forbid! She was the noblest of creatures, the kindest, most loving person and capable of any kind of sacrifice, although I must, between ourselves, admit that, if I had not had the misfortune to lose her, I would probably not be in a position to talk to you today, because in my earth-floor barn you will find to this day in good shape the beam on which I had more than once intended to hang myself!'

'Some pears,' he began after a short silence, 'need to lie a while covered with earth in a cellar to enable them, as they say, to acquire their true taste; my late wife, apparently, belonged to such types of natural produce. It is only now that I can do her full justice. It is only now, for instance, that the memory of certain evenings spent in her company before our marriage not only does not arouse in me the least bitterness but, to the contrary, touches me almost to the point of tears. They were not rich people; their house, very ancient, of wooden construction, but comfortable, stood on a hill between a garden buried under weeds and an overgrown courtyard. At the foot of the hill ran a river and it was scarcely visible through the thick foliage. A large terrace led from the house into the garden, and in front of the terrace there arrayed itself in all its splendour a lengthy flower-bed covered with roses; at each end of the flower-bed grew two acacias which had been twined as young bushes into a screw shape by the late owner of the property. A little farther away, in the very depths of a neglected and wild raspberry patch, stood a summer-house, decorated with exceeding cleverness inside, but so ancient and dilapidated on the outside that it gave one the shivers to look at. From the terrace a glass door led into the drawing-room; while inside the drawing-room the following items met the curious gaze of the onlooker: tiled stoves in the corners, a flat-sounding piano on the right-hand side piled with sheets of handwritten music, a divan upholstered in a faded, pale-blue material with broad whitish patterns, a round table, two cabinets containing china and bead trinkets of the time of Catherine the Great, on the wall hung a well-known portrait of a fair-haired girl with a dove on her breast and upraised eyes, on the table stood a vase with fresh roses. . . . Note in what detail I describe it all. In that drawing-room and on that terrace was enacted the entire tragic comedy of my love.

'The widow herself was a dreadful woman, with the continuous rasp of malice in her throat, a burdensome and cantankerous creature; of her daughters one of them – Vera – was in no way distinguishable from the ordinary run of provincial young ladies, the other was Sofia and it was with Sofia that I fell in love. Both sisters had another little room, their common bedroom, which contained two innocent little wooden beds, some yellow little albums, some mignonette, some portraits of friends of both sexes, drawn rather poorly in pencil (among them there stood out one gentleman with an unusually energetic expression on his face who had adorned his portrait with a still more energetic signature and had aroused in his youth unusual expectations, but had ended like all of us by doing nothing), busts of Goethe and Schiller, some German books, some withered garlands and other objects preserved for sentimental reasons. But I entered that room on few occasions and then unwillingly: somehow or other it made me gasp for breath. Besides, strange though it may be, Sofia pleased me most when I was sitting with my back to her or again, if you will, when I was thinking or, more likely, dreaming about her, particularly in the evening, out on the terrace. I would gaze then at the sunset, the trees, the tiny green leaves which, though already darkened, were still sharply outlined against the rosy sky; in the drawing-room Sofia would be seated at the piano endlessly playing over some favourite, exceedingly meditative phrase from Beethoven; the wicked old woman would be peacefully snoring on the divan; in the dining-room, illumined by a flood of crimson light, Vera would be fussing over the tea; the samovar would be hissing fancifully to itself, as if enjoying some secret joke; pretzels would break with a happy crackling, spoons would strike resonantly against teacups; the canary, mercilessly chirping away all day long, would suddenly grow quiet and chirrup only now and then as if asking a question about something; one or two drops of rain would fall from a translucent, light cloud as it passed by. . . . But I would sit and sit, listening and listening and watching, and my heart would fill with emotion, and it would again seem to me that I was in love. So, under the influence of just such an evening I asked the old woman for her daughter's hand and about two months later I was married.

'I suppose that I was in love with her. Even though by now I should know, yet – my God! – I don't know even now whether I loved Sofia or not. She was a kind creature, intelligent, quiet, with a warm heart; but God knows why, whether from having lived such a long time in the country or from some other cause, she secreted at the bottom of her soul (if the soul may be said to have a bottom) a wound or, better, a festering hurt which it was impossible to cure and which neither she nor I was able to give a name to. Naturally, I did not perceive the existence of this trauma until after our marriage. What I didn't do to help her, but nothing was any good! In my boyhood I had a little finch which the cat once got her claws into; we rescued it, nursed it, but my wretched finch didn't get right again; it began to droop and ail and stopped singing. The matter ended one night when a rat got into its open cage and bit off its beak, as a result of which it finally decided to die. I don't know what cat had got its claws into my wife, but she also started to droop and ail like my luckless finch. Sometimes she herself obviously wanted to flutter her wings and frolic in the fresh air, in sunlight and freedom; she'd try it and then curl up into a ball again. Yet she certainly loved me: she assured me time and again that she had nothing more to wish for – oh, the devil take it! – and yet there she was with her eyes already fading. Is there something in her past? I wondered. I sought around for information, but there was nothing to be found. Well, then, judge for yourself: an original fellow would have given a shrug of the shoulders, perhaps, sighed once or twice and then settled down to live his life in his own way; but I, unoriginal creature that I am, began looking for suitable beams. My wife had become so profoundly imbued with all the habits of an old maid – Beethoven, nightly strolls, mignonette, writing letters to friends, keeping albums and so on – that she was quite incapable of accustoming herself to any other form of life, particularly to the life of a lady of the house; and yet it's ridiculous for a married woman to languish from some nameless heart-break and spend her evenings singing: "Awaken her not till dawn has broken."[7]

'However, sir, in such a manner we passed a blissful three years. In the fourth year Sofia died in childbirth and – strange though it may be – I had literally had a premonition that she would be in no condition to present me with a son or daughter and the earth with a new inhabitant. I remember her funeral. It happened in the spring. Our parish church is not large and it is ancient, with a blackened icon screen, bare walls and a brick floor with holes in it; each choir stall has a large antiquated icon. They brought in the coffin, set it down in the very middle of the church before the holy doors, draped it with a faded cloth and placed three candlesticks round it. The service began. A frail sexton, with a little plaited knot of hair on the nape of his neck, wearing a green girdle tied low down, made sad mumblings before the lectern; the priest, also elderly, with a small, kindly, purblind face, in a mauve cassock with yellow patterning, officiated both for himself and for the sexton. The entire area of the open windows was filled with the shimmerings and rustlings of the young, fresh leaves of weeping birches; a smell of grass wafted in from the graveyard; the red flames of the wax candles paled in the gay sunlight of the spring day; sparrows chirruped throughout the whole church and occasionally the noisy twitterings of a swallow that had flown in resounded beneath the cupola. In the golden dust of the sun's rays the auburn heads of the sparse peasant congregation rose and fell in quick obeisances as they uttered earnest prayers for the soul of the departed; incense rose from the opening in the censer in a delicate, pale-blue stream. I looked at the dead face of my wife. My God! Even death, death itself, had not freed her, not healed her wound: her face wore the same sickly, timid, dumb look, as if she literally felt awkward lying in her coffin. My blood stirred bitterly within me. Kind, kind being that you were, but you still did well for yourself in dying!'

The speaker's cheeks reddened and his eyes lost their brightness.

'Having rid myself finally,' he started to say again, 'of the weight of despondency which settled on me after my wife's death, I thought I ought to get down to work, as they say. I entered the service in the provincial centre, but the large rooms of the government building made my head ache and also had a bad effect on my eyes; other convenient reasons also came along. . . . So I retired. I had wanted to go to Moscow, but, in the first place, I hadn't enough money, and in the second place . . . I have already mentioned to you that I had become reconciled. Such reconciliation came to me both suddenly and gradually. In spirit, so to say, I had long ago become reconciled, yet my head was still unwilling to bow down. I used to ascribe the humble mood of my feelings and thoughts to the influence of country life and my misfortune. On the other hand, I had long ago noticed that almost all my neighbours, both old and young, who were cowed to begin with by my show of learning, foreign travel and other perquisites of my education, not only succeeded in becoming quite used to me but even began to treat me not so much rudely as off-handedly, not bothering to hear my discourses through to the end and failing to address me in a proper manner when speaking to me. I also forgot to tell you that during the first year of my marriage I attempted out of boredom to turn my hand to writing and even sent a small piece – a short work of fiction, if I'm not wrong – to a journal; but after a certain lapse of time I received from the editor a polite letter, in which mention was made, among other things, of the fact that it was impossible to deny me intellect but it was possible to deny me talent, and talent was the one thing needed in literature. Over and above this, it came to my knowledge that a certain Moscovite who was passing through the province – the kindliest young man imaginable, by the way – had made a passing reference to me at a Governor's *soirée* as a person of no consequence who had exhausted his talents. But I still persisted in maintaining my partially voluntary blindness; I didn't feel, you know, like pulling down my ear-flaps. Eventually, one fine morning, I had my eyes opened.

'This is how it happened. The local police inspector called on me with the object of directing my attention to a broken-down bridge on my property, which I definitely had no means of repairing. Tasting a tot of vodka along with a piece of cold sturgeon, this condescending pillar of the law reproached me in a fatherly way for my lack of scruple, entered none the less into my position and advised me simply to order my peasants to spread some muck by way of repairs, lit up his little pipe and started talking about the forthcoming elections. The honourable title of provincial marshal of nobility was being sought at that time by a certain Orbassanov, an empty loud-mouth and, what is more, a bribe-taker. Besides, he was distinguished neither for wealth nor lineage. I expressed my opinion about him, and even rather freely: I confess that I looked down on Mr Orbassanov. The inspector looked at me, fondly tapped me on the shoulder and declared benevo-lently: "Now, now, Vasily Vasilych, it's not for you and me to discuss such people, so what's it got to do with us? Every cricket should know its own hearth." "But kindly tell me," I protested in annoyance, "what difference there is between me and Mr Orbassanov?" The inspector took his pipe out of his mouth, screwed up his eyes – and burst into spluttering laughter. "Well, you're one for a joke!" he uttered eventually, through his tears. "What a thing to say, what a thing to let drop just like that! You're a one, aren't you?" – and right up to his departure he kept on making fun of me, from time to time nudging me with his elbow and adopting an extremely intimate form of address in talking to me. He left finally. His attitude was all I needed: the cup of my humiliation was full to overflowing. I walked several times about the room, stopped before the mirror, gazed for minutes on end at the look of confusion on my face and, slowly sticking out my tongue, shook my head in bitter derision. The scales had fallen from my eyes: I now saw clearly, more clearly even than I saw my own face in the mirror, what an empty, worthless, unnecessary, unoriginal person I was!'

The speaker fell silent.

'In one of Voltaire's tragedies,'[8] he continued despondently, 'some gentleman or other is overjoyed at having reached the extreme limit of unhappiness. Although there is nothing tragic in my fate, I admit that at that time I experienced something of the same kind. I learned to know the poisoned joys of chill despair; I learned to know how sweet it was, during the course of a whole morning, lying in bed and not hurrying over it, to curse the day and hour of my birth. I could not become reconciled at once. I mean, judge for yourself: lack of money tied me down in the country, which I hated; neither management of my estate, nor the service, nor literature – nothing had proved suitable; I avoided the local landowners like the plague, and books were repugnant to me; in the eyes of watery-puddingy, chronically sensitive young ladies who had a habit of shaking their curls and feverishly reiterating the word "life" (pronounced almost like "leaf") I ceased to be an object of interest once I had stopped chattering and going into raptures; I simply didn't know how to cut myself off completely and was physically incapable of it. . . . So I began – guess what? – I began dragging myself round from neighbour to neighbour. Literally drunk with self-disgust, I deliberately laid myself open to all sorts of petty humiliations. I was overlooked by the servants at table, greeted coldly and arrogantly, and finally, I wasn't noticed at all; I wasn't even allowed to add my bit to the general conversation, and I myself, it so happened, would deliberately nod agreement from my corner at some crass chatterbox or other who in the past, in Moscow, would have been delighted to lick the dust from my feet and kiss the hem of my overcoat. . . . I did not even allow myself to think that I was submitting to the bitter pleasure of irony – after all, there's no such thing as irony in isolation! So that's the sort of life I've led for several years in a row and that's how things are up to the present time. . . .'

'I've never heard anything like it,' the sleepy voice of Mr Kantagryukhin grumbled from the next room, 'who's the fool that's decided to talk away at this time of night?'

My room-mate swiftly plunged under the counterpane and, glancing out timorously, shook his finger at me.

'Tut, tut,' he whispered, and as though literally apologizing and bowing in the direction of Kantagryukhin's voice murmured respectfully: 'Of course, sir; of course, sir. Forgive me. ... His lordship must be allowed to sleep, he should sleep,' he continued again in a whisper, 'he must gather his strength, well, at least so that he can eat tomorrow with the same enjoyment as he has eaten today. We have no right to disturb him. Besides, it seems I've told you all I wanted to tell; no doubt you also want to go to sleep. I wish you good night.'

The speaker turned away in feverish haste and buried his head in his pillow.

'Permit me at least to know,' I asked, 'with whom I've had the pleasure ...'

He swiftly raised his head.

'No, for God's sake,' he interrupted me, 'don't ask me or anyone else for my name. Let me remain for you an unknown person, a Vasily Vasilyevych who has been crippled by fate. At the same time, as an unoriginal person, I don't deserve any particular name. But if you earnestly want to give me some kind of title, then call me ... call me Hamlet of the Shchigrovsky District. There are many such Hamlets in every district, but perhaps you haven't come across any others. ... And so farewell.'

He again buried himself in his feather-bed, and the next morning, when they came to wake me, he was no longer in the room. He had left before daybreak.

Living Relic

Homeland of longsuffering –
Thou art the land of Russia![1]
                         F. Tyutchev

THERE is a French saying which runs: 'A dry fisherman and a wet hunter have the same sad look.' Never having had a fondness for catching fish, I am unable to judge what a fisherman must experience at a time of fine, clear weather and to what extent, when the weather is bad, the pleasure afforded him by an excellent catch outweighs the unpleasantness of being wet. But for a hunter rainy weather is a veritable calamity. It was precisely to such a calamity that Yermolay and I were subjected during one of our expeditions after grouse in Belev county. The rain did not let up from dawn onwards. The things we did to be free of it! We almost covered our heads completely with our rubber capes and took to standing under trees in order to catch fewer drips – yet the waterproof capes, not to mention the way they interfered with our shooting, let the water through in a quite shameless fashion; and as for standing under trees – true, at first it did seem that there were no drips, but a little later the moisture which had gathered in the foliage suddenly broke its way through and every branch doused us with water as if it were a rainpipe, cold dribbles gathered under my collar and ran down the small of my back. . . . That was the last straw, as Yermolay was fond of saying.

'No, Pyotr Petrovich,' he exclaimed eventually, 'we can't go on with this! We can't hunt today. All the scent's being washed out for the dogs and the guns are misfiring. . . . Phew! What a life!'

'What do we do, then?' I asked.

'This is what. We'll drive to Alekseyevka. Perhaps you don't know it, but there's a small farm of that name belonging to your mother, about five miles away. We can spend the night there, and then tomorrow . . .'

'We'll come back here?'

'No, not here . . . I know some places on the other side of Alekseyevka. They're a lot better than this for grouse!'

I refrained from asking my trusty companion why he had not taken me straightaway to those places, and that very same day we reached the farm belonging to my mother, the very existence of which, I admit, I had not suspected until that moment. The farm-house had an adjacent cottage of considerable antiquity, but not lived-in and therefore clean; here I spent a reasonably quiet night.

The next day I awoke pretty early. The sun had only just risen and the sky was cloudless. All around glistened with a strong, two-fold brilliance: the brilliance of the youthful rays of morning light and of yesterday's downpour. While a little cart was being got ready for me, I set off to wander a little way through the small, once fruit-bearing but now wild, orchard, which pressed up on all sides against the cottage with its richly scented, luxuriantly fresh undergrowth. Oh, how delightful it was to be in the open air, under a clear sky in which larks fluttered, whence poured the silver beads of their resonant song! On their wings they probably carried drops of dew, and their singing seemed to be dew-sprinkled in its sweetness. I even removed my cap from my head and breathed in joyfully, lungfuls at a time. . . . On the side of a shallow ravine, close by the wattle fencing, a bee-garden could be seen; a small path led to it, winding like a snake between thick walls of weeds and nettles, above which projected – God knows where they had come from – sharp-tipped stalks of dark-green hemp.

I set off along this path and reached the bee-garden. Next to it there stood a little wattle shed, a so-called *amshanik*, where the hives are put in winter. I glanced in through the half-open door: it was dark, silent and dry inside, smelling of mint and melissa. In a corner boards had been fixed up and on them, covered by a quilt, a small figure was lying. I turned to go out at once.

'Master, but master! Pyotr Petrovich!' I heard a voice say, as faintly, slowly and hoarsely as the rustling of marsh sedge.

I stopped.

'Pyotr Petrovich! Please come here!' the voice repeated. It came to me from the corner, from those very boards which I had noticed.

I drew close and froze in astonishment. In front of me there lay a live human being, but what kind of a human being was it?

The head was completely withered, of a uniform shade of bronze, exactly resembling the colour of an ancient icon painting; the nose was as thin as a knife-blade; the lips had almost disappeared – only the teeth and eyes gave any gleam of light, and from beneath the kerchief wispy clusters of yellow hair protruded on to the temples. At the chin, where the quilt was folded back, two tiny hands of the same bronze colour slowly moved their fingers up and down like little sticks. I looked more closely and I noticed that not only was the face far from ugly, it was even endowed with beauty, but it seemed awesome none the less and incredible. And the face seemed all the more awesome to me because I could see that a smile was striving to appear on it, to cross its metallic cheeks – was striving and yet could not spread.

'Master, don't you recognize me?' the voice whispered again: it was just like condensation rising from the scarcely quivering lips. 'But how would you recognize me here! I'm Lukeria. . . . Remember how I used to lead the dancing at your mother's, at Spasskoye . . . and how I used to be the leader of the chorus, remember?'

'Lukeria!' I cried. 'Is it you? Is it possible?'

'It's me, master – yes, it's me, Lukeria.'

I had no notion what to say, and in a state of shock I gazed at this dark, still face with its bright, seemingly lifeless eyes fixed upon me. Was it possible? This mummy was Lukeria, the greatest beauty among all the maid servants in our house, tall, buxom, white-skinned and rosy-cheeked, who used to laugh and sing and dance! Lukeria, talented Lukeria, who was sought after by all our young men, after whom I myself used to sigh in secret, I – a sixteen-year-old boy!

'Forgive me, Lukeria,' I said at last, 'but what's happened to you?'

'Such a calamity overtook me! Don't feel squeamish, master, don't turn your back on my misfortune – sit down on that little barrel, bring it closer, so as you'll be able to hear me. . . . See how talkative I've become! . . . Well, it's glad I am I've seen you! How ever did you come to be in Alekseyevka?'

Lukeria spoke very quietly and faintly, but without pausing.

'Yermolay the hunter brought me here. But go on with what you were saying . . .'

'About my misfortune, is it? If that's what you wish, master. It happened to me long, long ago, six or seven years ago. I'd just then been engaged to Vasily Polyakov – remember him, such a fine upstanding man he was, with curly hair, and in service as wine butler at your mother's house. But by that time you weren't here in the country any longer – you'd gone off to Moscow for your schooling. We were very much in love, Vasily and I. I couldn't get him out of my mind; it all happened in the springtime. One night – it wasn't long to go till dawn – I couldn't sleep, and there was a nightingale singing in the garden so wonderfully sweetly! I couldn't bear it, and I got up and went out on to the porch to listen to it. He **was pouring** out his song, pouring it out . . . and suddenly I imagined I could hear someone calling me in Vasya's voice, all quiet like: "Loosha! . . ." I glanced away

213

to one side and, you know, not awake properly, I slipped right off the porch step and flew down – bang! – on to the ground. And, likely, I hadn't hurt myself so bad, because – soon I was up and back in my own room. Only it was just like something inside – in my stomach – had broken. . . . Let me get my breath back. . . . Just a moment, master.'

Lukeria fell silent, and I gazed at her with astonishment. What amazed me was the almost gay manner in which she was telling her story, without groans or sighs, never for a moment complaining or inviting sympathy.

'Ever since that happened,' Lukeria continued, 'I began to wither and sicken, and a blackness came over me, and it grew difficult for me to walk, and then I even began to lose control of my legs – I couldn't stand or sit, I only wanted to lie down all the time. And I didn't feel like eating or drinking: I just got worse and worse. Your mother, out of the goodness of her heart, had medical people to look at me and sent me to hospital. But no relief for me came of it all. And not a single one of the medicals could even say what kind of an illness it was I had. The things they didn't do to me, burning my spine with red-hot irons and sitting me in chopped-up ice – and all for nothing. In the end I got completely stiff. . . . So the masters decided there was no good in trying to cure me any more, and because there wasn't room for a cripple in their house . . . well, they sent me here – because I have relations here. So here I'm living, as you see.'

Lukeria again fell silent and again endeavoured to smile.

'But this is horrible, this condition you're in!' I exclaimed, and not knowing what to add, I asked: 'What about Vasily Polyakov?' It was a very stupid question.

Lukeria turned her eyes a little to one side.

'About Polyakov? He grieved, he grieved – and then he married someone else, a girl from Glinnoye. Do you know Glinnoye? It's not far from us. She was called Agrafena. He loved me very much, but he was a young man – he couldn't be expected to remain a bachelor all his life. And what sort of a companion could I be to him? He's found himself a good wife, who's a kind woman, and they've got children now. He's steward on the estate of one of the neighbours: your mother released him with a passport, and things are going very well for him, praise be to God.'

'And you can't do anything except lie here?' I again inquired.

'This is the seventh year, master, that I've been lying like this. When it's summer I lie here, in this wattle hut, and when it begins to get cold – then they move me into a room next to the bath-house. So I lie there, too.'

'Who comes to see you? Who looks after you?'

'There are kind people here as well. They don't leave me by myself. But I don't need much looking after. So far as feeding goes, I don't eat anything, and I have water – there it is in that mug: it always stands by me full of pure spring water. I can stretch out to the mug myself, because I've still got the use of one arm. Then there's a little girl here, an orphan; now and then she drops by, and I'm grateful to her. She's just this minute gone. . . . Did you meet her? She's so pretty, so fair-skinned. She brings me flowers – I'm a great one for them, flowers, I mean. We haven't any garden flowers. There used to be some here, but they've all disappeared. But field flowers are pretty, too, and they have more scent than the garden flowers. Lilies-of-the-valley now – there's nothing lovelier!'

'Aren't you bored, my poor Lukeria, don't you feel frightened?'

'What's a person to do? I don't want to pretend – at first, yes, I felt very low, but afterwards I grew used to it, I learned to be patient – now it's nothing. Others are much worse off.'

'How do you mean?'

'Some haven't even got a home! And others are blind or dumb! I can see perfectly, praise be to God, and I can hear everything, every little thing. If there's a mole digging underground, I can hear it. And I can smell every scent, it doesn't matter how faint it is! If the buckwheat is just beginning to flower in the field or a lime tree is just blossoming in the garden, I don't have to be told: I'm the first to smell the scent, if the wind's coming from that direction. No, why should I make God angry with my complaints? Many are worse off than I am. Look at it this way: a healthy person can sin very easily, but my sin has gone out of me. Not long ago Father Aleksey, the priest, was beginning to give me communion and he said: "There can't be any need to hear your confession, for how can you sin in your condition?" But I answered him: "What about a sin of the mind, father?" "Well," he said and laughed, "that kind of sin's not very serious."

'And, it's true, I'm not really sinful even with sins of the mind,' Lukeria went on, 'because I've learned myself not to think and, what's more, not even to remember. Time passes quicker that way.'

This surprised me, I must admit.

'You are so much by yourself, Lukeria, so how can you prevent thoughts from entering your head? Or do you sleep all the time?'

'Oh, no, master! Sleep's not always easy for me. I may not have big pains, but something's always gnawing at me, right there inside me, and in my bones as well. It doesn't let me sleep as I should. No . . . I just lie like this and go on lying here, not thinking. I sense that I'm alive, I breathe – and that's all there is of me. I look and I smell scents. Bees in the apiary hum and buzz, then a dove comes and sits on the roof and starts cooing, and a little brood-hen brings her chicks in to peck crumbs; then a sparrow'll fly in or a butterfly – I enjoy it all very much. The year before last swallows made a nest over there in the corner and brought up their young. Oh, how interesting that was! One of them would fly in, alight on the little nest, feed the young ones – and then off again. I'd take another look and there'd be another swallow there in place of the first. Sometimes it wouldn't fly in but just go past the open door, and then the baby birds'd start chirping and opening their little beaks. . . . The next year I waited for them, but they say a hunter in these parts shot them with his gun. Now what good could he have got from doing that? After all, a swallow's no more harm than a beetle. What wicked men you are, you hunters!'

'I don't shoot swallows,' I hastened to point out.

'And one time,' Lukeria started to say again, 'there was a real laugh! A hare ran in here! Yes, really! Whether dogs were chasing him or not, I don't know, only he came running straight in through the door! He sat down quite close and spent a long time sniffing the air and twitching his whiskers – a regular little officer he was! And he took a look at me and realized that I couldn't do him any harm. Eventually he upped and jumped to the door and looked all round him on the door-step – he was a one, he was! Such a comic!'

Lukeria glanced up at me, as if to say: wasn't that amusing? To please her, I gave a laugh. She bit her dried-up lips.

'In the winter, of course, things are worse for me. I'm left in the dark, you see – it's a pity to light a candle, and anyhow what'd be the good of it? I know how to read and was always real keen on reading, but what's there to read here? There are no books here, and even if there were, how would I be able to hold it, the book, I mean? Father Aleksey brought me a church calendar so as to distract me, but he saw it wasn't any use and picked it up and took it away again. But even though it's dark, I've always got something to listen to – maybe a cricket'll start chirruping or a mouse'll begin scratching somewhere. That's when it's good not to be thinking at all!'

After a short rest, Lukeria continued: 'Or else I say prayers. Only I don't know many of them, of those prayers. And why should I start boring the Lord God with my prayers? What can I ask him for? He knows better than I do what's good for me. He sent me a cross to carry, which means he loves me. That's how we're ordained to understand our suffering. I say Our Father, and the prayer to the Blessed Virgin, and I sing hymns for all who sorrow – and then I lie still without a single thought in my mind. Life's no bother to me!'

Two minutes went by. I did not break the silence and I did not stir on the narrow barrel which served as a place for me to sit. The cruel, stony immobility of the unfortunate living being who lay before me affected me also, and I became literally rigid.

'Listen, Lukeria,' I began finally. 'Listen to what I want to propose to you. Would you like it if I arranged for you to be taken to a hospital, a good town hospital? Who knows, but maybe they can still cure you? At least you won't be by yourself . . .'

Lukeria raised her brows ever so slightly.

'Oh, no, master,' she said in an agitated whisper, 'don't send me to a hospital, let me alone. I'll only have to endure more agony there. There's no good in trying to cure me! Once a doctor came here and wanted to have a look at me. I said to him, begging him: "Don't disturb me for Christ's sake!" What good was it! He started turning me this way and that, straightening and bending my legs and arms and telling me: "I'm doing this for learning, that's why. I'm one who serves, a scientist! And don't you try to stop me, because they've pinned a medal on me for my contributions to science and it's for you, you dolts, that I'm working so hard." He pulled me about and pulled me about, named what was wrong with me – and a fine name it was! – and with that he left. But for a whole week afterwards my poor bones were aching. You say I'm alone, all the time by myself. No, not all the time. People come to see me. I'm quiet and I'm not a nuisance to anyone. The peasant girls come sometimes for a chat. Or a holy woman will call in on her wanderings and start telling me about Jerusalem and Kiev and the holy cities. I'm not frightened of being by myself. Truly it's better, truly it is! Let me alone, master, don't move me to hospital. Thank you, you're a good man, only leave me alone, my dear.'

'Just as you wish, as you wish, Lukeria. I was only suggesting it for your own good . . .'

'I know, master, it was for my own good. But, master, my dear one, who is there that can help another person? Who can enter into another's soul? People must help themselves! You won't believe it, but sometimes I lie by myself like I am now – and it's just as if there was no one on the whole earth except me. And I'm the only living person! And a wondrous feeling comes over me, as if I'd been visited by some thought that seizes hold of me – something wonderful it is.'

'What do you think about at such times, Lukeria?'

'It's quite impossible to say, master – you can't make it out. And afterwards I forget. It comes just like a cloud and pours its rain through me, making everything so fresh and good, but what the thought was really you can never understand! Only it seems to me that if there were people round me – none of that would have happened and I'd never feel anything except my own misfortune.'

Lukeria sighed with difficulty. Like the other parts of her body, her breast would not obey her wishes.

'As I look at you now, master,' she began again, 'you feel very sorry for me. But don't you pity me too much, don't you do that! See, I'll tell you something: sometimes even now I. . . . You remember, don't you, what a gay one I was in my time? One of the girls! . . . D'you know something? I sing songs even now.'

'Songs? You really sing?'

'Yes, I sing songs, the old songs, roundelays, feast songs, holy songs, all kinds! I used to know many of them, after all, and I haven't forgotten them. Only I don't sing the dancing songs. In my present state that wouldn't be right.'

'How do you sing them – to yourself?'

'To myself and out loud. I can't sing them loudly, but they can still be understood. I was telling you that a little girl comes to visit me. An orphan, that's what she is, but she understands. So I've been teaching her and she's picked up four songs already. Don't you believe me? Wait a moment, I'll show you . . .'

Lukeria drew upon all her reserves of energy. The idea that this half-dead being was preparing to sing aroused in me a spontaneous feeling of horror. But before I could utter a word, a long-drawn, scarcely audible, though clear sound, pitched on the right note, began to quiver in my ears, followed by another, then a third. Lukeria was singing 'I walked in the meadows of green grieving for my life'. She sang without altering the expression on her petrified face, even gazing fixedly with her eyes. But so touchingly did this poor, forced, wavering little voice of hers resound, rising like a wisp of smoke, that I ceased to feel horror: an indescribable piteousness compressed my heart.

'Oh, I can't any more!' she uttered suddenly. 'I've no strength left . . . I've rejoiced so very much already at seeing you.'

She closed her eyes.

I placed my hands on her tiny cold fingers. She looked up at me and her dark eyelids, furred with golden lashes like the lids of ancient statuary, closed again. An instant later they began to glisten in the semi-darkness. Tears moistened them.

As before, I did not stir.

'Silly of me!' Lukeria uttered suddenly with unexpected strength and, opening her eyes wide, attempted to blink away the tears. 'Shouldn't I be ashamed? What's wrong with me? This hasn't happened to me for a long time – not since the day Vasya Polyakov visited me last spring. While he was

sitting with me and talking it was all right. But when he'd gone
– how I cried then all by myself! Where could so many tears
come from! For sure a woman's tears cost nothing. Master,'
Lukeria added, 'if you have a handkerchief, don't be finicky,
wipe my eyes.'

I hastened to do what she asked, and left the handkerchief
with her. She tried to refuse at first, as if she were asking why
she should be given such a present. The handkerchief was very
simple, but clean and white. Afterwards she seized it in her
feeble fingers and did not open them again. Having grown
accustomed to the darkness which surrounded us both, I
could clearly distinguish her features and could even discern
the delicate flush which rose through the bronze of her face
and could make out in her face – or so at least it seemed to me
– traces of her past beauty.

'Just now you were asking me, master,' Lukeria started
saying again, 'whether I sleep. I certainly don't sleep often,
but every time I have dreams – wonderful dreams! I never
dream that I'm ill. In my dreams I'm always so young and
healthy. . . . I've only one complaint: when I wake up, I want
to have a good stretch and yet here I am, just as if I were
bound in fetters. Once I had such a marvellous dream! Would
you like me to tell it to you? Well, listen. I dreamt of myself
standing in a field, and all around me there was rye, so tall
and ripe, like gold. . . . And there was a little rust-red dog with
me, wickedly vicious it was, all the time trying to bite me.
And I had a sickle in my hand, and it wasn't a simple sickle,
but it was the moon when the moon has the shape of a sickle.
And with the moon itself I had to reap the rye until it was all
cut. Only I grew very tired from the heat, and the moon
blinded me, and a languor settled on me; and all around me
cornflowers were growing – such big ones! And they all
turned their little heads towards me. And I thought I would
pick these cornflowers, because Vasya had promised to come,
so I'd make myself a garland first of all and then still have time

to do the reaping. I began to pluck the cornflowers, but they started to melt away through my fingers, to melt and melt, no matter what I did! And I couldn't weave myself a garland. And then I heard someone coming towards me, coming close up to me and calling: "Loosha! Loosha!" Oh dear, I thought, I'm too late! It doesn't matter, though, I thought, because I can put the moon on my head instead of the cornflowers. So I put the moon on my head, and it was just like putting on one of those tall bonnets – at once I glowed with light from head to foot and lit up all the field around me. I looked, and there, through the very tips of the heads of rye, someone was smoothly approaching ever so quickly – only it wasn't Vasya, it was Christ Himself! And why I knew it was Christ I can't say – He's never depicted as I saw Him – but it was Him! He was beardless, tall, young, clad all in white, except for a belt of gold, and He put out a hand to me and said: "Fear not, for thou art My chosen bride, come with Me. In My heavenly kingdom thou shalt lead the singing and play the songs of paradise." And how firmly I pressed my lips to His hand. Then my little dog seized me by the legs, but at once we ascended up into the heavens, He leading me, and His wings stretched out to fill the heavens, as long as the wings of a gull – and I followed after Him! And the little dog had to leave go of me. It was only then that I understood that the little dog was my affliction and that there was no place for my affliction in the Kingdom of Heaven.'

Lukeria fell silent for a minute.

'But I also had another dream,' she began again, 'or perhaps it was a vision I had – I don't know which. It seemed that I was lying in this very wattle hut and my dead parents – my mother and my father – came to me and bowed low to me, but without saying anything. And I asked them: "Why do you, my mother and my father, bow down to me?" And they answered and said: "Because thou hast suffered so greatly in this world, thou hast lightened not only thine own soul but hast also lifted a great weight from ours. And for us in our world the way has been made easier. Thou hast already done with thine own sins and art now conquering ours." And, having said this, my parents again bowed low to me – and then I couldn't see them any longer: all I could see were the walls. Afterwards I was very full of doubt whether such a thing had happened to me. I told the priest of it, only he said it couldn't have been a vision, because visions are vouchsafed only to those of ecclesiastical rank.

'Then there was yet another dream I had,' Lukeria continued, 'I saw myself sitting beside a big road under a willow, holding a whittled stick, with a bag over my shoulders and my head wrapped in a kerchief, just like a holy wanderer! And I had to go somewhere far, far away on a pilgrimage, offering prayers to God. And the holy wanderers, the pilgrims, were continually going past me; they were walking quietly past me, as if unwillingly, all the time going in the same direction; and their faces were all sad and very much alike. And I saw that weaving and hurrying among them was one woman, a whole head taller than all the others, and she wore a special kind of dress, not our kind, not like a Russian dress. And her face was also of a special kind, stern and severe, like the face of one used to fasting. And it seemed that all the others made way for her; and then she suddenly turned and came straight towards me. She stopped and looked at me. Her eyes were like the eyes of a falcon, yellow and big and bright as could be. And I asked her: "Who are you?" And she said to me: "I am your death." I should've been frightened, but instead I was happy as a child, I swear to God I was! And this woman, my death, said to me: "I am sorry for you, Lukeria, but I cannot take you with me. Farewell!" O Lord, what sorrow there was for me then! "Take me," I cried, "beloved mother, dear one, take me!" And my death turned to face me and began to speak. . . . And I understood that she was appointing the hour when I should die, but I couldn't quite grasp it, it wasn't clear, except that it would be some time after Saint Peter's Day. . . . Then I woke up. Such surprising dreams I've been having!'

Lukeria raised her eyes to the ceiling and grew reflective.

'Only I have this one trouble, that a whole week may pass and I never once go to sleep. Last year there was a lady who came by, saw me and gave me a little bottle with some medicine to make me sleep. She told me to take ten drops each time. That was a great help to me, and I slept. Only now that little bottle's long ago finished. Do you know what that medicine was and how to get it?'

The lady who came by obviously gave Lukeria opium. I promised to procure such a little bottle for her and again could not restrain myself from remarking aloud at her patience.

'Oh, master!' she protested. 'What d'you mean by that? What sort of patience? Now Simon Stilites' patience was really great: he spent thirty years on a pillar! And there was another of God's servants who ordered himself to be buried in the ground up to his chest, and the ants ate his face. . . . And here's something else that an avid reader of the Bible told me: there was a certain country, and that country was conquered by the Hagarenes, and they tortured and killed all who lived therein; and no matter what those who lived there did, they could in no way free themselves. And there appeared among those who dwelt in that country a holy virgin; she took a mighty sword and arrayed herself in heavy armour and went out against the Hagarenes and did drive them all across the sea. But when she had driven them away, she said to them: "Now it is time that you should burn me, for such was my promise, that I should suffer a fiery death for my people." And the Hagarenes seized her and burned her, but from that time forward her people were freed for ever! Now that's a really great feat of suffering! Mine's not like that!'

I wondered to myself in astonishment at the distance the

legend of Joan of Arc had travelled and the form it had taken, and after a brief silence I asked Lukeria how old she was.

'Twenty-eight . . . or twenty-nine. I'm not thirty yet. What's the good of counting them, the years, I mean! I'll tell you something else . . .'

Lukeria suddenly coughed huskily and gave a groan.

'You are talking a great deal,' I remarked to her, 'and it could be bad for you.'

'That's true,' she whispered, hardly audible. 'Our little talk's got to end, no matter what happens! Now that you'll be going I'll be quiet as long as I wish. I've unburdened my heart to the full . . .'

I began to take leave of her, repeating my promise to send her the medicine and imploring her again to give careful thought to my question whether there was anything that she needed.

'I don't need anything, I'm quite content, praise God,' she uttered with the greatest of effort, but moved by my concern. 'God grant everyone good health! And you, master, tell your mother that, because the peasants here are poor, she should take a little less in rent from them! They haven't enough land, there isn't an abundance of anything. . . . They'd give thanks to God for you if you did that. . . . But I don't need a thing – I'm quite content.'

I gave Lukeria my word that I would fulfil her request and was already on the way to the door when she called to me again.

'Remember, master,' she said, and something wondrous glimmered in her eyes and on her lips, 'what long tresses I had? Remember, they reached right down to my knees! For a long time I couldn't make up my mind. . . . Such long hair! . . . But how could I comb it out? In my state, after all! . . . So I cut it all off. . . . Yes, that's what I did. . . . Well, master, forgive me! I can't go on any more . . .'

That very day, before setting out for the hunt, I had a talk about Lukeria with the farm overseer. I learned from him that she was known in the village as the 'Living Relic' and that, in this regard, there had never been any trouble from her; never a murmur was to be heard from her, never a word of complaint. 'She herself asks for nothing, but, quite to the contrary, is thankful for everything; a quiet one, if ever there was a quiet one, that's for sure. Struck down by God, most likely for her sins,' the overseer concluded, 'but we don't go into that. And as, for instance, for passing judgement on her – no, we don't pass judgement. Let her alone!'

*

A few weeks later I learned that Lukeria had died. Her death had come for her, as she thought – 'after Saint Peter's Day'. There were rumours that on the day of her death she heard a bell ringing all the time, although from Alekseyevka to the church is a matter of three miles or more and it was not a Sunday. Lukeria, however, said that the ringing did not come from the church but 'from above'. Probably she did not dare to say that it came from heaven.

Clatter of Wheels

'WHAT I want to tell you,' said Yermolay, coming
into the hut – while I, for my part, had only just had
dinner and stretched myself on a little travelling bed
to rest for a short while after a fairly successful, but tiring,
grouse shoot (it was some time in mid-July and the prevailing
heat was awful) – 'What I want to tell you is that all our
shot's used up.'

I jumped up from the bed.

'The shot's all used up! That's impossible! Surely we
brought with us from the village by any reckoning about
thirty pounds of it! We had a whole sackful!'

'Right. And it was a large sack, enough for two weeks.
Who knows what's happened to it! Maybe the sack got a hole
in it, but whatever it was, the fact is there's no shot left – ten
more charges and that'll be it.'

'Well, what on earth are we going to do now? The best
places are ahead – they've promised us six coveys for tomorrow. . . .'

'Send me into Tula. It's not far from here – only about
thirty miles. I'll fly like the wind and bring you back, if you
like, a whole ton of shot.'

'All right, but when'll you be able to go?'

'Right now. Why delay? 'Cept there's only one thing –
we'll have to hire some horses.'

'Hire some horses! What's wrong with our own?'

'We can't use ours. The shaft-horse's gone lame. . . .
Something awful.'

'When did this happen?'

'Just the other day. The driver took him off to be shod. So
he was shod. But the blacksmith must've been poor at his job.

Now the horse can't even stand on his leg. It's a front leg. He carries it lifted up, like he was a dog.'

'What's been done about it? At least he's been unshod, hasn't he?'

'No, he's still the same, but it's high time he was unshod. I reckon a nail's been driven into the fleshy part.'

I ordered the driver to be brought to me. It transpired that Yermolay had been telling the truth: the shaft-horse could not in fact stand on its leg. I at once arranged for the horse to be unshod and placed on damp clay.

'What about it now? Will you order horses to be hired for going to Tula?' Yermolay badgered me.

'Do you really think it's possible to hire horses in this back of beyond?' I cried out in a fit of vexation.

The village where we had found ourselves was out of the way and dead; all its inhabitants seemed to be poverty-stricken and it was only with difficulty that we had come across even so much as a hut with a chimney, let alone one that was in the least spacious.

'It's possible,' Yermolay answered with his usual imperturbability. 'It's true what you've said about this village, and yet in this very place there was once a peasant living – the cleverest man, he was! Rich, too! He had nine horses. He himself is dead and it's now his eldest son who looks after everything. As a person he's a real fool, but still he hasn't yet managed to get rid of all his father's property. From him we'll be able to fit ourselves out with horses. You give the order and I'll bring him along. They say his brothers are real bright lads, but he's still their boss.'

'Why so?'

'Because he's the eldest! That means the younger ones've got to kow-tow!' At this point. Yermolay expressed himself strongly and unprintably about younger brothers in general. 'I'll bring him along. He's a bit simple. You should be able to make a deal with a man like that, eh?'

While Yermolay was fetching this 'simple' man, the thought occurred to me: wouldn't it be better if I went into Tula myself? Firstly, schooled by experience, I had learned to put little faith in Yermolay: I had sent him into town once to make some purchases, he promising to do everything he was told in the course of a single day – and he had disappeared for a whole week, drunk away all the money and returned on foot, whereas he had gone there in a racing buggy. Secondly, there was a horse-dealer I knew in Tula, and I could buy a horse from him in place of the lame shaft-horse.

'That's decided then,' I thought. 'I'll go myself and I can sleep on the way – which is the blessing of having a comfortable carriage.'

*

'I've brought him!' Yermolay exclaimed a quarter of an hour later as he tumbled into the hut. He was followed by a tall peasant in a white shirt, blue trousers and blue bast shoes, with a head of tousled fair hair and a myopic look, a light-coloured and wedge-shaped little beard, a long puffy nose and a gapingly open mouth. He looked exactly like a simpleton.

'Here he is,' Yermolay said. 'He's got horses and he's agreed to help.'

'It's like this, see, I . . .' the peasant stammered in a hoarse voice shaking his wispy locks and running his fingers along the band of the hat which he held in his hand. 'I, you see . . .'

'What is your name?' I asked.

The peasant lowered his head and literally started to ponder the question.

'What's my name?'

'Yes, what name have you?'

'My name will be Filofey.'

'Well, that's it, then, my good friend Filofey – I've heard that you have horses. Bring along three of them, if you would, and we'll harness them to my carriage – it's a light one – and you can take me into Tula. It's a moonlit night tonight, bright and fresh for travelling. What's the road like in your parts?'

'The road? Not bad. It'll be about fifteen mile to the main road – no more'n that. There's one little part where it's bad, but that's nothing really.'

'What's this bad part?'

'It's where we'll be needin' to cross a river.'

'Does this mean you yourself'll be going into Tula?' inquired Yermolay.

'Yes, I'll be going myself.'

'Well!' declared my trusty servant, and gave a shake of the head. 'Well, well, well!' he repeated, spat and left the hut.

A journey into Tula obviously no longer offered any attractions for him; it had become an empty matter of no interest.

'Do you know the road well?' I asked, addressing myself to Filofey.

'For sure I know the road! Only I, you see, beggin' your pardon, I can't go . . . seein' as it's so sudden-like. . . .'

It transpired that Yermolay, in hiring Filofey, had declared to him he had no doubt that he, the fool, would be paid – and that would be all! Filofey, although a fool, in Yermolay's estimation, had not been satisfied by this declaration in itself. He began by demanding from me fifty roubles in notes – an enormous sum; I offered him ten toubles – a small sum. We set about bargaining; Filofey was stubborn to start with, then he began to give way, albeit slowly. Yermolay, who had come in for a moment, began to assure me that 'This fool' ('See how fond he is of that word!' Filofey remarked under his breath) 'this fool has no idea of the value of money', and incidentally reminded me how twenty years ago a coaching inn which had been established by my mother at a busy point at the intersection of two main roads had proved a complete failure because the ancient house-serf who had been put in charge of it literally did not know the value of money, but valued the coins according to number – that is to say, he would, for instance, give a silver quarter for half a dozen five-copeck coppers and swear strongly into the bargain.

'Damn you, Filofey, you're a right Filofey, you are!' Yermolay exclaimed finally and, going out, slammed the door angrily behind him.

Filofey did not answer him, as if acknowledging that it was certainly no easy matter to be called Filofey, that a man could even be held blameworthy for having such a name, although the real blame lay with the priest at his christening who had not been properly paid for his services.

Eventually, however, we agreed on twenty roubles. He went off to get the horses and an hour later brought five of them for me to choose from. The horses turned out to be suitable, although they had tangled manes and tails and large bellies stretched tight as drums. Filofey was accompanied by two of his brothers, who were quite unlike him. Small of stature, dark-eyed and sharp-nosed, they did indeed produce the impression of being 'bright lads', talking a great deal and at great speed – 'Shooting their mouths off', as Yermolay expressed it – but they still deferred to the eldest.

They pulled the carriage out from under the lean-to and for a whole hour and a half fussed round it with the horses. At one moment they would loosen the shaft fastenings, at the next they would do them up as tight as could be! Both the brothers insisted on harnessing a roan as shaft-horse because 'that un'd run mighty fine downhill', but Filofey decided on a shaggy horse and that was the horse they finally harnessed in the shafts.

The carriage was stuffed with hay and the collar from the lame shaft-horse was pushed under the seat – in case it became necessary to drive the horse into Tula in exchange for a newly purchased one. Filofey, having managed to dash home and return dressed up in his father's long, white, loose-fitting coat, tall hat and blackened boots, climbed solemnly up on to the box. I sat down, noting that my watch showed the time as a quarter to eleven. Yermolay did not even say good-bye to me, but took it upon himself to beat his dog Valetka. Filofey gave a jerk of the reins, called out: 'Gee up, there, my pretties!' in the most high-pitched of voices – his brothers jumped up on either side of us and lashed the underbellies of the outer horses – and the carriage started away, turning through the gate into the street. The shaggy horse would have turned back into the courtyard if left to its own devices, but Filofey admonished it with a few blows of the whip; and soon we had sped briskly out of the village and were travelling along a fairly smooth road between thick lines of nut trees.

The night was quiet and splendid, perfect for a journey. A wind would rustle occasionally in the bushes, set the branches quivering and then die away. Motionless, silvery clouds were visible here and there in the sky. The moon floated high up and bathed the countryside in its clear rays. I stretched myself out on the hay and was on the point of dozing when I suddenly remembered the 'bad part' and roused myself.

'Hey there, Filofey. Is it far to the ford?'

'To the ford? It'll be about five miles.'

'Five miles,' I thought. 'In that case it'll be an hour before we get there and I can have a sleep in the meantime.'

'D'you know the road well, Filofey?' I asked again.

'And why shouldn't I know her well – the road, I mean? It's not the first time I've been along here. . . .'

He added something else, but I had already stopped listening. I was asleep.

*

I was awakened not by my own intention of waking up in an hour's time, but by some kind of unfamiliar, though faint, splishings and sploshings right beside my very ear. I raised my head.

What on earth had happened? I was lying in the carriage as

before, but all around it, and barely more than a foot below its edge, a flat area of water, illuminated by the moon, was fragmented and criss-crossed by tiny, distinct ripples. I looked toward the front and there was Filofey sitting on the box, his head fallen forward, his back bent, solemn as an idol, and further ahead still, above gurgling water, I could see the bent line of the shaft and the horses' heads and backs. And everything was so still, so soundless, as if it were in an enchanted kingdom, a dream, a fairy-tale sleep. Fantastic! Then I looked towards the back from under the hood of the carriage. We were indeed in the very middle of a river, with the bank a good thirty paces from us!

'Filofey!' I exclaimed.

'What d'you want?' he answered.

'How can you say "What d'you want"? For heaven's sake, where are we?'

'In the river.'

'I can see we're in the river. And any minute now we'll drown. So you're crossing by the ford, are you? Eh? Filofey, you're sleeping. Answer me!'

'I made a wee mistake,' my driver announced, 'and went a little to one side, you know, took the wrong way, sad to tell, but we'll have to do some waiting now.'

'Why've we got to do some waiting? What're we going to wait for?'

'Let the shaggy horse look around 'isself, 'cause where 'e turns is where we'll be going.'

I raised myself on the hay. The head of the shaft-horse was motionless above the water. All that could be seen by the bright light of the moon was one of his ears moving slightly backwards and forwards.

'And he's asleep as well, that shaggy horse of yours!'

'No,' answered Filofey. 'What he's doing now is sniffing the water.'

And everything again fell quiet, with only the water giving

faint splashings. I also froze into immobility. The moonlight, the night, the river and ourselves in the middle of it . . .

'What's that hissing?' I asked Filofey.

'That? It's ducklings in the reeds . . . or maybe it's snakes.'

Suddenly, the shaft-horse began shaking its head, pricked up its ears, started snorting and fussing.

'Gee up, gee-gee-gee!' Filofey unexpectedly howled at the top of his voice, rose up and began wielding his whip. The carriage at once jolted from the place where it had been standing and thrust itself forward against the flow of the river. It went a short way, jerking and wobbling. To start with, it seemed to me that we were sinking, going in deeper, but after two or three jolts and slips, the surface of the water appeared suddenly to grow lower. It went farther and farther down and the carriage rose out of it. Then the wheels appeared and the horses' tails and then, raising large, powerful splashes of water that exploded in the moon's dull white brilliance like flashing sheaves of diamonds – no, not of diamonds but of sapphires – the horses all pulling happily together drew us out on to the muddy bank and followed the road uphill, stepping out in irregular strides on their glittering, wet legs.

'What,' it occurred to me, 'will Filofey say now: You see, I was right! or something on those lines?' But he said nothing. For that reason I did not consider it necessary to blame him for carelessness and, bedding down in the hay, attempted once again to go to sleep.

*

But I couldn't sleep – not because I wasn't tired from hunting, not because the alarm which I had experienced had driven away my sleepiness – but simply due to the extremely beautiful regions through which our route took us. These were free-ranging, expansive, well-watered grassy meadowlands with a host of small pastures, miniature lakes, streams and large ponds overgrown at each end with willows, absolutely Russian, places dear to the heart of the Russian people, like the places to which the legendary warriors of our old folk sagas used to travel to shoot white swans and grey-hued ducks. The smooth road unwound behind us like a yellowish ribbon, the horses were going at an easy pace and I couldn't close my eyes for joy at my surroundings. And everything flowed past so softly and surely under the friendly moon. Even Filofey was affected by the scene.

'Them there meadows are named after Saint Yegor,' he said, turning to me. 'And beyond 'em there'll be the Grand Duke's. You'll not see any other meadows the likes of these in the whole of Russia. There's real beauty for you!' The shaft-horse snorted and shook its mane. 'The Lord be with you!' Filofey declared gravely in a low voice. 'There's real beauty for you!' he repeated and sighed, but went on to make a protracted clearing of his throat. 'Soon the haymaking'll be beginning, and they'll rake in a whole heap of hay from them meadows. And there's a whole lot of fish in them ponds. Such bream you've never seen,' he added in a singsong. 'That's what life's worth living for!'

Suddenly he raised his hand.

'Hey, look over there! On the other side of the lake, isn't that a heron standing there? Can that be a heron catching fish at night? Blast it, it's a bough of a tree, sticking up, not a heron! I made a muck of that one! It's the moon fools you.'

So we travelled on and on. Then the meadowlands came to an end, and woodlands and ploughed fields appeared; to one side there twinkled two or three lights of a village. There still remained about two miles to the main road, and I drifted off to sleep.

Again, I did not wake of my own accord. On this occasion I was roused by the voice of Filofey.

'Master. . . . Hey, master!'

I raised myself up. The carriage was standing on a level place in the very centre of the main road. His face turned to me from the box with wide open eyes (I was astonished, because I had not imagined that he had such big eyes), Filofey was whispering meaningfully and mysteriously:

'There's a clattering!... A clattering!'

'What are you talking about!'

'I say there's a clattering. Lean outside and listen. Do you hear it?'

I stuck my head out of the carriage and held my breath – I did, in fact, hear somewhere very far off behind us a faint, intermittent clattering, as of turning wheels.

'D'you hear it?' Filofey repeated.

'Yes, I do,' I answered. 'It sounds like a carriage on the road.'

'But don't you hear it! Listen... there! The bells... and also a whistling.... Hear it? Take your cap off and you'll be able to hear it better.'

I did not take my cap off, but bent my ear to the sound.

'Well, yes... perhaps so. What about it?'

Filofey turned to face the horses.

'It's a cart on it's way, travelling light, with iron-shod wheels,' he said and took up the reins. 'There's bad people travelling in it, master. Hereabouts, around Tula, there's many people up to no good.'

'What nonsense! What makes you suppose they're bound to be bad people?'

'I am telling you the truth. With bells on 'em... and in an empty cart.... Who else would it be?'

'Well, then, is it far yet to go to Tula?'

'It'll still be 'bout 'leven miles and there's none living round these parts.'

'Well, let's get a move on. There's no need to loiter about.'

Filofey gave a wave of his whip and the carriage once more rolled on its way.

*

Although I gave no credence to Filofey, I was still not able to get to sleep. And what if he was, indeed, telling the truth? An unpleasant feeling stirred within me. I sat up in the carriage – for until this time I had been lying down – and began looking about on either side of me. While I had been sleeping a light mist had gathered – not a ground mist but one that obscured the sky. It stood high up in the sky and the moon hung in it like a whitish blur, as if surrounded by smoke. Everything up in the sky had grown blurred and confused, but closer to the earth, it was clearer. All around there was a flat, despondent landscape: all fields and more fields with here and there a bush or a ravine – and then more fields, chiefly lying fallow and dotted with patches of weed. It was empty and dead. I only wished that a quail would cry.

We drove for about half an hour. Filofey all the while waved his whip and smacked his lips, but neither he nor I exchanged a single word. Then we ascended a slight rise in the terrain, Filofey stopped the three horses and announced at once:

'There's the clattering . . . it's clattering, master!'

I again stuck my head out of the carriage, but it would have been just as well if I had stayed under the hood of the carriage so clearly now, although still far off, could be heard the clatter of the cart-wheels, people whistling, the jingling of harness bells and even the thud of horses' hooves. I even thought I could hear singing and laughter. The wind, it is true, was coming from that direction, but there was no doubt that these strange travellers had grown a mile or more closer to us.

Filofey and I exchanged looks. All he did was to tilt his hat from the back of his head on to his brow and at once, crouching over the reins, started whipping up the horses. They broke into a gallop, but they were unable to gallop for long and settled once again into a trot. Filofey continued to lash at them. For we simply had to get away!

I could not explain to myself why, this time, after having at first rejected Filofey's suspicions, I now suddenly felt convinced that those travelling in our wake were in fact bad people. There was nothing new to be heard: the same jingling bells, the same clatter of an unladen cart, the same whistling, the same vague clamour. . . . But now, I was no longer ready to doubt. Filofey couldn't be wrong!

About another twenty minutes went by. Towards the end of these twenty minutes there grew audible above the clatter and rumble of our own carriage another clattering and another rumbling.

'Stop, Filofey!' I said. 'It doesn't matter – it'll have to come to an end some time!'

Filofey called a cowardly halt. The horses stopped instantly, as if glad of the opportunity of resting.

Good heavens! By this time the harness bells were simply thundering at our very backs, the cart was roaring and rattling, the people whistling and shouting and singing, the horses snorting and beating the earth with their hooves. . . . They'd caught up with us!

'Glo-o-ory be!' Filofey uttered in a soft voice, elongating the syllables, and after clicking his tongue irresolutely, started urging on the horses. But at that instant there was a loud tearing sound, a roaring and thundering – and an outsize rickety cart, pulled by three wiry horses, overtook us like a whirlwind, swerving sharply, galloped on beyond us and at once slowed down to a walking pace, blocking the road.

'That's the way robbers do it,' Filofey whispered.

I confess that a chill tremor seized my heart. I started peering tensely into the semi-darkness of the mist-veiled light of the moon. The cart in front of us contained – not exactly lying, not exactly in sitting positions – six men in peasant shirts and open cloth coats; two of them were hatless; huge, booted legs hung dangling between the cart's side supports, arms flopped up and down, bodies shaken against each other. It was clearly a case of a cart-load of drunks. Some were bellowing the first thing that came into their heads at the tops of their voices; one of them was whistling very piercingly and clearly; another was using foul language; and a giant of a man in a sheepskin coat was sitting on the box and driving. They went along at walking pace as though paying no attention to us.

What could we do? We drove along behind them also at walking pace, despite ourselves. For about a quarter of a mile we travelled in this fashion. The waiting was sheer torment. There was no way of saving or defending ourselves, in such a situation. There were six of them, and I didn't even have a stick! Turn the shafts round? They'd catch up with us at once. I recalled the line from Zhukovsky (where he is speaking about the murder of Field Marshal Kamensky):

> The robber's axe, despiséd thing . . .[1]

Or if they didn't use an axe, then they'd throttle you with a dirty piece of rope and hurl you into a ditch to croak and beat about like a hare caught in a snare. . . . The whole thing was foul!

All the while they continued to travel at walking pace and paid no attention to us.

'Filofey,' I whispered, 'try going to the right and see if you can get past them.'

Filofey tried. He went to the right, but they at once went to the right as well and it was impossible to pass them. Filofey tried again, going to the left this time, but here again they wouldn't let him pass the cart. They even laughed. So they were not going to let us pass.

'Exactly like robbers,' Filofey muttered to me over his shoulder.

'What are they waiting for?' I asked, also in a whisper.

'Up there ahead of us, in a hollow, there's a little bridge over a stream – that's where they'll do for us! That's where they always do it – close to bridges. We're in for it, master, plain as anything!' he added with a sigh. 'They'll surely not let us get away alive. 'Cos the main thing for 'em's to have water to hide the remains in. What's worrying me, master, is that my three horses'll be lost and won't be passed on to my brothers.'

I should have been amazed at the way Filofey could be worried about his horses at such a time, but I must confess that I didn't have much thought for him. 'Surely they're not going to kill us?' I went on repeating to myself. 'What for? I'll give them everything I've got with me.'

Meanwhile, the little bridge continued to grow closer, becoming all the while more clearly visible.

Suddenly there were piercing shouts and the trio of horses drawing the cart literally wound themselves up, dashed forwards and, having galloped to the little bridge, stopped dead as if rooted to the spot a little to one side of the road. My heart quite simply sank within me.

'Oh, Filofey, my good fellow,' I declared, 'you and I're going to our deaths. Forgive me if I've been the cause of it all.'

'What fault is it of yours, master! One can't escape one's fate! Hey there, shaggy one, faithful horse o' mine,' said Filofey, addressing the shaft-horse, 'move on, there's a good chap! Perform a final service for me! It's all the same. . . . O Lord! Bless us!'

And he sent his three horses off at a trot.

We began to approach the little bridge, began to approach the motionless, threatening cart. . . . As if intentionally, everyone in it had grown quiet. Not so much as a whisper! In just the same way a pike, a hawk, any predator becomes quite still as its prey draws close. We drew level with the cart. Suddenly the giant in the sheepskin coat jumped down from it and came straight towards us!

He said not a word to Filofey, but Filofey at once reined in the horses. Our carriage came to a stop.

The giant placed both hands on the doors of the carriage

and, leaning his tousled head forward and screwing up his mouth in a grin, uttered in a soft, level voice and factory dialect the following speech:

'Guv'nor, sir, we're on our way from a real good party, a wedding party. We've married off one of our mates, see. Put him to bed, real and proper. They're all young lads 'ere, a bit wild – we've downed a lot, but haven't got nuthin' for the hair of the dog, see. So maybe it'll be your pleasure you'll let us have just a little bit o' small change, so as there'll be a round for each of us? We'd drink your health, sir, and raise a toast to your highness. But if it isn't to your liking – don't get mad at us!'

'What's this?' I asked myself. 'A joke? Is he putting one over?'

The giant continued to stand there, his head lowered. At that moment the moon broke through the mist and lit up his face. It wore a grin, the face did, a grin of the eyes and lips. But there was nothing threatening to be discerned in it, except that it seemed to be literally on its guard, and the man's teeth were so large and white. . . .

'With pleasure I'll . . . here, take this,' I said in a hurry and, having extracted my purse from my pocket, took out two silver roubles; at that time silver coins were still in circulation in Russia. 'Here it is, if that'll be enough.'

'Mighty thankful!' the giant barked out in military fashion and his large fingers instantly seized from my hands – not the whole purse, but only the two roubles. 'Mighty thankful!' He shook back his hair and ran to the cart.

'Lads!' he shouted. 'The guv'nor in the carriage's given us two roubles!' The rest of them at once made a fine uproar. The giant tumbled on to his box.

'The best o' luck to you!'

And that was all we saw of them! The horses started away, the cart thundered off uphill – it flashed into sight once more against the dark line of horizon dividing the earth from the sky, sank from view and disappeared. Soon even the clattering and shouting and jingling bells were no longer audible.

Deathly silence reigned.

*

Filofey and I did not come to our senses immediately.

'You're a right joker, you are!' he said eventually and, removing his hat, began to make the sign of the cross. 'A right joker, that's for sure,' he added and turned to me, radiant with joy. 'But he must've been a good chap, that's for sure. Gee-up, gee-up, my pretties! Get wheeling! You'll be whole! We'll all be whole! He didn't let us pass, you see, 'cos he was driving the horses. A right joker that lad was! Gee-up, gee-up, get along there! God's speed to you!'

I did not say anything, but I began to feel much happier. 'We'll be whole!' I repeated to myself and spread myself out in the hay. 'We got off cheaply!' I was even a little ashamed of having recalled the line from Zhukovsky.

Suddenly, a thought occurred to me:

'Filofey!'

'What is it?'

'Are you married?'

'I am.'

'And have you children?'

'I have.'

'How is it you didn't think of them? You worried about the horses, but what about your wife and children?'

'What would've been the good of worrying about them? After all, they wouldn't have fallen into the hands of thieves. Still I had them in mind all the time, and I still do . . . sure I do.' Filofey paused. 'It may be, 'cos of them, the good Lord had mercy on the two of us.'

'And what if they turned out to be robbers after all?'

'How's that to be known? D'you think it's possible to get inside another's soul, eh? Another's soul sure is a mystery. It's always best to be on God's side. No. . . . I keep my family always. . . . Gee-up, gee-up, my pretties! God's speed!'

It was almost quite light by the time we began to approach Tula. I lay in the oblivion of a half sleep.

'Master,' Filofey said to me suddenly, 'take a look over there! That's them standing by the tavern – and there's their cart.'

I raised my head – true enough, it was them; and their cart and horses. All of a sudden the familiar giant in the sheepskin coat appeared on the threshold of the drinking house.

'Guv'nor!' he exclaimed, waving his cap. 'It's your money we're drinking! But as for the driver,' he added, giving a nod of the head towards Filofey, 'you most likely had a fright, eh?'

'Highly divertin' fellow,' remarked Filofey, driving a good fifty yards on beyond the tavern.

Finally we reached Tula. I purchased some shot, also some tea and spirits, and I even procured a horse from the dealer friend of mine. At midday we set off on our return journey. Travelling past the place where we had first heard the clattering of the cart behind us, Filofey, who, having had a drink in Tula, turned out to be a man of extremely garrulous disposition (he even regaled me with fairy-tales) – travelling past that place, Filofey suddenly burst out laughing.

'Remember, master, how I kept on saying to you: There's a clattering . . . a clattering, hear it, clatter-clatter?'

He made several sweeping, dismissive gestures with his hand. The word 'clattering' seemed to be a source of special amusement to him.

That evening we got back to his village.

I informed Yermolay of what had occurred to us. Being in a sober condition, he expressed no sympathy, simply grunted – whether approvingly or scornfully he did not know himself, or so I believe. But a couple of days later he took pleasure in letting me know that on the very same night Filofey and I had been travelling to Tula, and on the very same road, some merchant or other had been robbed and killed. At first I did not believe this news. But later I had occasion to change my mind, the truth of it being confirmed for me by the local police-officer who had galloped up to attend the investigations. Was it not perhaps from this 'wedding' that our 'wild ones' had been returning, and was this not the 'mate' that, as the jocular giant expressed it, they had been putting to bed real and proper? I remained in Filofey's village another five days or so. It happened that each time I met him I would ask him:

'There's a clattering, eh, a clattering?'

'A divertin' fellow,' he would answer me each time and burst out laughing.

Forest and Steppe

... Little by little he felt his desire harden,
Drawing him back to the village and shady garden,
Where lindens stood in stately dark magnificence,
And lilies of the valley spread their virgin fragrance,
Where round-shouldered willows by the weir,
Bend in a row above the water clear,
Where a stout oak grows above the fat-eared wheat,
Where hemp and nettles make the air smell sweet ...
He was drawn back to those broad fields so lush,
Where the earth like velvet is so black and plush,
So that, no matter where you may direct your eye,
Everywhere is a rustling of soft waves of rye,
And through transparent clouds, so round and white,
Fall heavy beams of sunshine's golden light;
There is it good ...

(From a poem consigned to the flames)

THE reader, perhaps, has already had enough of my Sketches, but I hasten to allay his fears with the promise that they are to be limited to these printed extracts; and yet, in making my farewell, I must say a few words about the sport of hunting.

Hunting with a gun and a dog is a delight in itself, *für sich*, as they used to say in the past. But let us suppose that you are not a born hunter, though you still love nature; in that case, you can hardly fail to envy the lot of your brother hunters. ... Pray listen awhile.

Do you know, for instance, how delightful it is to drive out before a spring dawn? you walk out on to the porch and here and there on the dark grey sky stars wink at you, light waves of a moist breeze occasionally stir the air about you, the muffled, indistinct murmurs of the night can be heard and the trees rustle softly, immersed in shadow. A cover is drawn over the cart and a box with a samovar is placed at your feet. The trace-horses fret, snort and affectedly stamp their hooves; a pair of newly awakened white geese make their way slowly and silently across the road. In the garden, on the other side of the fencing, the night-watchman snores peacefully from time to time. Every sound hangs as if frozen upon the still air – hangs there frozen and motionless. Then you take your seat; the horses start away at once and the cart clatters off on its journey.... You drive past a church, downhill and to the right across a dam; a mist is just beginning to rise from a pond. The air chills you slightly and you cover your face with your coat collar; you are pleasantly drowsy. The horses' hooves squelch in the puddles and the driver whistles to himself. By the time you've travelled two miles or so the rim of the sky is beginning to crimson; in the birches jackdaws are awakening and clumsily fluttering from branch to branch; sparrows twitter about the dark hayricks. The air grows brighter, the road clearer, the sky lightens, suffusing the clouds with whiteness and the fields with green. Lights burn red in the cottages and sleepy voices can be heard beyond the gates. In the meantime dawn has burst into flame; stripes of gold have risen across the sky and wreaths of mist form in the ravines; to the loud singing of skylarks and the soughing of the wind before dawn the sun rises, silent and purple, above the horizon. Light floods over the world and your heart trembles within you like a bird. Everything is so fresh, gay and lovely! You can see for miles. Here a village glimmers beyond the woodland; there, farther away, is another village with a white church and then a hill with a birchwood; beyond it is the marsh to which you are driving.... Step lively there, horses! Forward at a brisk trot!... No more than two miles to go now. The sun is rising quickly, the sky is clear.... The weather will be perfect. You meet a herd of cattle coming in

a long line from the village. Then you ascend the hill. . . .
What a view! The river winds away for seven miles or more, a
faint blue glimmer through the mist; beyond it are water-
green meadows; beyond them, low-lying hills; in the distance lapwings veer and cry above the marsh; through the
gleaming moisture which pervades the air the distance emerges
clearly . . . there is no summer haze. How freely one breathes
the air into one's lungs, how buoyant are one's limbs, how
strong one feels in the grip of this fresh springtime atmosphere!

*

And a summer morning in July! Has anyone save a hunter
ever experienced the delight of wandering through bushes at
dawn? Your feet leave green imprints in grass that is heavy
and white with dew. You push aside wet bushes – the warm
scent accumulated in the night almost smothers you; the air is
impregnated with the fresh bitter-sweet fragrance of wormwood, the honeyed scent of buckwheat and clover; far off an
oak forest rises like a wall, shining purple in the sunshine;
the air is still fresh, but the coming heat can already be felt.
Your head becomes slightly dizzy from such an excess of
sweet scents. And there's no end to the bushes. . . . Away in
the distance ripening rye glows yellow and there are narrow
strips of rust-red buckwheat. Then there's the sound of a cart;
a peasant drives by at walking pace, leaving his horse in the
shade before the sun gets hot. You greet him, pass on, and after
a while the metallic rasping of a scythe can be heard behind
you. The sun is rising higher and higher, and the grass
quickly dries out. It's already hot. First one hour, then another
passes. The sky darkens at the edges and the motionless air is
aflame with the prickly heat.

'Where can I get a drink, friend?' you ask the peasant.

'There's a spring down there in the ravine.'

You make your way down to the floor of the ravine

through thick bushes of nut which are entwined with bind-weed. There it is; at the very bottom of the ravine hides the spring; a small oak has greedily spread its webbed branches over the water; large silver bubbles rise in clusters from the spring's bottom nestling in a thin, velvety moss. You fling yourself to the ground and drink your fill, but have no wish to rise again. You are in a shady place, breathing in the pungent dampness; you're glad to be here while beyond you the branches burn with heat and literally turn yellow in the sun. But what's that? A breeze has suddenly risen and scurried by you; the surrounding air shudders. You leave the ravine. . . . What's that lead-grey strip running along the horizon? And the heat's thicker, isn't it? Is there a cloud forming? . . . Then comes a faint lightning flash – yes, it's a storm all right! Yet the sun is still shining brightly and hunting's still possible. But the cloud grows: it's nearest edge is stretched out like a sleeve and looms like an arch. Bushes, grass, everything sud-denly darkens. . . . Quick, quick! There's a hay barn over there. Quick! . . . You reach it, go in and come rain, come lightning, it makes no difference. . . . Here and there water drips through the straw roof into the fragrant hay; soon the sun's out again. The storm passes and you step outside. Oh, how gaily every-thing glitters around you, how fresh and liquid is the air, how sweet the scent of mushroom and wild strawberry!

But now evening is approaching. The sunset has burst into flame and covered half the sky with fire. The sun sinks. The air near by is somehow particularly lucid, exactly as if made of glass; in the distance a soft haze is settling, warm as heat-haze in appearance; along with the dew a crimson glow is descending on the open fields which were so recently in-undated by torrents of liquid gold; from trees, from bushes, from tall hayricks have run long shadows. . . . The sun has set; a star ignites and twinkles in the fiery sea of the sun's sinking. . . . Now the sun pales; the sky grows blue; separate shadows

vanish away and the air fills with dusk. It is time to go home,
to the village, to the hut where you are spending the night.
Slinging your gun over your shoulder, you walk at a brisk
pace despite your tiredness. And in the meantime night de-
scends; you can hardly see twenty paces ahead of you; your
dogs are barely visible in the murk. Over there, above the
blackness of the bushes, the rim of the sky shines dimly. . . .
What's that? Is it a fire? No, it's the rising of the moon and
there below you, to your right, the lights of the village are
already glimmering. Finally, you reach your hut. Through the
little window you see a table covered with a white cloth, a
lighted candle and supper. . . .

Or you order the racing buggy to be harnessed and off you
go into the forest after grouse. It is a happy feeling to be
making your way along a narrow track between two high
walls of rye. The heads of grain gently strike you across the
face, while cornflowers catch at your feet, and quail cry in the
vicinity and the horse goes at a lazy trot. Then comes the
forest. Shade and silence. Stately aspens murmur high above
you; the long hanging branches of the birches hardly stir; a
powerful oak stands like a warrior beside a gracious linden.
You travel along a green track that is dappled with shadows;
large yellow flies hang motionless in the gold-dust air and
suddenly fly away. Gnats weave in spirals, glittering in the
shade, darkening in the sunlight; birds sing peacefully. The
small golden voice of the robin makes a sound of innocent
prattling gaiety: it accords with the scent of lilies of the
valley. You go farther and farther, deeper into the forest. The
forest thickens. An inexplicable quietude begins to descend
on your soul; and all around it is so dream-like and still. But
now a breeze has sprung up and the tips of the trees have begun to rustle like tumbling waves. Through last year's rust-
brown fallen leaves tall grass grows here and there; mushrooms
stand individually under their little hats. A white hare jumps

suddenly into view and the dog races after it with loud barks. . . .

And how fine that very same forest looks in late autumn, when the snipe fly in! They do not frequent the forest depths, but must be sought along its outskirts. There is no wind, nor is there any sun, any brightness, any shade, any movement, any noise; the soft air is saturated with an autumnal fragrance, like the bouquet of wine; a thin mist hangs in the distance over the yellow fields. Through the naked, dark-brown branches of the trees the still sky peacefully shines; here and there on the lindens hang the last golden leaves. The damp earth is springy under your feet; the tall dry blades of grass are perfectly still; long threads gleam in the pale-hued grass. Your breathing is calm, though a strange anxiety invades your soul. You walk along the edge of the forest, keeping your eyes on the dog, but in the meantime there come to mind beloved images, beloved faces, the living and the dead, and long-since dormant impressions unexpectedly awaken; the imagination soars and dwells on the air like a bird, and everything springs into movement with such clarity and stands before the eyes. Your heart either suddenly quivers and starts beating fast, passionately racing forward, or drowns irretrievably in recollections. The whole of life unrolls easily and swiftly like a scroll; a man has possession of his whole past, all his feelings, all his powers, his entire soul. And nothing in his surroundings can disturb him – there is no sun, no wind, no noise. . . .

And a clear, autumnal, slightly cold day with frost in the morning, when the birch, literally a tree out of a fairy-tale arrayed all in gold, stands out in beautiful outline against a pale-blue sky, when the sun, low on the horizon has no more power to heat, but shines more brightly than the sun of summer, when the small aspen wood glows through and through as if it were delighted and happy to stand there naked, when the hoar-frost still whitens the floors of the valleys, but a fresh breeze ever so quietly rustles and drives before it the fallen twisted leaves, when blue waves race gaily along the river, making geese and ducks scattered on its surface bob evenly up and down; when in the distance a watermill, half hidden by willows, makes a clattering sound and, colourfully flickering in the bright air, pigeons circle swiftly above it. . . .

Wonderful also are hazy summer days, although hunters dislike them. It is impossible to do any shooting on such days: a bird, though it rises from beneath your very feet, immediately disappears into the whitish murk of the motionless haze. But how quiet, how unimaginably quiet is everything around you! Everything is awake and everything is silent. You walk past a tree – it does not even so much as stir: it simply swoons in the stillness. Through the fine mistiness with which the air is evenly suffused a long strip of something black emerges in front of you. You take it for a nearby forest; you approach – and the forest turns into a high bank of wormwood on the boundary of a field. Above you and all about you, everywhere there is haze. But then a breeze stirs faintly – and a patch of pale-blue sky vaguely emerges through the thinning mist, which has literally begun to rise like smoke; a golden-yellow ray breaks through suddenly, streams out in a long flood, strikes across the fields, runs up against a wood – and then once more everything clouds over. This struggle continues for a long while; but how indescribably magnificent and lucid is the day itself, when the sunlight finally triumphs and the last waves of sun-warmed haze either roll away and spread themselves out smooth as tablecloths, or spiral upwards and vanish in the deep, gently gleaming atmosphere. . . .

But now you've set off into the distant fields and the steppe-land. You've made your way for six or seven miles along country roads and now, at last, you've reached the main road.

Past endless lines of carts, past little wayside inns with samovars hissing under the lean-to out front, with their wide-open gates and well-holes for water, from one village to another, through endless expanses of fields, beside plantations of green hemp, you travel for hour after hour. Magpies flit from one clump of broom to another; women with long rakes wander in the fields; a traveller on foot wearing a worn nankeen coat, with a small bundle over his shoulder, plods on his way at a tired pace; a bulky landowner's carriage, harnessed with six full-grown and jaded horses, trundles towards you. The corner of a cushion is sticking out of a window, but on the rear step, on a mat, holding on by a rope, a lackey in an overcoat sits sideways, spattered with mud up to his eyebrows. Then there is a little county town with small lop-sided wooden houses, endless fences, vacant merchants' dwellings built of stone and an ancient bridge over a deep ravine. . . . Farther, farther! The steppelands are approaching. You look down from a hill – what a view! Round, low hillocks, ploughed and sown right up to their tips, billow in all directions like broad waves; ravines overgrown with bushes weave among them; small woods are scattered here and there like elongated islands; from village to village run narrow tracks; churches gleam white; between thickets of willow glitters a small river, its flow staunched in four places by dams; far off in the field wild cranes stick out as they waddle in file; an antiquated landowner's mansion with its outbuildings, orchard and threshing floor is settled comfortably beside a small pond. But you go on travelling, farther and farther. The hillocks grow shallower and shallower and there is hardly a tree to be seen. Finally, there it is – the limitless, enormous steppe no eye can encompass!

And on a wintry day to go walking through the high snow-drifts in search of hares, to breathe in the frosty, sharp-edged air, to crinkle one's eyes unwillingly against the dazzling, finely speckled glitter of the soft snow, to wonder at the green hue of the sky above a reddening forest! . . . And then there are the first spring days, when all around everything gleams and crashes down, and the smell of the warmer earth begins to rise through the heavy steam of melting snow, and skylarks sing trustingly under the sun's oblique rays on patches where the snow has thawed, and, with a gay noise, a gay roaring, the torrents go whirling from ravine to ravine. . . .

It is time, however, to finish. Appropriately I have mentioned the spring; in springtime it is easy to say good-bye, in the spring even the happy are enticed to far-off places. . . . Farewell, my reader; I wish you lasting happiness and well-being.

Appendix

THE RUSSIAN GERMAN

ONCE I followed my dog into a field of buckwheat which did not belong to me at all. In our obliging Fatherland anyone is free to shoot where he likes, on his own land or on his neighbour's. Apart from a few elderly and shrewish ladies, and landowners who have perfected themselves on the English pattern, no one so much as thinks of forbidding strangers from hunting on their lands. I had barely succeeded in taking a few steps when I heard loud shouts from behind me. It did not occur to me that I was being shouted at in person, and I continued very calmly, with all the thorough conscientiousness of a hunter, walking backwards and forwards across the field, until I finally heard quite clearly:

'What're you doing, master, trampling down the buckwheat? You mustn't, it's not allowed . . .'

I turned round and saw a peasant in a cloth coat, with an unusually picturesque and wavy beard, who was walking directly towards me and waving his arms wildly. I stopped.

'T'ain't right for you to be walking through the buckwheat. Stop, or I'll take you to the bailiff. A fine's laid down for this and there's an order issued about it,' the peasant said as he walked, shaking his head.

Eventually he came up to me. I apologized. He made a grumbling sound. But the prohibition against walking through the buckwheat seemed to me so strange in our beautiful Russia, the more so since it was a steppe province, that I could not refrain from asking the peasant who had given him such an order.

'Who?' the peasant retorted with displeasure. 'Who? The master himself.'

'And who's your master?'

The peasant did not answer at once and played with his belt. 'Makarat Ivanych Shvokhtel . . .'

'Who on earth . . .?'

The peasant repeated his master's name. 'But maybe,' he added, 'you'd be having some snuff?'

'No, I don't, but take this to buy some with.'

The peasant thanked me, took off his cap and became much happier.

'So it's not allowed, is it?' I asked him.

''S not allowed,' he replied smiling, like a man who, though he is doing what his master orders, feels for his own part that the orders are in fact ridiculous. ''Course,' he continued, 'buckwheat's not peas; no point in having someone to guard it, seein' as someone might start eatin' it raw. . . . But that's the sort of master we have. He'd grind rye in a thimble, he would, the Lord forgive us.'

That same week it happened that I became acquainted with this very man. Mr Leberecht Fochtlender was born, so rumour had it, in the glorious German township of Guzbach. In his twenty-fifth year he entered the Russian civil service, occupied various posts for a period of thirty-two and a half years, retiring with the seventh-grade rank of aulic councillor and the Order of St Anne. He had married at forty. He was small in stature and on the thin side; he used to sport a brown frock-coat of old-style cut, grey trousers, a small silver watch attached by a string of blue beads and a high white cravat which gathered in folds right up to his ears. He held himself very straight and walked about with a prim haughtiness, now and then turning his small head. He had a small, smooth face, light-blue eyes, a sharp little nose, semicircular sideburns, a forehead covered with tiny wrinkles and thin, tightly closed lips.

THE REFORMER AND THE RUSSIAN GERMAN

I was sitting in the so-called 'clean' room of a wayside inn on the main Kursk road and asking the inn-keeper, a stout man with wavy grey hair, bulging eyes and sagging stomach, about the number of hunters who had recently visited the Telegin marsh, when the door was suddenly flung wide open and a traveller entered the room, a tall, graceful gentleman in a stylish travelling coat. He removed his cap.

'Yevgeny Alexandrych!' I cried. 'What luck, eh?'

'Ah, ★ ★ ★!' he exclaimed in his turn.

We shook each other's hands. 'How pleased I am, how pleased,' we both babbled, not without a certain tenseness.

'Where in God's name are you going?' I asked at last.

'To Kursk . . . I've come into an inheritance.'

'Has your aunt died?' I asked with a modest show of sympathy.

'She's died,' he answered with a faint sigh. 'Inn-keeper!' he added in a loud voice, 'the samovar – and quick about it! Yes,' he continued, turning to me again, 'she's died. I'm just now on my way to receive what she's left me.'

Yevgeny Alexandrych's servant came in, a young man with reddish-coloured hair and dressed in the manner of a *chasseur*.

'Hans!' my acquaintance declared. '*Geben Sie mir eine Pfeife.*'

Hans went out.

'Is your valet a German?' I asked.

'No, he's – er – a Finn,' answered Yevgeny Alexandrych, leaving intervals between the words. 'But he understands German.'

'And he speaks Russian?'

Yevgeny Alexandrych paused briefly before saying: 'Oh, yes, he speaks it!'

Hans returned, respectfully set the pipe directly between his master's lips, placed a square-shaped scrap of white paper on the bowl and touched a match to it. His master began to smoke, taking the pipe with the side of his mouth, and contorting his lips over the amber stem like a dog seizing a hedgehog. The inn-keeper brought in a hissing and bubbling samovar. I took a seat beside Yevgeny Alexandrych and struck up a conversation with him.

I had known Yevgeny Alexandrych Ladygin in St Petersburg. He was a tall, personable man with large bright eyes, an aquiline nose and a resolute expression of the face. All who knew him, and many who did not, spoke of him as a 'practical' man. He expressed himself without grandiloquence, but powerfully; while listening to others, he used to clench his jaws in impatience and let his cheek twitch; he was self-assured in his speeches and he would walk about the streets at a brisk pace without moving either his arms or his head, darting his eyes rapidly from side to side. Seeing him, more than one passer-by no doubt exclaimed despite himself: 'Phew, there's a man for you, by God! Where's that fellow off to?' But Yevgeny Alexandrych was simply on his way to dinner.

Rising from the table, he used to button his coat right up to the neck with such chill and concentrated resoluteness that he might have been setting off at that very moment to fight a duel, having just put his signature to his will. And yet, despite this, there was not a trace of boastfulness to be discerned in him; he was a stubborn man, one-sided and insistent in his opinions, but no fool, not malicious, looking everyone straight in the eye and fond of justice. . . . True, he would have found it much pleasanter to punish oppressors than alleviate the lot of the oppressed, but there can be no accounting for people's tastes. He did four years or so of service in a guards regiment, and the remainder of his life was fearfully busy – with what? you may ask. . . . With nothing save various futile matters, which he always set about in a fever of activity and with systematic stubbornness. He was a type of Russian pedant – Russian, take note, not Little Russian. There is an enormous

difference between the two, to which attention should be paid
more than ever now that, since Gogol's time,[1] these two related, but opposed, nationalities have often been confused.

'Are you going to spend a long time in the country?' I
asked Ladygin.

'I don't know – perhaps it'll be a long time,' he answered me
with concentrated energy and glanced away indifferently, like
a man of strong character who has taken an irrevocable de-
cision but is ready, notwithstanding, to take account of that
fact.

'You must have a host of plans in mind?' I remarked.

'Plans? It depends what you call plans. You don't think, do
you,' he added with a grin, 'that I belong to the school of
young landowners who find difficulty in telling the difference
between oats and buckwheat and dream of English winnowing machines, threshing machines, rotation of crops, sugar-
beet factories and brick huts with little gardens facing on to
the street? I can assure you that I have nothing in common
with those gentlemen. I'm a practical man. But I do have a
number of ideas in mind . . . I don't know whether I'll succeed in doing everything I intend doing,' he added with
modest arrogance, 'but, in any case, I'll try.'

'It's like this, you see,' he continued, transferring his pipe
with dignity from his right hand to his left and grandly emitting
smoke through his whiskers, 'it's time for us landowners to
start using our brains. It's time to look into the way our
peasants live and, having once understood what their needs
are, to lead them firmly along a new road towards a chosen
aim. . . .' He fell into a reverential silence in the presence of his
own phrase. 'That's my basic idea for you,' he started up
again. 'Russia in general must have – and consequently the
way of life of the Russian peasant must have – its own in-
digenous, characteristic, so to speak, aim for the future. Isn't
that true? It must, mustn't it? In that case you must strive to
perceive it and then act in accordance with its spirit. It's a

...fficult task, but nothing is given us for nothing. I will gladly devote myself to it . . . I'm free to do it and I sense in myself a certain firmness of character. I have no preconceived system: I'm not a Slavophil and I'm not a devotee of the West . . . I, though I say it again, I am a practical man – and I know . . . I know how to get things done!'

'That's all very fine,' I protested. 'You – if I may be so bold as to say so – you want to be a little Peter the Great of your own village.'

'You're laughing at me!' Yevgeny Alexandrych said animatedly. 'Though,' he added after a short pause, 'what you've said has an element of truth in it.'

'I wish you every possible success,' I remarked.

'Thank you for wishing . . .'

Yevgeny Alexandrych's servant entered the room.

'*Sind die Pferde angespannt, Hans?*' my acquaintance asked.

'*Ja . . . Sie sind.* They're ready, sir,' Hans answered.

Yevgeny Alexandrych hastily finished his tea, rose and drew on his overcoat.

'I don't dare to invite you to stay with me,' he declared. 'It's more than seventy miles to my village. However, if it should occur to you to . . .'

I thanked him. We said good-bye. He drove off.

For the space of a whole year I heard nothing of my St Petersburg friend. Once only, I recall, at a dinner given by the Marshal of Nobility a certain eloquent landowner, a retired chief of the fire brigade called Sheptunovich, referred in my presence (between swigs of Madeira) to Yevgeny Alexandrych as a member of the nobility given to daydreaming and a man readily carried away by his own ideas. The majority of the guests at once expressed agreement with the fire-brigade chief, but one of them, a stout man with a purplish face and unusually wide teeth, who vaguely reminded one of some sort of healthy root vegetable, added for his own part that he, Ladgyin, had something wrong with him up there

(indicating his temples) – and gave regretful shakes of his ⌐
remarkable head. Apart from this instance, no one even
much as uttered Yevgeny Alexandrych's name in my presence. But on one occasion, in the autumn, it happened to me,
while travelling from marsh to marsh, to land up a long way
from home. A fearful thunderstorm caught me out on the
open road. Happily, a village could be seen not far off. With
difficulty we reached the outskirts of the village. My driver
turned towards the gates of the nearest hut and shouted for
the hut's owner. The man, an upstanding peasant of about
forty, let us in. His hut was not remarkable for its neatness,
but it was warm inside and not smoky. In the entrance-way a
woman was frantically chopping up cabbage.

I seated myself on a bench and asked for a jug of milk and
some bread. The woman set off to get the milk.

'Who is your master?' I asked the peasant.

'Ladygin, Yevgeny Alexandrych.'

'Ladygin? Are we already in Kursk Province here?'

'Kursk, of course. From Khudyshkin it's all Kursk.'

The woman entered with a jug, produced a wooden spoon
that was new and had a strong smell of lamp-oil attaching to
it, and pronounced:

'Eat, my dear sir, to your heart's content,' and went out,
clattering in her bast shoes. The peasant was on the point of
going out behind her, but I stopped him. Little by little we
started talking. Peasants for the most part are not too willing
to chat with their lords and masters, particularly when things
are not right with them; but I have noticed that some peasants,
when things are going really badly, speak out unusually
calmly and coldly to every passing 'master' on the subject that
is close to their heart, just as if they were talking about someone else's problem – save that they may occasionally shrug a
shoulder or suddenly drop their eyes. From the second word
the peasant uttered I guessed that Yevgeny Alexandrych's
wretched peasants made a poor living.

ɔo you're not satisfied with your master?' I asked.

'We're not satisfied,' the peasant answered resolutely.

'How so? Does he oppress you, is that it?'

'Fagged us right out, worked us to the bone, that's what he's done.'

'How's he done it?'

'This is how. The Lord knows what sort of a master he is! Not even the old men in the village can remember such a master. It isn't that he's ruined the peasants; he's even reduced the quit-rent of those who pay it. But things don't go no better, God forbid. He came to us last autumn, at the Feast of the Saviour – arrived at night, he did. The next morning, just as soon as the sun'd started to show, he'd jumped out of bed and – dressed, he had, real lively – and he came running from house to house. He's a one for dashing here and there; dreadful fluttery he is, like he's got a fever shaking him. And so he went from house to house. "Fellow," he says, "all your family in here!" An' he stands there in the very middle of the hut, not shifting at all and holding a little book in his hands, and looks all round him, he does, like a hawk. Fine eyes he's got, bright ones. An' he asks the man o' the house: "What's your name? How old are you?" Well, the peasant answers, of course, and he notes it down in his book. "And what's your wife's name? Children's names? How many horses have you? Sheep? Pigs? Sucking-pigs? Chickens? Geese? Carts? Ploughs and harrows? Are the oats in? The rye? How much flour? Give me some of your *kvas* to try! Show me your horse-collars! Have you got boots? How many jugs? Basins? Spoons? How many sheepskin coats? How many shirts?" By God, yes, he even asked about shirts! An' he notes everything down, just like he was making an investigation. "What d'you trade in?" he asks. "D'you go into town? Often? Precisely how many times each month? Are you fond of drinking? D'you beat your wife? D'you also beat your children? What's your heart set on?" Yes, twice, by God, he asked that,' the peasant added, in response to my involunt. smile.

'And he went round all the yards, all the huts, he did. He quite wore out Tit, the elder, and Tit even fell on to his knees in front of him and said: "Good master, have mercy on me! If I've done something wrong in your eyes, then I'd rather you ordered me to be flogged!" The next day, again before it was light, he got up and ordered all the peasants there are here to come to an assembly. So we all came. It was in the yard of his house. He came out on to the porch, greeted us and started talking. Talk, he did, talk and talk. The strange thing was we didn't understand what he was saying though he seemed to be talking Russian. "Everything," he said, "is wrong, you're doing everything the wrong way. I'm going to lead," he said, "in a different way, though I don't want at all to have to force you. But," he said, "you're my peasants. You fulfil all your obligations," he added. "If you fulfil them, fine; if you don't, I shan't leave a stone unturned." But God knows what he wanted done!'

'"Well," he said, "now you've understood me. Go back to your homes. My way's going to start from tomorrow." So we went home. We walked back to the village. We looked at each other and looked at each other – and wandered back to our huts.'

Notes

(With the exception of the two fragments in the Appendix, the *Sketches* translated in this selection are all taken from I. S. Turgenev, *Polnoye sobranie sochinenii i pisem*, izd. Akad, nauk (M-L, 1963), Vol. IV, which is the most complete and fully annotated edition of the *Zapiski okhotnika* so far published. The ensuing notes are drawn largely from this edition.)

KHOR AND KALINYCH

1. Zhizdra: a region of Kaluga Province (in pre-revolutionary Russia), in which Turgenev owned seven villages containing a peasant population of more than 450 'souls'.
2. *Corvée:* unpaid labour which serfs were obligated to perform for their masters.
3. Nakhimov, Akim: (1783–1815), second-rate satirist, versifier and prose-writer.
4. *Pinna:* a sentimental romance by M. A. Markov (1810–76), first published in 1843.
5. *Kvas:* a kind of cider made from rye-bread.

KASYAN FROM THE BEAUTIFUL LANDS

1. Beautiful Lands: *Krasivaya mech*, a tributary of the river Don and regarded as one of the most beautiful regions in European Russia.
2. Gamayun: a legendary bird associated with falconry.

BAILIFF

1. *Wandering Jew, The (Le Juif errant)*: a novel by Eugène Suë popular in the mid 1840s.
2. *Lucia*: a reference to the opera of 1831 by Donizetti, in which Pauline Viardot sang the leading role during her first visit to St Petersburg in the 1843-4 season.

Somnambules, Les: an opera (1835) by Bellini, in which Pauline Viardot also sang.

4. Carême, Marie-Antoine (1784–1833): famous French cook, who worked for Talleyrand and later at the Russian and Austrian imperial courts.

TWO LANDOWNERS

1. Saadi (1184–1291): the Persian poet, referred to by Pushkin in the last stanza of Ch. VIII of *Eugene Onegin*.

DEATH

1. Zusha: a tributary of the river Oka, situated about three miles from Turgenev's estate of Spasskoye.
2. Schopenhauer, Johanna: German novelist and mother of Arthur Schopenhauer, the philosopher.
3. '. . . had supplanted them but not replaced them': paraphrase of a line from Ch. I, stanza XIX of Pushkin's *Eugene Onegin*.
4. Koltsov, A. V.: (1809–42), Russian poet, many of whose poems, written in the manner of the folk-song, have been set to music. The lines are from his poem 'The Forest' of 1838.
5. 'What if a falcon's . . .': quoted from the third stanza of Koltsov's 'Dream of a Falcon' (1842).

HAMLET OF THE SHCHIGROVSKY DISTRICT

1. 'sideburn-ites': by a decree of April 1837 Tsar Nicholas I forbade the wearing of beards and whiskers by officials in the civil service. The interdiction also extended to students. This explains the reference to 'the distant past', since *Hamlet of the Shchigrovsky District* is known to have been written in 1848, and it also explains the 'ravening hunger' of disapproval with which the dignitary later glances at Prince Kozelsky's beard. It must be assumed that the Prince was not in the civil service.
2. 'With my fate is no one much concerned . . .': from 'Testament' (1840), a poem by M. Yu. Lermontov (1814–41).
3. *Mon verre n'est pas grand, mais je bois dans mon verre*: from a dramatic poem *Coupe et les livres* (1832) by A. de Musset (1810–57).

4. Encyclopedia of Hegel: a reference to Hegel's *Enzyklopädie de philosophischen Wissenschaften im Grundrisse* (1817). Turgenev possessed a copy of this work in its third edition (Heidelberg, 1830).

5. Moscow sages: a reference to the Slavophils.

6. '*Gefährlich ist's den Leu zu wecken*': a slightly inaccurate quotation from Schiller's *Das Lied von der Glocke*.

7. 'Awaken her not till dawn has broken': from a lyric by A. A. Fet (1820–92), supposed to have been set to music by A. E. Varlamov.

8. 'In one of Voltaire's tragedies . . .': the reference is possibly to Act II of Voltaire's *Mérope* (1743).

LIVING RELIC

1. 'Homeland of longsuffering . . .': from the first stanza of a short poem of 1855 entitled 'These wretched hamlets'. F. Tyutchev (1803–73), a remarkable philosophical and nature poet, was first brought to the notice of a wide reading public through a collection of his lyrics which Turgenev prepared for publication in *The Contemporary* in 1854.

CLATTER OF WHEELS

1. 'The robber's axe, despiséd thing . . .': a line from a poem on the death of Field-Marshal Count Kamensky by V. A. Zhukovsky (1783–1852), leading exponent of Russian Romanticism and well-known for his translations of German and English Romantic poetry.

THE REFORMER AND THE RUSSIAN GERMAN

1. . . . since Gogol's time . . .: a reference presumably to the Little Russian (Ukrainian) extraction of Nikolay Gogol (1809–52), whose first successful work *Evenings on a Farm near Dikanka* (1831) was devoted to stories about life in Little Russia. Gogol's descriptions of life in Little Russia have been compared with – or, more aptly, contrasted with – Turgenev's description of life in the Russian countryside in his *Sketches*.

MORE ABOUT PENGUINS
AND PELICANS

For further information about books available from Penguins please write to Dept EP, Penguin Books Ltd, Harmondsworth, Middlesex UB7 0DA.

In the U.S.A.: For a complete list of books available from Penguins in the United States write to Dept CS, Penguin Books, 625 Madison Avenue, New York, New York 10022.

In Canada: For a complete list of books available from Penguins in Canada write to Penguin Books Canada Ltd, 2801 John Street, Markham, Ontario L3R 1B4.

In Australia: For a complete list of books available from Penguins in Australia write to the Marketing Department, Penguin Books Australia Ltd, P.O. Box 257, Ringwood, Victoria 3134.

In New Zealand: For a complete list of books available from Penguins in New Zealand write to the Marketing Department, Penguin Books (N.Z.) Ltd, P.O. Box 4019, Auckland 10.

IVAN TURGENEV

Fathers and Sons

Translated by Rosemary Edmonds, with the Romanes Lecture
'Fathers and Children' by Isaiah Berlin

Fathers and Sons is generally agreed to be Turgenev's masterpiece,
and its hero, Bazarov, is one of the most remarkable figures in
Russian literature. Turgenev's creation of the first literary nihilist and
his demonstration of the failure of communication between genera-
tions succeeded in enraging both fathers and sons in the Russia of
his time; they also help to explain the appeal of this work to
Europeans today. Yet *Fathers and Sons* also contains some of the
most moving scenes in the literature of any language.

Also published in Penguin Classics:

ON THE EVE
Translated by Gilbert Gardiner

HOME OF THE GENTRY
Translated by Richard Freeborn

RUDIN
Translated by Richard Freeborn

FIRST LOVE
*Translated by Isaiah Berlin
and introduced by V. S. Pritchett*

SPRING TORRENTS
Translated by Leonard Schapiro

PENGUIN CLASSICS

'Penguin continue to pour out the jewels of the world's classics in translation . . . There are now nearly enough to keep a man happy on a desert island until the boat comes in' – Philip Howard in *The Times*

Some recent and forthcoming titles

Théophile Gautier

MADEMOISELLE DE MAUPIN

Translated by Joanna Richardson

Murasaki Shikibu

THE TALE OF GENJI

Translated by Edward G. Seidensticker

THE GREEK ANTHOLOGY

Edited by Peter Jay

Three Sanskrit Plays

SAKUNTALĀ/RĀKSHASA'S RING
MĀLATĪ AND MĀDAVA

Translated by Michael Coulson

ORKNEYINGA SAGA

Translated by Hermann Pálsson and Paul Edwards